PRAISE FOR SARAH BAMFORD SEIDELMANN

"Sarah Seidelmann is a true medicine woman, and everything she creates is good for what ails us."

—**Martha Beck**, author of *Expecting Adam* and *Finding Your Way in a Wild New World*

"[*Swimming with Elephants*] is an exceedingly vulnerable, beautifully written book and one of the most genuine spiritual memoirs I have ever read. It is also—in many hilarious moments—laugh out loud funny."

—**Maria Bamford**, Comedian and star of Netflix Original Series *Lady Dynamite*

"*Swimming with Elephants* is an entertaining and moving front row seat in the drama that unfolds when a western-trained physician does the work required to become a true healer."

—**Christiane Northrup, MD**, NY Times best-selling author of *Goddesses Never Age*

"*The Book of Beasties* guides readers into a profound understanding of the personal messages offered through spirit animals. Detailing the techniques for applying their transformative, healing medicine, Seidelmann empowers us to dissolve the boundaries between what is seen and interpreted by the outer physical eye and the inner eye of the soul."

—**Michael Bernard Beckwith**, author of *Life Visioning*

"What happens if you marry legend, lyricism, and practicality? You create a doorway of light: *The Book of Beasties*. In a fresh and beautiful style, Sarah introduces you to all things beastie, describing the dozens of spirit animals ready to grant you advice, guidance, and a sprinkling of magic . . . This book is sure to become a daily source of inspiration and insight."

—**Cyndi Dale**, intuitive, healer, teacher, and author
of *The Subtle Body* and *The Subtle Body Coloring Book*

"*Swimming with Elephants* is a fascinating, amusing, and wise account of how someone born with a shaman's predilections, raised in a rationalist culture, finds her way back to her true self."

—**Martha Beck**, New York Times best-selling
author of *Expecting Adam*

"Seidelmann is an often irreverent narrator whose memoir is as transformative as it is off-the-wall. Told with a mix of humor, raw honesty, and gentleness, *Swimming with Elephants* is a journey of healing. Though becoming a shamanic healer is at the core of the book, it's about much more than just this one route to becoming whole. Seidelmann's struggles will be familiar to anyone who has tried to balance a career with family and personal fulfillment. What stands out is Seidelmann's unique way of bucking tradition and finding her own way. Memoirs work best when the author is ready to lay it all out on the table, and Seidelmann does this in *Swimming with Elephants*. Her willingness to be herself and to follow her path—no matter how non-traditional and wacky it might seem at first—makes for an endearing and illuminating adventure."

—*Foreword Reviews*

"Sarah Bamford Seidelmann has amassed heaps of wisdom in her courageous leap from the safe realm of medical science into the unknown—the world of spirit. In *Swimming with Elephants*, this incredibly honest and compassionate memoir, you feel as though you're soaking in her courage and wisdom on every page. Even better, you do so laughing."

—**Jaimal Yogis**, Author of *Saltwater Buddha* and *All Our Waves Are Water*

Where
the Deer
Dream

OTHER BOOKS AND THINGS
BY SARAH BAMFORD SEIDELMANN

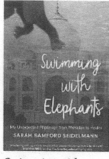

Swimming with
Elephants: My
Unexpected
Pilgrimage
from Physician
to Healer

The Book of
Beasties: Your
A-Z Guide to
the Illuminating
Wisdom of
Spirit Animals

Born to FREAK:
A Salty Primer for
Irepressible Humans

**What the
Walrus Knows**
app for
iPad and iPhone

**How Good
Are You Willing to
Let it Get?**
Card Deck

Available at
www.FollowYourFeelGood.com

Where the Deer Dream

A Coming of
Age Adventure
in Spirit

SARAH BAMFORD SEIDELMANN

Where the Deer Dream
Sarah Bamford Seidelmann

FIRST EDITION
ISBN 978-0-9860692-8-4 (paperback)
ISBN 978-0-9860692-6-0 (ebook)

Printed in USA

Cover concept by Josephine Seidelmann

Cover design by the author

Interior design by charlyn_designs @fiverr.com

www.followyourfeelgood.com

For Maria Sabina and all the medicine women:

Gini, Sarah, Luzma, Leela, Jen, Maria, Kim, Aviva,
Monique, Lauren, Benesiskwe, Carly, Barbara,
Kaweah, Alicia, Danit, Simon, Emily and Meera.

May your path always be blessed and protected.

"When you reach the end of what you should know,
you will be at the beginning of what you should sense."
–Kahlil Gibran, *Sand and Foam*

"The rose of the world was breathing out smell.
It followed her through all her waking moments
and caressed her in her sleep."
–Zora Neale Hurston, *Their Eyes Were Watching God*

Chapter One

They say that everything happens for a reason. Even bad things. Especially bad things. I'm not sure if that's true, but there is *something* that wants to help. I'm not saying it's God or that I fully comprehend it, but *it's there*. This *thing that wants to help* has been talking to me in my dreams and through animals and birds. My Aunt Jill gave me a book when I was ten that says that the animals that cross our path, especially the wild ones, are here to help us. I loved *The Book of Beasties* so much that I doodled and colored in practically every page of it, and I still have the book today. It made me feel like I wasn't weird. I'm no fucking Dr. Dolittle, but I have been learning to listen and to trust, and it's made all the difference.

In ninth grade, I had a terrible dream. Unlike most of my complicated dreams, this one was oddly simple. Just one scene. I saw white pills, some sort of medicine, sitting on a dresser, and *I knew* that something awful had happened. I couldn't say what. But in the dream I also felt the sensation of the deepest, calmest peace you can imagine. And I knew that *the peacefulness was where we come from and where we return to when we die.* Death, the dream showed me, is natural and it's not just OK...it's absolutely beautiful. Joyful. I knew that no matter what the bad thing was, things were going to be OK. When I woke up, I sketched a picture in my journal of the tablets on the dresser, and I wrote, "Everything is going to be fine" in my loopy script.

Just as I had finished writing, I saw an unusual shadow on my wall and did a double-take. It looked exactly like a fawn's head with large, tapered ears. The cedar tree outside my window was creating it in the morning sun. Immediately I *knew* it was Sweetie, and even though I felt upset by the dream, the shadow made me feel like I was not alone. Sweetie, my special animal-spirit companion, was there with me. Hours later, my uncle called my mom on the phone to tell her that his daughter, my beautiful cousin Lexi, had died of an overdose.

At first, it felt utterly surreal. How could Lexi be dead? She was one of the most alive people I knew. Initially, I felt kind of numb. Yet because of my dream and because of Sweetie, I felt confidant to immediately hug and console my mom that morning as she fell apart. And I didn't hesitate to go with her to my aunt and my uncle's house that morning to be with them. That day, I felt like I experienced the whole world underwater, as if my emotions were quieted and muffled, temporarily. I felt terrible that Lexi was gone. I missed her so much, but I truly felt, as the dream seemed to communicate, that she would be OK. That dream about my cousin Lexi was the beginning of me learning *how to know things*. I've never told anybody about the dream, but I put it in my journal. It's proof to me of this thing that wants to help.

Two weeks before she died, Lexi and I watched the movie *Legally Blonde* together. We hadn't seen each other in about a month, so I was thrilled when she suggested the idea. She was my "older sister" and I loved being around her.

"Meera, it's my absolute favorite movie. You're gonna love it!" she enthused.

I was surprised as we sat watching the uber buoyant and irrepressible character of Elle Woods in her sorority house. Lexi was so unlike Reese Witherspoon's straight-A-student character. Lexi was smart, but school was never her thing.

I thought of how Lexi lied sometimes. It never made sense to me. She didn't need to lie. Like once, during middle school, she and a friend told a whole camp of girls that she was the niece of the King of Sweden…that she was royalty. All the girls bought the story…hook, line and sinker. Lexi loved the attention, but then all the campers found out it wasn't true. They turned on her. Lexi laughed when she told the story, and I always wondered why she did it. She was so interesting already. I loved Lexi, but parts of her made me uneasy.

In the movie, Elle Woods begins to take the older manicurist under her wing, the one with an abusive boyfriend. I suddenly got why Lex loved the movie. She was always fighting for the underdog. She loved rescuing people and animals.

Lexi was always encouraging me to stop standing on the sidelines and to try new things…even if I was going to be uncomfortable or look like a fool. "What have you got to lose?" was her constant anthem. She was the one who got me to try paddleboarding for the first time. Without her dragging me onto the board, I never would have done it. I was happy just to lie in the sun on the warm sand, away from the ice-cold water of Lake Superior. I didn't want to be uncomfortable. But, when I finally surrendered to her, that board took me for my first glide atop the water, and I was hooked! It was the most magical feeling to fly across the surface of the lake. I felt so light and free.

Since Lexi's been gone, I promised myself that I wouldn't resist new things. I'd say YES more often instead of playing it safe and staying warm and dry on the shore. In a weird way, her death (and that dream) inspired me to stop hesitating. And to trust myself and whatever it was that brought the dream of those white tablets to me.

It still feels like Lexi is cheering me on towards my biggest dream, to become an interior designer. Since I was really little, I've loved houses. My Grandma Max brought me back a few dog-eared copies of *World of Interiors*, a European interior-design magazine that she found on her garden tour of England when I was a junior. It showcases some of the best rooms I've ever seen…so personal and filled with fascinating, unusual objects that reveal so much about the individual who lives there. Personally, I love a room that's comfy, but sophisticated, with a sense of history. My favorite section of *Elle Decor* (my other favorite design publication) is the page where famous designers speak about their most beloved possessions. When they call to feature me, I will be ready.

Future Issue of *Elle Decor*

Things That Designer Meera Townsend Cannot Do Without

In a featured photo of my bedroom, walls painted in Farrow & Ball's Dayroom Yellow No. 233 and ceiling in Farrow & Ball's sky-blue Skylight (color matched at the Hardware Hank) are:

1. **A photo of me (age five), my mom and my Grandma Max that Uncle Mitch took.** We all have huge smiles on our faces, and we are at Stony Point, my favorite Lake Superior beach. Our faces are basking in the glow of a sunrise.

2. **My vintage Japanese paper parasol** in jade covered in faded pink peonies. It hangs upside down below the ceiling light over my bed, creating a distinctive light shade.

3. **My crazy, beautiful, yellow Chinoiserie secretary desk** that I found on Craigslist and bought with birthday money. It was originally owned by a prominent Duluth socialite. The inside is painted in lapis lazuli blue. I keep perfume, a couple photos of me and my BFF Penn, jewelry and a little Colombian flag in there.

4. **My Lee Jofa "Pugs and Petals" throw pillows** my grandma helped me make out of one precious yard of fabric (provenance: eBay). If you can't have a pug (my mom Lorraine is allergic), at least you can have a pug pillow.

5. **My brass dragon incense burner with pinon wood incense** my Aunt Jill gave me. She found the burner at Goodwill. I love incense, and my mom decided this is safe enough to actually use in my room. The incense smells like the most exotic campfire you can imagine.

6. **My simple modern bed (IKEA Malm)** "canopied" by ivory-colored burlap drapery panels (hung on suspended drapery cables that Mom and I attached to the ceiling) and adorned with navy-blue pom-pom fringe (hot glued on because I hate to sew).

7. **The strawberry toleware chandelier,** which hangs over my desk. My grandma saved it for me from her friend's dining room remodeling project.

I'm on my way back home from a run. I stop and stand momentarily, watching hundreds of hawks flying in rising spirals. It's a clear October day, and thousands of raptors…hawks, vultures and eagles… can be seen over the bluffs arriving from as far away as the Arctic, heading for their winter homes. Reluctant to cross large expanses of open water, they turn southwest and trace the shore of Lake Superior. They soar upward in these "kettles" to conserve energy for their long journey. The higher they ride the thermals of warm air coming off the ridge, the longer they can coast without effort. Sometimes for miles.

Maybe I was a hawk in a previous life, because I can almost feel what it's like to ride those warm currents. Who wouldn't want to harness the wind like that? Mentally, I make a note to look up the message of hawk in *The Book of Beasties* when I get back home.

As I'm walking along the trail, a small irregular path catches my eye. I check my phone. I'm still OK for time. I turn off the main route and enter what I recognize as the deer's irregular passage. After a few hundred feet of travelling, I can't see a thing on either side of me. I begin to feel claustrophobic with the grasses rising taller and taller. It's as if my options and possibilities are being taken away. I also feel more vulnerable–like I could be ambushed. What's lurking behind these silent walls of grass? I stop. Just as I'm about to turn back, I sense Sweetie tracking gracefully ahead of me, and she says, wordlessly, *Do you trust me?*

Sometimes I invite Sweetie to hike with me, but this time she showed up on her own. She always runs ahead of me, and so I just "see" her white tail pointed up. From time to time she'll stop and turn her head back to me like "Are you coming already?" When I remember her, I don't ever have to be alone. That's what Grandma Max says that her faith does for her.

Her easygoing grace comforts me as I see her long legs disappear down the trail before me. Encouraged by her presence, the part of me that's willing to endure uncertainty proceeds, and I move forward a few more yards.

As I'm willing to take just a few more steps, the trail suddenly opens into an amazing space. A small clearing lies before me, sheltered beneath a grove of towering white pines. A half dozen or so deer have just been resting here. The soft impressions their warm bodies left on the grass are all that remain. The lingering sweetness of those wide-eyed and gentle creatures is so palpable and powerful, and I stand still, taking it all in for a moment. Enchanted. It's so inviting; I'm tempted to lie down and curl up on the ground too. To soak up the feeling here. But what if somebody comes up the trail…how would I explain? This sweet discovery reminds me that I need to trust my strange inner nudges to explore unfamiliar things.

⟋⟋⟋⟋⟋

"We're going to be late!" Mom says in an exasperated tone as she heads toward the front door. "Meera, *you have got to pay more attention;* get your head out of the clouds. We had to LEAVE five minutes ago."

Ugh. Lorraine is a nurse and she's super practical. I'm the dreamy one in our little family of two. When I was really little, I remember her being more playful and fun. I kept all of these little love notes that she used to write me with her funny sketches of sweet little animals on them. That part of Mom seemed to disappear all at once.

She used to paint all the time too. She would set a little easel for me next to her sometimes so I could paint alongside her using my kids paints. I loved being with her like that. One of her bright oil paintings, lush with wildness, still hangs above our fireplace, and there are more at my grandma's and aunt's houses. She stopped painting when I was nine to go to nursing school. Sometimes I wish I could get to know the person who painted the abstract, jungly and blossoming paintings she made. They look like otherworldly planets plumbed with strange rivers and inhabited by trees ripe with magical fruit. The colors are so juicy and vibrant. When I ask her about her art and why she doesn't paint these days, Mom always acts mildly irritated, like she doesn't want to remember.

"Oh yes...art is wonderful, Meera. I wish I had more time for it, but it's not that easy for me...," and then she usually launches into a lecture about how I should be thinking about going to law school like Grandpa. Her paintings are so amazing, I wish she'd paint more again. I know it's partially because she has had to take care of me and, sometimes, I feel guilty about that.

My mom says that when I was little I was "full of beans" and covered in bruises and scrapes. I was always trying to climb something tall and jumping off it. I've seen video footage of that "little me" and it's pretty hilarious. There's barely a frame where I am standing still, except when I'm hamming for the camera and making faces.

I guess we don't change much, and to this day I constantly seem to be injuring myself. My mom says it's because I don't stop and think. My "not thinking" has gotten me a broken arm (first grade: fall from the top of the monkey bars after my friend Penn and I gave each other our first "manicures" complete with hand lotion), a broken collarbone (fourth grade: going off a mogul my first night skiing at the local ski hill), and another broken arm (seventh grade:

rollerblading). My accident-prone nature makes my mom nervous. Sometimes, I wish I could have been an easier kid.

Lorraine says we balance each other out because she's an earth sign (Virgo), and I'm an air sign (Gemini). Sometimes, rather than it feeling like a balance, it seems like I'm an airy, problematic balloon on the loose and she is tasked with trying to drag me back down to earth. Despite her passion for all things astrological, Lorraine is science-based and logical. I guess that makes sense, she's a nurse. You probably don't want your nurse riffing creatively or consulting the stars and planets when your life is on the line. That's also why I could *never* be a nurse. Or a lawyer. I'm going to be an interior designer. Because there aren't really any rules—as long as a room "works"…it works.

After my third broken bone in seventh grade, Mom took me to the pediatrician and then the neurologist—she thought maybe I was ADHD/hyperactive. I am legit a pretty high-energy kid, but it's not like I'm a snorting-rocket-fuel Ty Pennington (*Extreme Makeover: Home Edition*) kind of person. I went through the tests and both physicians said the same thing: *She's normal.* This will probably be just something that Meera will grow out of when she finishes puberty and catches up with her body. I'm safely through puberty now, but I'm still a klutz.

I also got glasses at the end of seventh grade. I wish I would have had the courage to get the more outrageous Iris Apfel style frames I secretly wanted to rock, but I worried they were a little too weird. *And, maybe, I don't want that much attention?* So I have these more classic tortoise frames, which still go with my boho preppy kinda vibe. But someday I want to have the courage to go BIG. Iris is on my bulletin board. I want to be brave like her. And to give less of a damn about what other people think.

That pediatrician I saw in seventh grade also told Lorraine I should take up a sport or dance. "It would be a great way to help her connect her mind and body," she said.

I would rather die than do sports, but Mom insisted because the institute of medicine *is her religion*. So, at age thirteen, I joined the basketball team. My best friend Penn played, and I knew she'd have my back. Still, it was a total disaster. She tried to help me. But when the coach gave me my first big chance, I ended up shooting and getting a basket for the other team at a home game.

Apparently, I just didn't have it in me to remember which end of the court we were playing towards. How did people keep track of this unfascinating little detail? Name a famous interior designer in New York from the 1980s (Mario Buatta!) or the perfect pale pink from Farrow & Ball (Middleton Pink No. 245)–I'm in! But which end of the court's hoop should I put the basketball in? Who cares?

I never did understand how others could catch the ball so effortlessly. No matter what I tried, ball-handling skills eluded me. I had a hard-enough time trying to stay on top of whoever I was guarding. It was a relief when my mom let me quit–not because *I hated it,* but because she felt our coach was "not very supportive of girls" after she saw him yell at his own daughter.

I lasted just two Tuesdays in dance. The other girls were all *So You Think You Can Dance* wannabes since kindergarten. For me, it was a nightmare. Step-ball-change was like walking for these girls. And because Penn was so much more advanced, I had to endure class without her. To make matter worse, the instructor (a Norwegian Cruella Deville, in a white leotard, shiny panty hose and nude character shoes) shamed me for my poor posture several times. I wasn't sucking in my gut and throwing back my shoulders like I should. I told Lorraine that Cruella was extremely bad for my self-esteem. Lorraine believed me and let me quit. Sometimes my mom could be cool like that.

So, dance and basketball, things that my BFF Penn loves, are a BIG NO for me. Interior design is my thing. If I could, I'd do it all day, every day.

"Meeeeerahhhhh!" I hear the front door slam, and I know my mom is heading out to her car to wait for me. We're going to dinner at my aunt and uncle's house. I quickly pull out the book my aunt gave me so many years ago and flip to "Hawk," and my eye scans quickly and lands on this line: "The circular patterns Hawk traces in the sky are a reminder for you that everything in life is a circle. Like the earth itself, nothing remains fixed. In this moment, embrace the circle you are in and where you exist in it."

It's nice to think that things aren't fixed because lately I've been feeling stuck and scared. I'm a senior in high school and it feels like my childhood is nearly over. I'm a little worried that I don't have what it takes to do the things I want to do.

Chapter Two

There's a video of four-year-old me in my *Powerpuff Girls* pajamas squealing hysterically next to the Christmas tree. Seeing the dollhouse that Santa had brought me was life-altering in every way. I nearly lost my ever-loving mind. My Grandma Max said my reaction was a sign that décor was my destiny. I loved being in charge of my little family of three complete with a rubbery dad.

My dad died when I was nine. Now it's just me and Lorraine. Sometimes it feels like I've forgotten everything about him. I don't miss him like I once did, but my memory of my dad is more like this empty glass I am always trying to fill up with details. There's a hole in the bottom of the glass, so it never holds water. Weirdly, he's with me now in a way that's stronger than when he was *really* here. The best parts of him. It's complicated, but I feel his love. Always. He was a Pisces, and my mom says that they're dreamers.

At first, the dollhouse was mostly about my family and playing "make believe." For every birthday after that, I always asked for all things small. I remember my Aunt Jill and Uncle Mitch getting me a miniature Victorian porcelain bathtub, sink and toilet for my birthday in kindergarten. With my dad's help, I fashioned a wee roll of toilet paper with some Kleenex, a toothpick and Elmer's. Suddenly, my tiny house felt more real and legit. I was a little weird that way.

By third grade, it wasn't so much about my dollhouse family; I wanted to make my dollhouse *beautiful*. That year, before he died, Dad helped me shingle the roof, apply wood parquet flooring in the living room, and glue tiny subway tiles onto the bathroom walls. He also took me to the library. I would check out stacks of books about dollhouses and crafting. I remember he and my mom fighting because we were spending so much time working on it, and she wanted him to do other projects. Then he was gone. I worried that, somehow, it was my fault. After that, I stopped working on my dollhouse.

At eleven, I got a hankering to make our own home beautiful, starting with my room. I began sketching my own actual bedroom's layout in detail on graph paper with elevations and begging my mom for rolls of wallpaper for my birthday. Instead of pricey and more permanent wallpaper, she helped me paint the walls a soft yellow and then the ceiling sky blue. For my fifth-grade Christmas, I got two monogrammed pillowcases and a rose-colored toile quilted bedspread. This helped me create a funky French vintage vibe in my room that I still love.

At twelve, I spent my allowance and Christmas money on my first piece of furniture: a set of three vintage Italian gilded wood nesting tables with emerald-green tops (fifty-eight dollars at an estate sale). By thirteen, I had every single issue of *Domino* magazine that had ever been published lined up in my room on a special shelf. And I believe, like *Domino* does, in the democratization of design. Everybody deserves a beautiful room.

My real education about interiors and how other people adorn their spaces began way back in third grade though when I started going on sleepovers. One friend's house was granny-ish and matchy with color-coordinated faux flower arrangements and matching scented candles in every room. There was a clear plastic cover on the couch. They moved here from Florida; maybe that's a thing there? I remember it feeling really heavy. One friend's mom collected these weird Snowbabies that she kept in lighted glass cabinets in the living room. *Why?* It made me wonder what she liked about them. It felt suffocating. I wanted to set all the tiny ivory clad infants dressed in winter clothes FREE from their hot airless nursery.

As I got older, I realized that some families just didn't have any design awareness whatsoever. It wasn't about money. You don't need a lot of money to make a home interesting, but you do need to care about it...*and not everybody does.* One girl's split level's living room held a couple mismatched futons and a pair of heavily distressed Lack tables from IKEA with concert posters taped on the wall. It looked like they had moved in five minutes ago. Another girl's newish house was so *un-decorated* that I wondered if something was deeply wrong. It was minimalism bordering on sensory deprivation. There was no evidence of actual human life being lived: not a single appliance on the kitchen counter, a photo on a table or shelf. No art. Was somebody in the family accessory averse? I feel like I can sense things about people by being in their spaces. It was extremely unsettling to be there. I'll never know what was going on, sadly, because she moved away in fourth grade. A little clutter is good. I think it means you're normal.

Before sleepovers, I just knew a few houses: my grandma's and my aunt's and Penn's. Penn's is slightly crowded with overstuffed furniture, but it's really warm and friendly with lots of books on the shelves, handmade afghans that her grandma knit, and her dad's guitar is always lying out. They have cool Chinese calligraphy art on the wall in the dining room from the region where Penn was born. Penn's mom stays home and always keeps the cookie jar filled with home-made cookies. Penn's house isn't a designer house, but you definitely feel the love when you're there.

My aunt and uncle's house is still one of my favorites. Being there feels like stepping into an adventure. My aunt is a textile importer and has travelled all over the world. My uncle is a contractor and remodels houses. They have collected so many cool things: an amazing stone Ganesha (an elephant-headed deity my aunt loves!) statue from Bali, a big fluffy Greek flokati rug, a glam 1940s vintage mirrored table they inherited from my uncle's great aunt. They have these cool Turkish poufs they got from Istanbul (my uncle carried them back, unstuffed in his suitcase for my aunt). It sounds chaotic, but somehow she arranges it in a way that makes it totally cohesive.

If my style statement is Bohemian Preppy, I'd say hers is Bohemian Adventure. When she lights all the candles, you feel like you are transported to another place. Maybe it's all the travel, but my Aunt Jill is nothing like my mom. She's relaxed and I feel like nothing can knock her off her center. It's so easy to be around her. She's softer. She's also a floral genius. She can grab a bunch of stuff out of the woods, arrange it in a planter on her porch, and it looks like the cover of *Country Living* magazine. She's got skills.

Grandma Max's house is different. Not in a bad way, but you'd never know she was related to Jill. She's a minimalist. Every object in her house breathes and tells a story. It's also very, very neat. So it's a little too restrained for me but *it's her*, for sure. For example, there's a pair of simple brass candlesticks on her dining room table that belonged to her mom. And she has a photo on the wall of her mom standing in HER dining room (which looks almost identical) with the same candlesticks in the photo. A framed rosary that was my great-grandma's hangs in the hallway.

A few years ago, I asked Grandma Max about her minimalist tendencies.

"Hmmm, you know I fell in love with the people in Guatemala when I was in the Peace Corps after college…they were so content, despite the fact that they had so very little. That stuck with me…we don't need a lot of things to be happy. I grew up in a home with lots of "things" but not a lot of happiness. I've told you that my mom and dad fought a lot. It seems to me like stuff can distract me from what's important."

Mom says Grandma Max's home growing up had a fair degree of luxury; her dad owned a paper mill. Seeing my grandma's simplicity makes me worry that I'm wrong to want so much! I mean, my fantasy home is pretty chock full of fabulous things!

Thankfully, Grandma Max isn't an absolute minimalist. Each summer, her house gets lush with cut flowers from her garden, fuzzy lamb's ears and peonies, in tiny little vases in the windows, on tables and in the bathrooms and bedrooms. Each tiny vase has a story too. My favorite is the green wine jug from her trip to Portugal that's covered in hand-painted vines and grapes. I'd say her style statement is Essential History; it suits her.

She also has a certain, organized way of doing things. We all defer to Grandma Max, even Lorraine. Mom says that her mom naturally leads because she's a Scorpio, and the shadow of Scorpio's leadership is that they can be controlling. They seem close now, but this makes me wonder if my mom ever fought with her mom.

Our house is pretty cute: a cozy Craftsman cottage in Lakeside. The outside could use paint, but my mom always keeps the window boxes filled with flowers or greens. Inside, with a modest budget, I could do so much with our living room. Under the carpet, I'm convinced there are wood floors which I would definitely refinish. Then I'd buy two pairs of black IKEA Billy bookcases and link them together on either side of the fireplace and accessorize them with books, art and baskets. Next, I'd get a neutral sisal rug and put it underneath the coffee table and couch to anchor the whole thing. A whole bunch of white orchids would fill in the deep window well perfectly. Boom–so LUXE. Of course the orchids would be real and bloom often. And I'd add a picture light to my mom's amazing jungly painting over the fireplace.

I believe your environment is EVERYTHING, and a room (and what is in it or not in it!) can tell you so much about a person. I love animals and I collect vintage ceramic birds that I keep on a bamboo shelf above my bed. I love the splashes of color they add, especially during the long winters. With them watching over me as I sleep, I feel a little like Snow White. At the foot of my bed, I've got a cool Shipibo textile from Colombia, where I was born. It's a small hand-stitched piece on cream fabric covered in beautiful vines, flowers and fine geometric patterns. The guy we bought it from explained that the jungle plants sing their songs to the artists who stitch the designs. So the geometric designs represent, visually, the plant's unique song. How amazing is that?

I really love the amazing strawberry chandelier my grandma rescued for me from a friend's dining room remodeling project. It's vintage Italian with bright red strawberries and green leaves made of painted metal. One summer, my mom and grandma and I got pick-ing strawberries...we went a little crazy. The berries that year tasted like heaven, they were so sweet and flavorful. We couldn't resist their juicy perfection. The next thing you know, we had abandoned the rest of the day's plan and picked a half dozen huge flats of them. The chandelier reminds me of that crazy beautiful day.

And I love desks! Mine is this yellow Chinoiserie type with glass doors and a lapis blue interior that we got off Craigslist. The intense yellow and blue are so perfect with my soft blue ceiling and yellow walls. I needed a desk, and my mom took me to the house of the lady who was selling it. The lady made me promise that I'd take good care of it and never sell it. It had belonged to her grandma, but her husband didn't like the style. It's covered in delicate hand-painted Chinese scenes, trees, birds, butterflies. I can hardly believe it's mine. I will never sell it.

I upholstered a bulletin board I scored at Goodwill with burlap and tucked it into an old, gilded frame. It holds my favorite things: a photo of me and Mom and Grandma, a picture of interior designer Diana Vreeland in the 80s in her amazing all red room, and a photo of me on my dad's shoulders at the Grand Canyon when I was little. So I guess in my room (Style Statement: Bohemian Preppy), you'd know that my family is everything, and I'm kind of a maximalist—*I want it all*. And sometimes I worry I want too much.

I love helping people fix up their rooms so they can be happier. I'm still learning, but a lot of it comes naturally. Every time I do it, I feel more like I am doing what I'm supposed to be doing. And sometimes I feel like I have magical powers. In eighth grade, Penn dubbed me "Makeover Meera" as I have helped a few girls rearrange their rooms to make them more awesome...*more true to their vibes*. Not that it is always super easy for me; I do get nervous about moving another people's stuff around. It's so personal.

A family friend, Lil, got one of my first room "makeovers." She's a couple years younger than me and liked my room. After finding out what she liked best, I gave her some ideas and she liked them too. While her dad painted her whole room this gorgeous deep blue gray, Down Pipe No. 26 (color matched at the Hardware Store from Farrow & Ball), we took all of her favorite photos of family and friends and had them blown up and printed in black and white at Walgreens. We mounted them together in a bunch of cool vintage frames that we found at Goodwill, and they really popped on that deep, watery gray. Her parents had this old funky rattan globe fixture that we spray-painted white and hung over her bed. It was unexpected and made an amazing pattern on the ceiling at night. We stenciled a cool vintage owl in simple grey onto a plain white comforter cover. She was so excited with the result. Lil still posts pics of her Vintage Natural styled room on her Instagram, and she hadn't moved or changed a thing, which really makes me feel good.

My mom's friend (she's a nurse with Mom) and her daughter Laura, age eleven, moved into a new apartment. I helped Laura make her room awesome. That felt especially amazing because it was a time when life for her (and her mom) truly sucked. Her parents were in the middle of a divorce. Laura loves bright colors and plants, and so we found this cool, old, multilevel plant stand that we painted bright yellow. With my mom and aunt's help, we made cuttings and created an amazing little garden for her window dormer. We kept her walls white except on one wall. There, inspired by an *Elle Decor* photo, she and I traced and painted big circles of her favorite primary colors on the wall across from her bed, and I found a cool vintage navy-blue wool blanket with stripes of red, yellow and blue to top her bed. Her style? Happy Modern! Her mom tells my mom that it still makes Laura so happy.

Probably the most fun project was helping Penn do her room. We created a super cool dressing table area for her with Hollywood style makeup lights. I painted some art that we framed for her walls using some acrylics. They are nothing fancy, just some super simple abstract art in the colors she wanted to pull in…the palest blush, cream and a few touches of neon pink. We even got super crafty and transformed these plain circular mirrors we found at Goodwill with hot glue guns and rattan "frames." We spray-painted them in metallic rose gold. They looked like those classic round mirrors with radiating sun beams but with a girly and modern twist.

I still get worried when I'm helping another person to redo their space. Grandma Max always tells me, "When you get nervous, think about service." She says that when you're all worried what other people are going to think of something you're doing or making, you should refocus yourself on how you can be helpful with your work. Remind yourself–it's not about you, *it's about them*. I relax when I remember that I just want the design to help the person feel better. I also love collecting quotes from kids' books. One of my favorites ones is related to all of this. It's from Winnie the Pooh: "Piglet was so excited about the idea of being Useful that he forgot to be frightened anymore…" I have that one pinned on my bulletin board.

Helping others with design is when I feel like I actually know what I am doing. Don't get me wrong. I'm not an expert, but I do have a good feeling for what works and what doesn't. I have an opinion (and usually it's a strong one). Doing design, I definitely feel useful, which is probably one of the best feelings in the world. Feeling like a complete spaz is one of the worst feelings.

Chapter Three

Sometimes it feels like something is wrong with me, and if I could just figure out what it is I could fix it. I used to pray that I could be that girl who loves basketball and could remember which end the team was shooting the ball towards, or that I could just be more loving and "normal" like Penn seems to be,

Penn and I are both adopted. She was born in China. I was born in Colombia. Maybe because of that, we get each other on a pretty deep level, and most of the time, I feel like I can be myself with her. Our moms took us to the same daycare. We literally grew up, side by side, in our infant car seats, and we have photos to prove it. In one picture, Penn looks serene, and I am crying and looking at her. She has always been the calm one. The one who knows everything is going to be fine. The one who isn't rocking the boat. And I feel like I'm always the one who's being difficult.

Despite growing up side by side, and being internationally adopted, we are also *really different*. Like, for instance, Penn is totally against searching for her birth family. She says she has no interest in going to visit China either. Even just for fun. I think going to China would be amazing and I wasn't even born there. I have desperately wanted to go to Colombia since the moment I fully understood that it was where I came from.

I finally had the opportunity to visit Colombia when I was fourteen. After I returned from that trip, I told Penn everything that had happened. What happened there was complicated. Then Penn asked me if I regretted travelling to Colombia. *That stung. A lot.* She really didn't understand my experience at all. *She had always thought it had been a bad idea for me to go.* I wanted her to understand that, though it was a difficult journey, I wouldn't change it for the world. Something in me changed; I definitely felt more at peace after going. I hated that she seemed to use my experience as more evidence that she shouldn't search. I wanted her to want the same things I did…to know where she came from.

We have other differences too. Penn, for example, is really close with her mom, and I hold Lorraine at arm's length a lot of the time. I am not dating a boy, and Penn is almost always dating a boy. Currently, she's with one that I really don't love. But I love Penn like a sister, and when you're an only child like me, you need friends like that. Maybe it's because I'm an "only," but I have another *different sort of friend* too—my spirit animal Sweetie. I've known this friend almost as long as Penn. Sweetie arrived unexpectedly, in the middle of the night.

I remember feeling really scared, I was maybe four years old. There was a loud summer thunderstorm with lots of lightening, and I heard my parents fighting down the hall. Then came a huge lightning strike. As the storm raged on and my parents kept fighting, I got more and more scared. I sat up on the edge of my bed. I felt paralyzed. Like that feeling in a dream where you can't move but you try to? And that was when Sweetie first appeared to me.

My whole bedroom became bathed in this beautiful light, and she appeared: A beautiful little fawn, with a spotted coat, staring straight into my eyes. There were many other more grown-up deer behind her. They were her family. It may sound like it would be scary to a four-year-old kid to have a whole mess of illuminated deer appear in their bedroom, but I wasn't scared at all. Her dark and sweet eyes made me feel so calm. They were so kind. Her delicate ears swiveled and twitched. Sweetie silently told me that she was my friend, and that the other deer were too. I told her I was scared about the yelling and the bad man cutting down the tree. She assured me that everything was going to be alright, and that they were here to help me. It was so vivid that I can feel the entire experience all over again right now. My body felt tingly all over. Then she and the other deer all knelt down and settled onto my bedroom floor to watch over me. Sweetie told me it was time for me to rest. And I fell back to sleep, completely relaxed.

When I woke up in the morning, my favorite huge tree in our front yard had fallen down in the storm, and I realized that I had Sweetie. *And she didn't leave my side.* Whenever I relaxed and closed my eyes, I could feel her with me. Though I have never fully "seen" her as intensely as I did that very first night, I do "see" her in my mind's eye. It's not like normal seeing. I feel her whole being with me whenever I bring her to my mind. It was about five years after her first appearance when my dad died, and Sweetie was there for me.

Maybe you have had an imaginary friend too? Most kids probably do, but I guess it's weird *that I still have one.* I can't say for sure, because I really don't talk about it with anybody. Not even Penn. I have a weird fear that if I talk about Sweetie to anybody—I'll jinx her…she might disappear. Like when you tell somebody about something magical that happened to you and they don't understand, and you suddenly feel stupid. A little of the magic you were feeling drains away. Or all of it does? Or like the way the sunset is so amazing, and when you grab your phone to take a photo or you turn your back for a moment to tell somebody, and it's changed and gone. Great things can be shy like that. And private. Maybe that's what makes them great.

Sweetie is like the best sort of friend. She comforts me, and she never tells me what I should do. She's my secret cheerleader. I don't ever have to feel alone. Whenever I think of her, I feel a little better. Lately, when I'm lying in my bed at home, sometimes I think of that amazing place I stumbled into at Hawk Ridge, where the deer had been sleeping beneath those pines. I imagine that heaven, where I picture that my dad and Lexi are, is a bit like that. And I'll feel Sweetie's cool wet nose against my cheek.

In *The Book of Beasties* that my aunt gave me, it says that deer's fast-growing antlers can symbolize intuition, and that deer can help me grow my connection to the wisdom everywhere that is lying in plain sight. I'm not sure about that, but Sweetie always makes me feel as if, no matter what, things are going to be OK. And I have learned, the hard way, that I can't ignore my intuition.

My sleepover career and informal community design education ended abruptly at age thirteen. I was staying over at Meredith Swenson's Victorian house with its sagging wood floors, flowery wallpaper and ruffled calico curtains from the *Vermont Country Store* catalog, and I went towards the stairs to the bathroom in the middle of the night. As I made my way, I missed where the steps began.

I fell down their main staircase. It was a long way to fall. The tears came as I lay there stunned, and blood trickled from my nose into the back of my throat. All I could think was *why?* Why was this happening to me? In an instant, Sweetie arrived. Her soft cool nose gently nuzzled my chin upward. *This is not where your story ends, Meera,* she whispered. *These moments of klutziness will not define you.* I let out a sigh. I then felt enveloped in the most intense blanket of love you can imagine. I didn't want it or the moment to end, but Meredith's parents had woken up to my cry (when I landed) and they discovered me.

Worried I had a concussion, they called my mom to come pick me up at two in the morning. Looking back, I believe that night was the beginning of me losing a bit of my confidence. If I couldn't trust myself to not fall down the stairs, I better be careful and that led to more carefulness in everything. And yet I remembered what Sweetie said: *These moments will not define you.* But what did she mean by that?

After my fall, I always made sure I had my phone charged and at the ready, so I'd have a flashlight (that night I had let it go dead). I pretty much stopped sleeping over at other people's houses. Even with my phone, I just felt like I couldn't trust myself. My anxiety got the best of me. I began waking up in the dark, and if my night light was unplugged or somehow blocked (by a pile of clothes), I would panic for a few moments. My heart would race until I was fully awake and I realized I was safe: I wasn't going to fall down the stairs. Though I felt unsure of myself in some ways (basketball, dance and being a klutz), I always had design.

I realize I'm weird, being so obsessed with design at a young age and knowing that's what I want to do. I guess that's why Penn and I get each other because she's always known she wants to be a nurse.

I believe that if everybody lived in a room that lit them up, the world would be a better place. I learned this truth in seventh grade. Dad had been gone for a few years already. I thought we were through the worst when my mom began to act strangely. I don't exactly remember when it started—it came on slowly. My aunt says it happened because my dad's death was a suicide. It wasn't just tragic, it was also traumatizing. Aunt Jill also thinks it happened because my mom pushed down her grief in order to go get her nursing degree and take care of me. Aunt Jill says if we would all just grieve properly, the world would be a lot easier to bear.

At first, it was just overcast. A few dark clouds around. Lorraine was kind of irritated by me, a little more than average. Then it became an eclipse in the middle of the day sort of thing. Suddenly, the sun disappeared midday and it had gone quiet. The birds stopped singing. Something was wrong. It was eerie, and our whole house got strangely dull when Mom was around.

Normally, my mom is Hummingbirdesque: A 5'1", she is an extremely fierce force of nature who barely weighs one hundred pounds. She never stops moving. I feel tall and strong standing next to her. I'm curvy, 5'4" and 140 pounds, with burnt caramel colored skin and my arms are covered in dark hair. On a very good hair day, people will tell me I'm a dead ringer for America Ferrera. In contrast, Mom is rail thin, blonde and has no visible arm hair. Which is kind of weird because, according to her, I'm supposedly the Gemini (air sign—the balloon) and she's the Virgo (earth sign) who's supposed to be bringing me back to earth.

That winter, when I was in seventh grade, she stopped doing my laundry. I started running out of underwear, and when I would ask when she'd get to it, she'd snapped at me. I knew something was wrong. She also stopped going out in the evenings after work. She stopped wanting to hang out together with me too. No more quick runs up to Walgreens for a new nail polish color and a pint of Ben and Jerry's to share while we watched *Modern Family*. Her bedroom door was closed a lot and it felt lonely at home. I worried that maybe I had caused the trouble as we had been fighting a little too. Nothing huge, but I thought maybe it was me.

When somebody you love changes, it's really confusing. I wanted her to be able snap out of it. To be my mother. I thought: *If you love me, then you will try to feel good again.* Like, how can you be feeling so different suddenly? *Isn't feeling good a choice?* And I also felt guilty for being able to feel so good myself.

My mom's sister Aunt Jill, the adventurous one with a Ganesha in her living room, told me that depression *is like snow*. She is an expert. Her daughter, my cousin Lexi, had struggled with it, on and off, since she was really young. But Lexi's death, thank God, wasn't a suicide, my Aunt Jill always points out. It was an accident. She never intended to die that night.

"For the person experiencing depression, Meer, some days the snow's like a few inches and they can quickly sweep off their sidewalks and get through the day. But other days...or maybe for months even...it's like a full-on blizzard. Now the drifts are up to the door and it's so overwhelming. The snow blower is broken, the power is out, and so they just crawl back into bed hoping conditions will clear. For some people, they never do."

Snow like that scares me. A blizzard like that is what killed my dad.

My aunt says, "Meera, in your dad's case, bad news during his blizzard triggered an avalanche. He was already depressed when he found out he'd be 'let go' from work. That was too much for him, and impulsively he decided we'd all be better off without him. Of course, he was so wrong. But people get confused…" My dad went out to a friend's hunting shack and shot himself in the head. I don't like to remember him like that, but sometimes I still think about it. It makes me mad that he was impulsive like that. The scene is so lonely and horrible in my mind. Why couldn't he see that there would be other jobs? Did he think about me?

That strange winter, I worried that my mom might do the same thing too if it ever got bad enough. When I would come bounding into the kitchen, excited about something, Lorraine would physically cringe. It felt like, in some way, my enthusiasm was all wrong. Or that I was a bad person. Was it wrong for me to feel good, somehow? When she was suffering? I tried to subdue myself, but squelching my own joy, I noticed, made *me* feel depressed.

One day I had a thought that fixing up her room might help. That winter I had been studying, with great intensity, the IKEA winter catalog, and I was filled with so much inspiration from the photos. I had organized the kitchen pantry that morning, and that had felt good. At least it was something I could improve. Mom's bedroom had always been drab, at least to me. It wasn't terrible. It was neat but crowded. Beige walls. Two huge old dressers that used to be my grandma and grandpa's in the 70s with her bed pushed up against the wall and one photo of me as a baby. On the bed was this old polyester quilt that was kind of a mash-up of colors. It looked like it was made of a dozen different fabrics from the 60s. Almost Pucci or Missoni cool, boho…but not quite…too many colors in the palette.

The overhead light fixture was one of those dusty etched-glass bowls with painted flowers on it. The light wasn't awful, but it was just meh. And there were those terrible sun-yellowed plastic mini-blinds on the windows.

In April, after I got my mom on board and asked what she might like, the two of us looked at a few magazines together. Meanwhile, with my Aunt Jill and Grandma Max's encouragement, she went to see the doctor. Lorraine got on medication and she got into counseling.

I sketched out my proposal for her room. I showed Mom how we could move things around so that she could have a little space to rest and put her feet up and read. I came up with the concept that it would be sort of "Swedish Farmhouse." She seemed to perk up at the idea of her room being like that. I showed her some inspo from the catalog. By adding a simple closet system, I explained, she wouldn't need both dressers. She agreed that we could remove the smaller dresser and use that as a little hall piece in our entryway. She gave me a budget of two hundred dollars, and my grandma chipped in with some birthday money for my mom. Mom was my first legit client. *Makeover Meera* was gaining momentum.

Armed with my list, Aunt Jill and I went to Minneapolis for the day in early May while my mom worked. We got her a new duvet and a beautiful, sunny-yellow comforter cover, the closet system, blinds, light fixtures and some frames at IKEA. All within budget. One weekend in June, after school was out, I made my mom sleep in my bed for two nights, and I slept in hers while we worked to get it all done. With my uncle's help, we installed her closet system and dropped two woven straw baskety lanterns on either side of the bed by screwing hooks into the ceiling. We pulled down the awful mini-blinds and put up simple soft Roman blinds (also IKEA!). My grandma donated a wonderful comfy neutral armchair from her basement for the corner. Next to it, I placed a mini-bookcase to hold Mom's favorite astrology books and her most treasured novels.

I painted wide horizontal stripes (Farrow & Ball, Borrowed Light No. 235 and All White No. 2005) of the palest blue and white on one wall, and a solid deep navy (Farrow & Ball, Hague Blue No. 30) behind her pale maple headboard to make it pop. I white-washed and mildly distressed the existing dresser in the garage, using spray paint and some steel wool. A sheepskin rug was placed where her feet would touch the floor at bedside (a gift from Aunt Jill that would have broken the budget!). Finally, I hung three photos in simple matching birch frames—one of me as a baby, a wedding photo of my grandma and grandpa, and one of my mom and her sister Jill.

For the final reveal, Aunt Jill brought the perfect vase of white lilacs (which smelled like heaven) mixed with a few tall yellow-budded forsythia branches from Grandma Max's yard, and I had a beeswax candle burning. It was a *Fixer Upper* TV-worthy reveal, as I had Mom uncover her eyes.

"Oh Meera—this is sooo perfect!" she gasped as my mom looked around with a hand covering her mouth. She smiled for the first time in a long time. Then, like a little kid, she flopped on her back onto the bed. It felt that my efforts really did work some kind of magic.

"Where did you learn to do this? You're amazing, Meera!" she said, still tired but it felt like something was shifting. My aunt and uncle beamed at me. It felt like I had done something impossible... made her smile again. The new room seemed to jumpstart Mom's return to her normal self. She was on meds too, and spring was on its way, but I *knew* the room helped.

Not too long after, I began to see glimpses of my hummingbird mother again. As the lilacs faded, she continued to keep the vase in her room filled with fresh flowers. It was as if the room's design had reminded her how to take better care of herself. She resumed doing my laundry a few weeks after this. I remember her saying later that summer, "Meera, thank you again; I never knew what a difference something like that could make!"

For years, she had been saying that, because I could write clearly, I could be a good lawyer like my grandpa was. Nothing sounded more boring or lethal than that! I didn't even like shows that featured lawyers on TV. I let her know this and she countered, "Whatever you do, Meera, you want to be sure you have a steady income and health insurance...something you can count on?" I always wondered where the artist part of her had gone. It didn't seem like the person who could paint those colorful worlds could be so practical or rule-oriented? It seemed that now she was driven by data and rules.

"But doesn't Jess your friend make a good living doing design?" I'd ask, as she seemed to be a big success.

"Yes, Jess does very well, but it has taken her decades to build her business, Meera, and she pays her own health insurance *which is not cheap*." She'd sigh, as if I just didn't get it.

But after I helped Mom with her room that year, it felt like she finally "got" me, and my devotion to all things beautiful, on some level? And I understood, a little more, the transformative power of beauty and good design. Maybe she believed a little in my dream.

When I was little, she read aloud to me a lot...up until Dad died. She read *The Secret Garden, Little Women, Little House on the Prairie*...all the books were filled with visions of these amazing and very different homes. Some were humble and others noble, but maybe it's how my imagination got ignited in the first place. The look of a room mattered, whether it was simple with muslin curtains and quilts or elegant with expensive furnishings. And it had the power to strengthen and comfort the people who lived there.

Chapter Four

Dried leaves blow across the bright sidewalk, now unburdened by shade. A part of me is ready to be done with high school already, and another part is a lot less sure. It is October, first quarter of senior is nearly over. Things are getting real. My college apps are all in, but I still have to submit my first-quarter grades with an updated transcript. I won't hear anything until next year. As I step off the bus and start walking towards home, a sharp pain shoots up through my knee reminding me of my horrible morning at school.

Lorraine texts as I enter our yard.

Mom: Can you please switch the Crockpot to warm when you get home. Did you bring home the cap and gown form?

Me: Yes—got form. When will u b home?

Mom: 7 unless we get an unexpected admission? Gotta run—my break is up!

Me: OK see you then.

Mom: Love u.

Me: Love u too.

I unlock the front door and lock it again behind me, and then I notice the chill in the air. It's already beginning to feel like winter in the house. Sometimes I wonder what it would have been like to grow up in a warmer place. Leaving my coat on, I head straight into the kitchen which smells warm and oniony, switch the Crockpot to low and then head to my room, closing the door behind me. The tears are already rising. I set my backpack on my desk chair, throw back my covers, slip off my coat and toss it over the foot of my bed, slide in and pull my comforter up to my chin. Beneath the covers I review the day as I begin to warm up. This is the spot where I feel the safest. I stare at my sky-blue ceiling (Farrow & Ball, Skylight No. 205) and my jade paper parasol with pink peonies on it. I listen to my own breathing, which is surprisingly fast.

As my breathing slows, I relive this morning's disaster...the crowded noisy hallway...my knee turning inside out (the sharp shock of the pain) on the cold metal arm of the bench that *I never saw coming*...the horrible laughter (Why?).

Warm tears trickle into my ears. A sob comes from deep in my chest and finally I let out a huge sigh. I remember the night of my final sleepover and getting a bloody nose from the fall down the stairs. Ever since then, I feel a little panicky just at the thought of a sleepover. It's so embarrassing. I want to control my environment. But, no matter what I do, it seems I can't avoid this Klutz gene I've got. And college? How will I ever?

I imagine Penn, who is normal, being able to tell her mom all about something like this. *I hate that I hold it all in.* But I don't want to burden my mom. And part of me won't let her back in. I wish I could tell Mom about my problems without worrying it's going to add a few inches of snow to her sidewalk...or, God forbid, trigger an avalanche.

All cried out, my breathing is now so soft it's nearly nonexistent. I'm remembering the dream I had a few nights ago. It's one I've had dozens of times recently. It's my favorite. Sometimes Sweetie is in it too. I'm a baby bird in an enormous nest. The nest is clown-ishly, cosmically HUGE. Or maybe it's that I am really tiny? Anyway, this crazy nest is somehow perched in the sky. And then a beautiful Momma bird lands on the nest and looks at me. Her eyes are huge and dark like Sweetie's are…and filled with SO MUCH LOVE that I almost need to look away. It's almost embarrassing…or overwhelm-ing…this love. Helpless to resist, I melt in her presence. My whole body buzzes and tingles with this enormously good feeling…kind of like waves of electricity that move through my whole body. That's where the dream always ends.

I must have fallen asleep. I check my phone, it's 5:00 pm. It will be getting dark pretty soon. This time of year is hard, because it's the time of year my dad died. We celebrated the anniversary of his death a few weeks ago by bringing flowers to the beach at Leif Erikson Park. Mom found the most beautiful dahlias in Grandma Max's garden that hadn't been ruined by the frost. We shared memo-ries of him and then put the flowers into Lake Superior one by one. The deep blood red and palest moon yellow of the dahlias was so striking against the silvery blue of the lake that cold day. I snapped a few photos because I wanted to remember the color combination.

Each year my mom and aunt tell a few stories. My uncle usu-ally comes too. I retell my memories of how Dad did my special tuck-ins at night by flipping my covers up and over me and then being sure I was snugged in on all sides. We laugh and talk about the funny things my dad did (he loved weird hats, and his favorite was a horse head my mom bought him for his birthday), and every year it seems to get easier. He loved us and we loved him, and the way his life ended becomes less important. After, we always go to dinner for Italian at 8, my dad's favorite restaurant. And when a person is gone for a very long time, it's harder to remember the part you didn't like. At least for me. I also just remember him helping me make things and always being so excited to see me after work. He made me feel so important. That's why it's still sometimes hard to understand that he chose death. Not life. It makes me want to choose life even harder.

My stomach is twisted in hunger now, but I just want to linger in the coziness of my bed a bit longer. I close my eyes and pull the covers higher. The world behind my eyes goes dark, and slowly as I relax again, tiny particles of light fill the dark screen behind my eyelids. They dance and vibrate. I have been seeing these dancing dots of light for a while now... *We love you,* they seem to say. Somehow, these little light particles are friendly. This is the comforting part of darkness that I love. It's so different than the darkness that's made me fall down staircases. Like two sides of the same coin. This light side of the darkness is friendly. It somehow holds potential. When I start to think about this friendly quality, the particles immediately disappear. It's always like that. Sort of like when I'm in the woods and I suddenly realize there's a beautiful bald eagle soaring above me and my mind thinks, "WOW!" and then the eagle suddenly careens out of sight. Without the friendly buzzing of those particles, I feel alone again. The act of thinking breaks the spell.

7:15 pm.

Lorraine is home, and now it is dark outside. I slowly wake up and come back to myself. I can hear the faucet at the kitchen sink running, and then a knife chopping carefully against the cutting board in the kitchen as a start of dinner. Her chopping is purposeful and determined. I wonder if she chopped differently before Dad died. I feel guilty that she's got to work so hard.

"Meera?! Meeraaaaah…!"

Long pause.

"Meera?"

"Yes Lorraine, I'm here tooooo!" I half-yell from my room with mild irritation. I wish I could reel my tone back. Too late. I should have been nicer.

I have been mostly calling my mom "Lorraine" since we got back from Colombia. It's my way of keeping her at a distance. A part of me still feels guilty for calling her that…like I should be loving and call her mom because that's what good daughters do. It's so fucking complicated sometimes, I don't even understand it. In my head, I love her so much and can't live without her, but, in actuality, I sometimes act like I don't care. I'm not saying it's right, but that's how it is.

I just wish that we could go back in time, and she could have just told me the truth. Or that she could be stronger, so that I could tell her everything without worrying she'll fall apart. Then I could be the Good Meera. When we returned from Colombia, I was so mad at her that I wanted to go live with my grandmother. I just needed some space so badly. That's saying a lot because I love Grandma Max, but she's pretty obsessed with cleaning. It would drive me batshit to live with her. Things between my mom and me have gotten better, but I still notice that I'm not letting her in.

After today's epic wipeout at school, I feel defeated more than usual. I have the same weird feeling that something is wrong. I've had it for a while. And I want to trust that feeling. It's those deer antlers, my intuition I think. It's been spot-on before and I didn't trust it. I'm not completely sure of it now either, but I don't want to ignore it. Something was off today when I had the accident. The smell of the garlic and onions cooking finally gets me out of my bed and into the kitchen.

"How was school today?" Lorraine asks, looking intently at the contents of the pot on the stove.

"Fine," I say, as I rub my eyes and yawn.

"We got our old unit-secretary back, thank God, and the number of patients is down so things weren't too shabby today. Dinner is ready."

My mom's Italian chicken isn't fancy, but it tastes really good—just garlic, onions and bright green peas added to cooked chicken with jarred sauce. She likes to use cloth napkins. We always put fancy curls of parmesan and fresh ground cracked pepper on it, which makes it taste so much better than a cold bowl of Cheerios.

After dinner, as we bring our dishes to the sink, I'm hoping she isn't going to ask me to help clean up.

"I've got homework, so I need to get going on that," I lie, ready to escape back to my room.

"No problem. I've got this. Do you want to watch something together when you're all done…? A little *Modern Family*?" she asks with a warm smile.

"No, I'm pretty tired—going to go to sleep after homework tonight. Penn is picking me up early for a study thing for English." With that, I shut possibility between us down.

Just as I'm saying no to my mom, a part of me is arguing, *Yes! I desperately want to hang out with you!* But I push that voice down, determined not to engage. I can't tell my mom what happened today. I don't want to be the three more inches of snow that collapses her roof, and I've also learned that oversharing leads to trouble. And I can't deal with that right now. When I bring up something that is bothering me, it's always a problem. My klutziness also triggers my mom, and for reasons that mystify me, she'll start asking me about my adoption. It's so annoying.

Adoption, for me, honestly feels like no big deal. I've known I was adopted since I was literally a baby. What's hard is having your mother ask you about it 24/7. It's like she sees me through adoption goggles. In her defense, I've heard of nightmare families where you don't dare bring up the subject to your adoptive parents because it will send your mother into a tizzy...because she's got issues. So, fine, maybe mention it to your kids at least annually, but leave it there. Penn's mom never asks her about it.

If, for example, I tell my mom I'm struggling in a class, or whatever else is bothering me, she will listen, and then, I kid you not, within three to four minutes (with no attempt to veil it whatsoever) she will say something like: "Now you know you can talk to me about adoption stuff any time, right sweetie?"

Or, if I cry at a Disney movie... "How does it make you feel when you see birth parents/adopted children portrayed like that in (fill in the blank Disney movie title)?"

Or (from the greatest adoptive parents' hits collection), if I am upset at any time around my birthday... "Sweetie–I know birthdays can be reaaaally hard when you're adopted so it's OK if you are feeling sad today." I wasn't even thinking about being sad on my birthday until NOW–ugh, thank you very much.

Newsflash to all adoptive parents out there. Whatever the hell your kid is doing that is weird or whatever they are experiencing–It's not *always* about their adoption. This is a common malady of adoptive parents...I know from talking to other girls at La Familia, an adoption camp I used to go to. Same story: every time they got a bad grade, got sick or cried about anything, the parents rush in with the adoption thing.

My mom has this belief that when I knock my head on a doorway, trip or fall down the stairs, *it's a cry for help*. Because I am adopted? Like somehow when I trip or fall, *I am doing it to show that I'm deeply messed up because of my adoption*. WTF. There's zero correlation.

Yes, I am adopted, but I don't think about it every day like I used to when I was younger…when I first figured out what it really meant: I wasn't being raised by the mother who gave birth to me. When you hear you are adopted from when you are two years old, it's like hearing you're Lutheran or Ukrainian. It's a bit of a foreign concept until you start to "get" it. When I started school, other kids began to point out that I didn't look like my mom. Eventually, I understood we did not share the same DNA. The truth is, I mostly feel lucky because I know I'm loved, and I have a great family. I am glad to be adopted.

I text Penn.

Me: Worst day ever.

Penn: What happened?

Me: I tripped during class change and fell so hard, Senorita had to help me get up. SO embarrassing.

(Senorita is our favorite teacher of all time. She keeps snacks in her room and we get to study Enrique Iglesias lyrics.)

Penn: Ugh. I'm sorry.

Me: It sucks being a clod.

Penn: Not a clod…u r AWESOME.

Me: I guess.

Penn: Sephora lady said they only need ppl who can work week-day mornings…so no job for me.

(Penn is obsessed with makeovers, hair and all beauty products. I was anxious to hear about her application at the Sephora at our mall.)

Me: Once you become YouTube famous, Sephora will come crawling.

(Penn has a YouTube channel with about fifty followers and growing.)

Penn: Yeah. Not quitting yet…working on a new look–a python eye!

Me: I wanna see!

Penn: Will do! Gotta study English vocab. Talk later?

Me: OK. Cya.

⸙

"Meera…?" Mom is knocking softly at my door.

"Y-e-a-h…?" I say slowly.

"Can I come in…?"

A pause. "Sure…"

My mom looks exhausted and distracted, and she's rubbing her temples. "I'm picking up an extra shift tomorrow, so I'll be late again, but I am off ALL WEEKEND! So maybe we can do something fun?" She finally smiles and looks at me hopefully.

My mom has been picking up extra shifts since last year; she says it's so she can help me pay for college. It makes me feel extra guilty and I wish she wouldn't.

"Mom, you don't have to work extra," I say. "I have told you that I can take student loans out for college. Everybody does." I am feeling simultaneously annoyed and guilty.

"Meera...I'm doing it because I want to do it. Anyway...I'll be home late tomorrow, just so you know. There is that chicken soup in the freezer or you can make something too." She pauses, looking around. "Your room looks so nice, did you do...?"

"Thanks," I interrupt her curtly. "Are we done talking? I have homework."

I look down at my backpack and begin pulling things out.

"Good night sweetie—I love you." Mom walks over and kisses me on the head.

"Love you too," I say, looking down, flipping the pages of my binder, pretending to be busy.

I wish she wasn't so focused on me. Or worried about paying for college. That's the downside of being an only. I wish she'd let herself have more fun. She has this great group of lady friends...The Brain Trust, she calls them. Whenever they come over for wine, I can tell my mom is happy and more relaxed, but they haven't been around in a while.

I grab my laptop and momentarily admire the custom case I ordered for it. The case was just delivered last week. It's the pattern of this beautiful carpet Stark makes called Antelope, which was a favorite of designer Mario Buatta's. It's spotted pattern reminds me of Sweetie's camouflage, and since I can't afford the actual carpet at this point, I thought it would be awesome to have a piece of it somehow. It felt like a splurge, and I worried it was wasteful. Grandma Max probably wouldn't ever spend money on something like this. But it makes me feel stronger somehow every time I open or close it. I'm glad I trusted it was the right thing to get. When I'm reminded that beauty make a difference, it feels good. When I doubt that, I get lost all over again.

I think I need new glasses because the board is getting fuzzy again at school. The optometrist told me that I might notice a change. I don't even want to bug my mom about that...more expenses. I hate having to ask for stuff. I hate being needy. I just want to be on my own but lately I feel weirdly uneasy. It feels a lot like I used to feel about my adoption before I traveled to Colombia. I don't want to ignore that feeling, that *inner knowing* ever again–if that's what it is. But what am I supposed to do? And if I get panic attacks just thinking of a sleepover now–how will I survive navigating a whole campus without Penn or my mom?

Just as I'm thinking about all this, I catch movement in my window. The sun is almost completely down, and I catch sight of the fox that we sometimes see crossing through our backyard. She pauses with her tail extended gracefully out behind her. Then she disappears, heading down a ravine towards the neighbor's house. I grab *The Book of Beasties* from the shelf and read an affirmation from the page on Fox. The line that catches my attention, this time, is this:

EXPOSE TRUTH
What is real? Find the piece.
And the peace.

Reading this line feels comforting. It's as if the fox is steering me towards the truth, whatever that is. I sure hope I can find it. I want to trust myself and be at peace with my mom too.

I stare at my face in the mirror as I carefully squeeze the water out of my wet curls with a flour sack dishtowel. Drying it like this keeps my curls from turning into a frizzy nightmare. When we visited Colombia a few years ago, the bossy (and a little judgy) social worker at the agency we worked with took one look at me, touched my curly hair and brown face and told me, "You are so beautiful, Meera…definitely you have mixed blood, some European and some Indian in you."

It was kind of weird to get a non-politically correct compliment while also being "assessed" like that (I never asked her in the first place) by a social worker. But she also kind of gave me something to fill in the blank of who I am. Could she be right that my ancestors were from Spain and also indigenous? I like my smooth brown skin and almond-shaped eyes.

Unlike most of the kids at my school in winter, I never need a spray tan. I love that about me. My hair is another story. I love it most when it's 40 below with zero humidity. I can actually blow dry it and flat-iron it and it will stay smooth. The rest of the year, all bets are off…it's curly, crazy and sometimes I just give up and braid it or wear it in a ponytail.

I wonder if my birth mother has hair like mine. Or what she looks like? Lorraine bought me a book last year about curly hair which annoyed me. But when I gave it to Penn, she got excited.

With her help and that book, I learned a few tricks. I still blow dry it and straighten it a lot, but now I have the option to go curly. When I do, I actually get tons of compliments on it. Lorraine's hair is flat and smooth 365 days a year...if I had been her biological daughter, maybe I could have had her hair too?

Chapter Five

I've always wondered about Nature versus nurture. Did my weird obsession with interior design and textiles come from one of my birth parents, or is it with me because I grew up around my Aunt Jill who has great style and has been importing indigenous textiles her whole life? For my Senior Honors Seminar, I'm thinking about designing an amazing one-of-a-kind fabric. I am considering a bird motif of some kind, but the design isn't coming together in my mind yet. Something is missing.

My Art teacher, Ms. Griffin, is cool, and she pretty much lets me do whatever I want. She's one of my favorites: she wears braids, a load of turquoise jewelry and converse high tops. She was born in Japan but moved here as a kid…she has a ton of cool Japanese art on the walls in her classroom. I had her for Art sophomore year too, and she was always encouraging me that I could be an artist. But I love interior design too much.

Whenever I ask Ms. Griffin which direction to go in or what I should create, she always looks at what I have and listens and then says some version of "Trust yourself, Meera." It's simultaneously annoying and flattering. I am thrilled she thinks I should trust myself, but sometimes I really want her input. I want her to tell me how to make something I'm creating better or what's missing.

In some areas of my life, I'm learning that I can trust myself. At least I've made some people happy with my work. Jess, my mom's friend and the awesome designer I worked with last summer, says I have "a good eye." Her words really encouraged me. I'd say her house's style statement is "Ralph Lauren Tomboy." It's filled with English antiques, with windowpane plaids in soft pastels and lots of rough-hewn textures thrown in. She's got two boys and six dogs, and despite all that chaos, it always feels so refined there…with candles burning, deep couches to sink into and lots of animal art, including a life-size horse photo looming over everything. That huge horse magically makes you feel like you're inside a barn. Being at Jess's house reminds me that *design is truly important.* It can make everything better.

As I set up to work in Art class today, I realize that I forgot the magazines I'd brought from home. A few of my prized *Elle Décors* had inspiring textile ideas, and they were back in my locker. Ms. Griffin gives me a hall pass. The quiet hall reeks of cedar shavings and floor wax. I spend five minutes at my locker staring at into my phone at the Pinterest board I created for the project. It's filled with textiles I love. I finger-comb my hair in my mirror and grab the magazines. I'm grateful for the quiet break.

As I stroll slowly back to Art, I pass by the Forestry class returning from outside, and as I scan, I spot Chris, the guy I asked to homecoming last winter. He's wearing a T-shirt with a silhouette of Lake Superior on it. I kind of hate myself for thinking he's hot. I wonder if he loves the Lake the way I do.

One night, the summer before Lexi died, I had just returned from Colombia and my Aunt Jill and my cousin Lexi were staying at our house with me because Mom was at a conference.

Lexi said there was a full moon, and suddenly my aunt got a wild look in her eyes. "Let's go down to Brighton Beach girls! Grab your sweatshirts."

She drove fast, rolling through stop signs, down to the lake, and we tumbled out of the car. Then we ran clattering across the beach of gray basalt stones in our flip-flops until we reached the enormous flat slabs of volcanic rock being quietly lapped by the water. The moon was huge and pinkish orange. Its glow cast an enormous shimmering "moon river" on the still lake's surface.

Aunt Jill showed us how to blow our wishes into a stone and send them into the sparkling moon river, so that the Universe would hear our requests. I made a silent wish into my stone that I could forgive my mom. So we could get along better. At the time, she was working a lot. In some ways, things did get better between my mom and me after that. I felt lighter. Not total forgiveness but closer.

I didn't want to leave the lakeshore that night. It felt like pure magic. Remembering this night makes me want to go to the beach now. I look down at my phone as I'm walking, pretending to ignore Chris walking towards me in the group of students. That's when I feel my right foot strike something with a dull thud. It's followed by a horrible loud CLAP-slap-CRASH, and I realize that I've walked right into one of those stupid folding bright yellow "wet floor" signs. *For the love of God, where did it come from?* Of course, my accident is so loud that the Forestry class people stop and stare. I look up to see Chris put a hand over his mouth like he is stifling a snicker.

Ugghhhh. Why did I ever invite him to Homecoming in the first place? Why is this my life?

I return to my table in Art, and by now I've plunged back into a full, all-over-body cringe remembering Homecoming. It started out great. I was in love with the gauzy, cream, vintage-80s Gunne Sax dress I found at a pop-up vintage clothing sale. I was trying to channel Rachel Zoe, my favorite fashion icon. I loved knowing I was wearing something nobody else would be, but I was also a little scared that it was weird. Of course, my hair and makeup were awesome thanks to Penn. She did this crazy romantic fishtail braided updo. That part was all good. But it all went south after we left the dance at the Convention Center.

Chris took me to his friend Nate's house. Outside, it was a nondescript split level. But the inside screamed: Elvis's dream gas station/sauna complete with two vintage fuel pumps, wall-mounted chrome fenders and car photos on the cedar paneling. All it needed (seriously!) was windshield washer fluid buckets and a Slurpee machine, and the kid's basement could have opened as a 7-Eleven. My group was supposed to include Penn, but she and her date hadn't arrived yet.

I was following Chris down the stairs in my long dress, carrying my backpack, hoping to find a bathroom in Elvis's time-warp sauna to change into my post-dance sweats. His friend's murky basement reeked of fake tans, enthusiastically applied Gucci Guilty and AXE body spray, clove cigarettes and sweat.

In a clipped tone, Chris told me, "Your phone's flashlight is still on–you should turn it off."

"Yeah I know..." I said, looking down.

Embarrassed and annoyed, I turned it off obediently, but it had been like my safety blanket down there in the dark basement. With the light gone, I felt even more vulnerable. I began to scan around. A few guys were gaming on the couch, while two girls, feigning curiosity, asked them questions about what they were playing. I didn't know anybody. I was trying not to be clingy but also did not want to make a fool of myself. I didn't stray from Chris's side.

I didn't exactly know what the status was between us…I mean he was cute, and I had always thought he was pretty nice. Chris and I had danced one slow dance together, but mostly we just danced as a group. I wasn't getting the vibe that he was into me, and I guess that made me even less into him. Being an only child, and never having a brother, I've never fully understood guys.

We stood awkwardly together. Just then, Penn texted me saying that Jared wanted to change his clothes, and they'd get there as soon as they could. But as they were out near Sunshine Lake, it would likely be an hour. Suddenly, I felt my heart start to race. I just couldn't wait any longer. The weirdness. The murky darkness of the sauna/basement, the overwhelming smell of it all…and my fear that I was going to do something stupid made me panic.

"Chris–ummm, can you take me home. I just don't feel good…" I offered weakly as my heart rate began to climb. I was beginning to feel like I couldn't catch a breath.

"What? You seem fine. What's wrong?" he retorted in a low voice.

He seemed annoyed. I couldn't blame him. We had just gotten there.

"Yeah–well, I'm not–and I think I might throw up, um…so I don't want that to happen," I said, with greater urgency. And I figured nobody was going to argue with a girl who was about to be sick.

Chris was now flat out irritated, like I was just a loser. "Sure–OK, but you're not going to…"

Ohmmmmygod. He thinks I'm going to puke on him. "It's not like I am going to puke *imminently*...I just think it could happen if I don't go home now," I explained, humiliated.

Chris sped off as soon as I closed the car door. Happy to be rid of me.

After his car pulled away (evidently he was not remotely chivalrous enough to be sure I made it in the door), I tripped on the curb, ripped a small hole in my awesome dress, and skinned my knee. It throbbed, and I looked down to see mud on my dress. *Ugh.*

As I entered the front door, Lorraine asked from the couch, "You're home early, Meera...was it fun?"

"Meh, it was OK. I just wasn't that into it," I replied, relieved to be back home.

"Oh no, Meera!" my mom said, wide-eyed with anxiety. She was staring at my dress. "...What's happened, sweetie?" she continued.

Then her expression turned more "Hey, I'm ON TO YOU" suspicious. "Where were you guys, Meera?!"

Lorraine was distrustful of me. I'm not a party person...but since my cousin Lexi died a few years ago, my mom has become super paranoid. No matter what I say to her, it's like she never believes me. And that sucks.

"Mom...I just tripped on the curb, that's all," I said, feeling frustrated.

"Where were you two?" she pressed, not satisfied.

"We were at Nate's house–he's a friend of Chris."

"Were his parents home?" The interrogation was continuing. "Have you been drinking, Meera Luz?" (She always uses my middle name when it's serious.)

"Oh my God, Lorraine. No!!! Just no," I answered, exasperated.

"If I find out you are drinking–or doing drugs…if I find out you're not telling the truth, I will bring you to Hazelden…and I am not kidding," my mom countered.

Mom's over-the-top remark made me think of my cousin Lexi and my dream about the white pills. Lexi was tall like her dad, loved running cross-country and country music. She had an super loud laugh and a rebellious streak. And, looking back, she had a hard time ever talking about herself. She was always more comfortable focusing on everybody else. The night she died, Lex and her fixer-upper boy-friend had no idea what they were getting into. The story goes that it was their first time trying these pills, and the stuff they bought was "cut" with another drug, fentanyl…and it was too strong. They had no idea that the pills were so dangerous. It made no sense because my cousin was beautiful and, yeah, she was a bit of a wild child. But never did I ever think something like that could happen to her.

"Lorraine, I wasn't drinking. I assure you," I repeated, hoping she'd change the subject. Then I added, "Mom, *I tripped–the sidewalk leapt up at me*–you know I'm a klutz?" I just wanted to go to my room.

Then I was trying to move past her towards my room, and she was coming even closer to me (trying to smell my breath).

"I just need to be sure, Meera," she said.

"Oh, my Goooooddddd!" I huffed, tears springing under my clenched lids. "Why can't you believe me? You make me crazy! And remember, I'm not the one who's a liar–YOU ARE."

I slammed my door behind me. A voice screamed in my head, *She's such a hypocrite! God!*

After getting out of my dress and into my pj's, I slipped beneath the covers and remembered the summer I got back from Colombia with my mom and Grandma Max. My social worker Christine at the Children's Home Society asked me if I'd speak as part of a teen panel that week at La Familia, this adoption camp I used to attend in Minneapolis every summer. The presentation would be for adoptive parents considering travel to their kid's birth country. These parents wanted to hear about our experiences.

I had agreed to do it, at the time, because I really liked Christine. But I was really nervous. I was feeling a lot of things after that trip. On the panel, there were two tenth-grade boys, a senior girl, plus me (it was the summer between my seventh and eighth grades). They went first. The boys both spoke about their searches. One of the boys met his birth family and his two siblings who had stayed behind in Colombia with their birth mother. He got to meet his siblings, who he was still connected with, but the experience left the boy wondering why it was him who got shipped away and not the other two children.

The other boy got to meet his birthmother and learned that she was a drug addict. Meeting her in person helped him to understand the dire situation she was in. He felt really sad for her, but he also realized how lucky he was to have been adopted into his family. He could no longer believe the fantasy in his mind that things would have been better if he'd stayed with her. He was still working out his feelings about his mom—wanting her to be happy.

The senior girl wasn't searching. She just spent time being a tourist in the birth country with her adoptive family. She talked about the Gold Museum of Bogota and taking the funicular to the top of Mount Monserrate.

We had a short bathroom break, and then I was up next.

My mom wasn't in the room because she was volunteering in the camp cafeteria that day, and this was good because I didn't have to worry about protecting her.

My social worker had coached me earlier. "Meera, they just want to hear your story in your words–you can't mess it up." Even so, I was so nervous that I did something I had learned to do when I was scared. I called on Sweetie. Before I went up to speak, I sat in my chair and closed my eyes and conjured her up in my mind. I begged her to be there with me. I felt her presence fill the room. Her four legs towered over the room and the whole building became encompassed and held by Sweetie. She was HUGE.

I breathed a sigh of relief and stood up. I could do this with Sweetie there.

I began, "When I was growing up, I asked my mom a lot of questions about my birth mother. What was she like? Can I see a photo of her? What do you know about her? My mom always answered with 'I don't really know much at all except that she loved you very much and someday, when you're a little older, we can learn more when we go to Colombia.' When she told me this again and again, I always had a funny feeling inside like something was wrong. It was like when you know something is off, but you aren't sure if it's just you or if it's real?

"My mom just acted strangely whenever I brought it up, and over time I learned not to talk about it because I could tell it made her very uncomfortable. My mom was prone to depression and had been very depressed at one time, so I really didn't want to do or say anything to upset her. And my dad committed suicide when I was younger, so there's that too..."

I watched a few of the parents in the audience flinch, and one put a hand to her mouth.

"Well, when we went to Bogota, we visited the orphanage where I stayed as a baby. When I met with the social worker, I was permitted to open my original adoption file and read the truth, exactly what my mom had seen fourteen years earlier. I discovered my adoptive mother had not told me the truth."

My voice had started to crack so I took a breath, then continued. "And the truth was that I had been abandoned..."

I paused for a moment. My body began to shake involuntarily.

"I'm sorry, I'm..." As I looked out and saw Christine's face, she was smiling and nodding vigorously, with both thumbs up... cheering me on.

I took another deep breath, then added, "I learned that I had been found in a cardboard box lined with blankets, a few days old, crying and hungry in a public park. There was no birthmother to meet...none that I could ever know. I will never know where I came from or who I came from. My adoptive mother had known this truth for fourteen years, but she decided to hide it from me."

By now I was crying and trembling all over. This wasn't my plan.

After a few moments of trying to get a grip on myself, I continued on. "To be lied to by the only person that matters to you?...I lost all my trust. So—if you know something about your child's history..."

I looked straight out at the group of a dozen or so parents through my tears and gazed right into their eyes. I felt a surge of confidence.

"If you know something. *Don't fucking lie to them.*"

My face was now hot, and I could see one mother visibly twitch. Next to her, Christine was beaming.

I was feeling a mild tingling all over, buzzing that I feel sometimes in my dreams…goosebumps all over. I was surprising myself.

On a roll, I continued. "Tell them the truth. My mom thought she was protecting me. Later, she told me that she had planned to tell me when I was older. She thought that I wouldn't be able to handle it after my dad committed suicide when I was nine. She said she had planned to tell me when the time was right…"

I paused for it to sink in. "But this secret-keeping didn't protect me…*instead, I felt destroyed.* I will probably never know who my birth mother is. But if I still felt that I could trust my mom, it would have made that easier…not harder. We are strong…"

I opened my hand and swept it towards the other kids on the panel and myself.

"We can handle truth," I said, with finality.

The parents in the audience were extremely quiet, and I would see a few were grabbing Kleenex out of their purses. A dad blew his nose hard. In that moment, I felt so free and so light. I felt an inner whoosh…like the part of me I lost that day in the orphanage–standing there and learning the truth about my story in Colombia–had come back to me. I was more fully Meera, a bit more of my confidence had returned.

Afterwards, there were questions, and several parents came up to tell me how brave I was. One woman said she was grateful that I told my story–she was definitely going to talk to her son about some of the details of his adoption that she had omitted. He was twelve years old and ready to hear them. My words had made her realize it was time. That made me glad. Maybe I helped somebody?

After learning that truth about my origins in Colombia, I knew that I couldn't afford to ignore my intuition. That little voice. The one that said, *Something is not right here.* Those growing antlers that pointed to the truth hidden around me.

⌇⌇⌇

The bell rings, and I gather my art stuff and put it in my folder. In Trig she passes out graded quizzes, and I see a red 40% circled at the top of my paper which blows. I had an 89% going into it, which helps. But lately this class is hard, and half the time I can't see or understand what she is doing on the board. I tried sitting closer, but the board has still been getting fuzzier. I am worried because I know I need a decent math grade to be accepted into the U of MN, my dream design school in Minneapolis.

Every time I try to imagine myself at the U next year, my brain goes into overwhelm. I can't wait to be independent, but what if I fail? What if being on my own in that huge campus is just too much for me and I hate it? Or what if I don't get in? Then what? My phone buzzes on silent mode and I look down at it.

Jess, the designer I worked for last summer, sends me a text with several photos of the new kids play area at the women's shelter downtown—it's completed now. I open up the images showing the different walls, the rug and the furnishings.

Jess: See how amazing this turned out! You are SO GOOD, Meera!

My mom had told Jess I was interested in interior design, and I finally got the guts up, last summer, to write her a letter about a job. I was thrilled but super nervous the first day. I knew little to nothing about the day-to-day workings of an Interior Design Studio, but I wanted to know everything. Thank God there was no trigonometry involved. At first, she had me organize her fabric wall by color and company, noting the samples we were missing and removing the ones that were discontinued. I loved that job! There were so many amazing samples!! My imagination went crazy thinking of all the chairs and curtains that could happen.

I must have done OK with that project, because next she assigned me the job of putting together design boards for the women's domestic violence shelter. She was creating a design proposal for their board of directors. I printed images of the furniture pieces, accessories, finishes and fabrics out on her color printer so I'd have them to glue onto poster boards to be presented at a board meeting.

Jess explained, "These kinds of projects are my feel goods, Meera...I love to create healing spaces for kids and families. Yeah we do high-end kitchens and luxury homes too, but this is when I feel like I'm really doing the work God put me here to do."

I love how confident Jess is...I want to feel that too.

As I started cutting out the images of selected furnishings and art, Jess hovered and said, "The boards of directors are kind of fussy—these presentations need to be perfect so we can show their leadership team our vision."

She gave me some examples of previous presentation boards and showed me what needed to go on my boards. "Leave a little room here, Meera." She indicated a space above the furnishings on the board. "We still need to find art for this playroom."

Yes I definitely admired Jess's confidence...she seemed to know exactly why she was here on Earth and how to do exactly what she was meant to do. She was warm and safe—just like her home. Around her I felt more capable, like anything was possible. It was different from being around my mom where I felt like things were possible, but only *some things* and not necessarily creative things. Jess broke the rules and didn't follow the path of anybody before her. She never even went to design school; she was self-taught. I was surprised when she told me that her actual degree was in social work. "I learned as I went! Each job taught me what I needed to know for the next one," she said.

I trimmed each image carefully and mounted it with double-stick tape, making sure everything was perfect. While I worked, I started thinking about this amazing artist in town named Adam Swanson. His Instagram was full of paintings of birds that were super playful and vibrant...alive somehow. His art seemed to come from that same place that Sweetie is from. Peaceful, vivid and unhurried. The art often featured owls, foxes and other wild animals—and sometimes imaginative things like penguins on the shore of Lake Superior. I thought his animals could bring a lot of life to this little windowless playroom and comfort to the kids living in such stressful homes. I shared some of his work with Jess from his Instagram feed. She loved my idea and ended up proposing an original Adam Swanson mural!

It was so wild to see a design that I had imagined inside my head become a reality. Addictive, actually. It wasn't exactly the same as I imagined...it was much better. Adam made this cool Lake Superior shoreline view with dozens of wild animals—penguins, giraffes, elephants and walruses all peeking out into the room. It was totally illogical and completely magical. The room felt so much more alive...like if these creatures could be all be living in Duluth, Minnesota, then what else might be possible?

Next summer, Jess has invited me to return as a full-time paid "intern." She knows I want to be a designer. She's going to teach me how to measure a room properly and get me started on CAD, the software they use to create construction drawings. In some ways, it seems like my dreams are already coming true, if I can just get through Trig and manage to keep up.

Though the fall colors and all leaves are gone, it's not too bitter cold yet. I decide to go for a long run around 5:00 pm, knowing Mom and I planned a late dinner after a training she has at work. I grab my phone, house key and a ten-dollar bill, just in case, and then tuck the bill and key into my sports bra. I slip my phone into the stretchy pocket at the back of the waistband and lock the door. I'm no speed demon but running helps keep me calm. I head up across the neighborhood, and I'm feeling pretty good by the time I get through the first big hill and onto the wide, flat, pea-gravel-packed Hartley nature trail. I get into my rhythm: inhale, four foot strikes, exhale, four foot strikes, inhale, exhale. Running also makes me feel more graceful, like I'm competent. I've tripped a few times on the trail but nothing as embarrassing as my basketball experience. Plus, it's just me. The team isn't depending on me.

There is something so reassuring in the cadence of running and breathing in this bright place. The grand old white pines whisper: *We've been here a couple hundred years and it's OK. Always has been. Always will be.* A few blocks into the trail, there's a little footbridge that crosses a small stream. I always stop there and put a wildflower or leaf in...it's my special wishing place. I hunt for three perfect leaves that say *pick me* as I approach the bridge.

I'm not sure about God, but I know that when I wish like this it always makes me feel lighter. Grandma Max says that praying is a kind of wishing and letting go that makes you feel calmer inside. When I remember to invite Sweetie along with me, I remember that I am never alone. And her company feels good in the same way making these little stream wishes does.

When I go with Penn to her Lutheran church or to Catholic mass with Grandma Max, I find the differences interesting. The regalia the priest or minister wears, the way the prayers are worded, and the hymns are so different and yet similar. But church can never compete with this sort of beauty: the sunlight flickering behind the fluttering, now bright-yellow birch leaves, the moss lined canyons steeply rising from shadowy creeks, and the tiny neon tangerine-colored mushrooms that rise from the dark forest floor like otherworldly visitors.

Lorraine still goes to church sometimes with my grandma. It makes Grandma Max so happy when we all go with her, but they don't make me go every week anymore. For this I am grateful. Plus, Grandma's church doesn't allow gay people or women to be ordained. Does God really think some people are more acceptable than others?

I stand by the bridge and look into the water. The stream's bottom is dark and hugged by mossy, emerald-green banks. Today's wish is "Thank you for this beautiful place, and please help me pay better attention so I can stop being such a klutz and help me do the college thing." And I add, "I want to be nicer to my mother." After making the wishes, I place the leaves as gently as I can onto the water's surface. Just watching them move so gently and surely always makes me feel better somehow. This favorite stream of mine has a tender confidence. It's not a loud roar…like the thawing Lester River crashing towards Lake Superior in April. But *it definitely knows where it's going*.

71

Even when it's mostly frozen and buried under in a foot of snow, you can feel its direction is there, if just in its tiniest trickle.

A little breeze kicks up, causing the dancing shadows of the surrounding trees' leaves on the water to flutter wildly, and a few yellow aspen leaves let go and settle onto the water's surface. I cross the bridge and reluctantly leave, slowly picking my pace back up again on the rolling trail. I keep my eyes ahead on the trail to look out for tree roots and loose rocks. I smile broadly as I pass a dad with a kid on the back seat of his bike.

I look at my watch, it's six o'clock. I decide to run back and do a loop through the University of Minnesota, Duluth campus before I head home. I'm in the best part of a run now, when everything feels effortless…like I could run forever. My breath is even, and my mind is free to wander and get good ideas. Strike, strike, strike, strike (exhale). Strike, strike, strike, strike (inhale).

I head back along the trail and zigzag through the quiet neighborhood streets until I am standing catty-corner from the UMD campus entrance. I quickly look both ways, and as I leave the sidewalk, there is a horrible screeching of tires as I jog across the pedestrian crosswalk. I'm almost to the other side of the street when it slowly registers…*I think I just missed being hit by a car.* But where did it come from? In shock, my adrenaline pumping, I keep moving. As I step up onto the opposite sidewalk, I hear my name being called.

"Meera!! Meera!!"

I turn to look, and it's my mom's friend, Mrs. Frye. Lorraine calls her Liz. She's a professor at UMD.

"Oh my God! You scared the hell out of me!" she yells, while standing by the car and putting a hand to her forehead. She motions for me to wait there at the other side of the road.

I'm suddenly annoyed and embarrassed.

I watch Mrs. Frye as she gets back into her car, pulls it over to park and puts the emergency flashers on. After exiting her vehicle, she carefully crosses the road and walks towards me. While approaching me, she has a hand on her chest and is out of breath, eyes wide.

"Meera, are you OK honey? I almost hit you. Did you see me at all?" She pauses, searching my face. "I thought you were waiting to cross and then the next thing I knew, you were walking right in front my car."

She looks back toward where I crossed and points. "I didn't have a stop sign. Didn't you see me?" This time she is sounding a little more irate than concerned.

I feel more irritated, while thinking, *It's not my fault you almost ran me over–Jesus!*

Wanting to be polite, I begin, "Oh my gosh. I'm so sorry, Mrs. Frye. I must have been lost in my thoughts. I get like that sometimes when I'm running–sorry...I didn't mean to scare you. Head in the clouds, I guess."

I just want to get out of there.

"It's OK," she tells me. "I mean...I am so glad I saw you in time, but be careful OK?"

"Yeah, I will for sure," I say, feeling a weight pressing down on my chest.

Mrs. Frye turns back to her car and I continue onto campus. My knees feel kind of shaky after a few blocks, and suddenly I feel extremely weak. I don't feel like running anymore. I'm crashing down from the adrenaline rush, and it feels like anything could happen. I want to cry. I walk more slowly and then stop, put my hands on my thighs, letting my head hang down between my legs and try to calm myself. There's a little ant there on the sidewalk I notice carrying a tiny grain of something. I watch him for a moment. He's just got that one task to do and I sigh feeling a little better. As I stand upright again, I notice the sign for the Tweed Museum of Art and decide I might as well go in...just to catch my breath and settle down for a moment.

As I push open the door to the museum, the expansiveness and hush of the all-white art space–so airy and bright–offers itself. I've been coming here since I was a little kid with Grandma Max. She's on their board. One of their focuses is Native American art and craft. It looks like I'm the only person in the whole place, except for the gift shop lady and a guard. I head upstairs for a little more privacy, and to look at the cases of Anishinaabe crafts. The floral beading always inspires me. Fat green leaves and wide flat jewel toned petals on a velvety black background. They remind me a little of the Shipibo embroidered cloth I brough home from Colombia. The ones with the designs that come from the singing plants.

The idea of a plant singing a song that could be translated into a design I could see is pretty amazing. If the local plants and trees here could sing, the lupine, cedar trees or birch, I wonder what the stitched design would look like? I love these moccasins and bags so much. It makes me wonder if my birth mom or her family were artists or craftspeople. These pieces have that same quality...of Nature itself...like my wishing brook...a cheerful fearlessness. I snap a few photos with my phone. Seeing those designs made me feel better somehow. Beauty does that.

As I leave that gallery and enter the dimmer hallway, I can see through the windows that it's already dark outside. Without consulting me, my heart begins to pound. I look at my watch: 6:50 pm.

Soon I push on the glass door at the entrance and step out into the courtyard, and I wait for my eyes to adjust. It gets a bit brighter. I can see the floodlights illuminating the sidewalks, but farther away from the building lies inky blackness. Total unknown. I can hear the voices of a few students passing in the courtyard. I don't know how many streetlights there are between here and home, but I know the little neighborhoods aren't so well lit.

I feel weak all over again. *What's my problem?* I could probably get home safely, but I'm still feeling shaky and weak. And more unsure of myself than usual. Plus, Mom is always telling me not to run in the dark alone. I lift my phone up, put it on flashlight mode and shine it on the ground to test it. Can I make it home like this? Then I notice my battery is on 6%...*figures.*

I text Penn.

Me: I'm stranded.

Penn: What's up?

Me: I'm stuck at UMD and need a ride.

Penn: Where are u? Can u wait a lil. I'm out at Jared's.

Me: UMD–the Tweed Museum…I can wait.

Penn: B there ASAP.

Twenty minutes later I get her arrival text. I move towards the glow of her headlights, climb in the car and sigh.

"Thanks for coming," I say with relief.

"No worries. One of these days' girl…you're gonna get your license and it'll be you saving me! What were you doing here?"

"It got dark so fast…and I just didn't want to run home alone in the dark. I panicked a little…it's like my anxiety is getting worse."

I don't tell her about my earlier near miss with the car and how it makes me worry about everything. I know she will just tell me I'm OK. I just want to get home.

"You were kind of walking funny just now, are you OK?" asks Penn.

"I was?" I say, wondering if it's that obvious that I'm anxious. Or is there something else weird about me?

She continues, "Yeah...like you were hesitating. Like my mom's horse Paulo does when he has to cross over something new or unknown, he acts afraid to step." Penn smiles. Her mom keeps the horse up at a stable because she grew up on a farm. He's super sweet.

"I think I'm just kind of shaky. My run was pretty long...I'm tired," I offer.

Then a part of me impulsively decides to plunge in and share more with her. "I guess I'm also kind of freaking out because of thinking about next year and college," I say to Penn. "What do you do when it gets dark outside and you're alone at the library or something?"

"Well, I wouldn't run home in the dark alone either...I'm paranoid that some guy is going to jump out of nowhere. I've watched too many *Hallmark Channel* movies...I think you're fine, Meer," Penn reassures me.

I don't feel fine and so her words kind of make me feel worse. Penn pulls over to the curb and puts the car in neutral.

I blink my eyes and look out. I must have forgotten to put the porchlight on.

"Home sweet home. Text me later?" asks Penn.

"Will do," I reply.

"Thanks for the ride," I say before shutting the car door.

As Penn pulls away, I put my phone flashlight on and use it to illuminate the walkway up to my porch. By the front door, I feel around in my sports bra for the key...I feel the ten-dollar bill, but no key. I pull the bra up and out hoping for the key to drop out, but it doesn't. It must have slipped out somehow. *Fuck.*

I head back down the porch stairs, with my phone now showing 2%. I make my way slowly down the overgrown side path around the house towards the back door and, after a moment of flashing the light around, find the fake plastic rock in the flower bed. It rattles dully when I shake it—thank God I put it back the last time. I start to slide open the back of the fake rock when my phone dies completely. I'm plunged into pure black. My heart starts to pound. The darkness had always been challenging but, somehow, this is a new level...I shut my eyes for a moment, willing them to adjust. When I reopen them after a minute, I look down and still can't see a thing.

I slip the black plastic slider off slowly and put my fingers where I think the key should be. And then the key falls from the holder landing with a musical ping onto the sidewalk. I begin to feel my way along the ground with my hands searching for the key when I hear a crunching of dry leaves. Something or someone is coming towards me. I wish Penn hadn't mentioned bad guys. Whatever it is, it's coming slowly and has now stopped. There had been bears back in our yard last fall. If it's a bear, am I supposed to freeze or make noise? My heart is now helplessly hammering away in my chest,

"Hello?" A low but friendly male voice has suddenly broken the silence. "Is that you, Meera? I saw somebody back here in the dark and didn't realize it was you. So I came over to see what was going on—there have been some break-ins in Kenwood, so..."

It's Steve from next door. I let out a sigh of relief and relax.

"Uh yeah…hi Steve. I dropped my door key and I can't seem find it."

I look up, hoping he would understand. He steps closer.

"Oh, I see it right there, at your feet," says Steve brightly.

"Where?" I ask a bit helplessly.

"Oh sorry, I thought you had it. It's right there," he repeats. Then there's a pause…

"If you open your hand, can I give it to you?" he asks slowly.

Suddenly, feeling like an idiot, I rise from my crouch with my palm open. He places the key in my hand.

"Thanks! I'm good now," I say, trying to act cheerful.

"OK. You sure? I didn't mean to scare you–I was just checking that everything was OK."

"Yes, thanks so much, Steve. I'm good now," I reply quickly, hoping he will just go.

"Alright–we're here if you need us," he tells me, then strolls away.

I pretend to dust myself off–buying time. Then I began to feel, exploring the ground with the tip of my shoe where the landscape border rocks are, and eventually get to the back door. I use the tip of the key to feel along where I think the keyhole is and, eventually, the key slips in. I unlock the door. I feel along the inside wall and flip the switch on, and light floods the hall. *Halle-fucking-lujah. Home at last.*

⁓ℓℓℓℓℓℓ⁓

About a half hour later, Mom is standing and staring at the fridge's slim contents, while talking to herself. "What are we going to have for our late dinner…?"

She starts hauling out some peppers and a bag of lettuce, bringing them to the cutting board.

"How was your day?" she asks.

I sit down at the kitchen table with pita chips and guacamole.

I look up. "Good–hey um–I know you're busy–but can you get me another eye appointment? It's getting kind of hard to see the board in Trig again...and I really want to do well in that class. I need it for my pre-reqs for next year. The doctor said to come back if things changed?"

My mom stops chopping, looks at me and says, "Sure–but I can't imagine you already need a new prescription. That was only two months ago when we saw him?"

She throws the peppers into the frying pan.

"I know but I'm squinting again, even in the front row. Remember he said to come back if my vision changed?" I remind her.

"Got it–I will get you the first appointment," she agrees.

My mom grabs a nearby cell phone to add it to her to-do list app.

"Thanks." Phew, that was easier than I thought it would be.

"Sweetie, *is everything else OK?*" she asks in a tone that I know is heading towards nowhere good.

Oh...God. Please God, don't let her bring up adoption.

"It's fine. *Everything is fine,*" I say with definiteness as I stand up to leave.

"Hey...before you go back in your room, I ran into Linnea, who has the driving school, and she said there are openings for the behind-the-wheel stuff you still need?"

Lorraine looks up at me from the stove.

"Yeah, OK...I'll look at my schedule," I tell her, chewing the inside of my cheek.

I'm still the only person I know in my group of friends without my license. Yet another reminder that I'm a freak. The idea of being strapped in and in control of a huge moving thing like a car seriously terrifies me. Even more than the dark.

"OK, well...she's ready for you when you are."

Lorraine throws the cooked pasta into the pan with the peppers.

"Yes, I got it. I'll let you know."

I need to face my fears...no more staying in my comfort zone. I need to learn to drive. I need to go away to college next fall. I also might need to walk home in the dark. I can feel my cousin Lexi encouraging me. Something keeps holding me back...it doesn't feel right yet. Is it my growing antlers, my intuition...or is it just plain old hesitation out of fear? I don't want to get stuck in my comfort zone, or I might never get to feel the magic like I did that day when Lex got me to get out on the paddleboard. It felt like walking on water. Pure freedom. I definitely want more of that.

Chapter Six

My mom pulls up in front of school at 11 am on Friday, just before lunch. I slide into the passenger seat and yank the door shut.

Lorraine hands me a hot drink in a paper cup with protective sleeve. "Got you a mocha from Amity," she says, smiling at me.

"Thank you," I reply. "What's the occasion?"

Lorraine is not one to splurge on fancy coffee drinks often.

"I just know you like them and wanted to do something nice." Mom smiles.

She turns out of the school parking lot and tells me, "So, I ran into Liz, Mrs. Frye? My friend who teaches at UMD? I was at the grocery today, and she said she nearly ran you over on campus last week?" My mom says this slowly, as if she had been waiting to mention it until now.

"In her car, Meer? She said you weren't watching when you crossed the road? She said it seemed like you never saw her coming?" Her voice is getting a little higher and tighter with each word.

Feeling embarrassed, I respond, "I *was* watching...I just didn't see her. I must have been thinking about other stuff. I *did* look both ways before I crossed but somehow...I told her I was sorry."

"Liz said there was no stop sign. If she hadn't stopped, you might have been seriously hurt. I just really worry that if you don't pay attention—one day something bad is going to happen…you need to be more careful."

She steps on the brake and halts the car at the red light.

"Meera…?" she presses, looking over at me now.

I shrug. Then I'm back at that street corner and reliving it a little. My body is tensed up, and a weight is growing on my chest. It is feeling harder to catch my breath.

"She said you looked pretty shaken up too, Meera. *Why didn't you tell me* what happened, Sweetie?"

The dam inside me breaks. Hot tears rise and I lay into her. "Do you think I want to get hit by a car? I was paying attention. Seriously—I LOOKED BOTH WAYS. And why do I have to tell you everything, but yet you hold things back from me? It was not a big deal, OK?" I am feeling defensive and wish we could change the subject.

"Meera, if you're talking about your birth mom, I have told you I'm sorry about holding back the truth. It was wrong of me. But…I'm just worried about you! When Liz told me this, I don't know—it scared me."

"The light is green by the way. Go!" I command, hoping she'll change the subject.

My mom turns forward and puts her foot on the gas again. I twist in my seat towards the window and drink my coffee, as I stare at the houses whizzing by. I pretend to scratch my eye, wiping away an escaped tear.

We ride the remaining blocks in silence (thank God!) and enter the parking structure. After a few moments of smugness, a part of me regrets lashing out at her. I silently decide I will try harder to be better. My mom seems to be willing to let this thing cool off for now, and she doesn't try to reopen the conversation.

After checking in at the reception desk, we find chairs in the waiting room of the eye doctor's office, and I flip through the latest *HGTV Magazine*, hoping to find a decent design idea. My mom gets up to go to the bathroom. When finished with scanning the magazine, I stare out at the view. From up here on the fourth floor, Lake Superior shimmers in the morning light. As I watch, a gust of wind strikes its silvery surface. A huge section of the lake is transformed into a glittering, hammered pewter oval that expands westward toward the aerial bridge. How effortlessly it changes. Never the same ever. Always beautiful.

I close my eyes for a moment and make a wish, standing on my secret wishing bridge. I drop an imaginary bright orange maple leaf into the stream, which I then can see gently moving calmly forward in the cool green shade.

Help me be different. Nicer?

"Meera?"

I open my eyes, and I see a woman in scrubs standing in the doorway and looking towards me. I stand up and approach her.

"How are you today?" she asks reflexively, holding the door open for me.

"I'm good, but...umm...my mom is with me. She just went to the bathroom?"

"No problem, I can let her know you're inside when she comes out and bring her in too. My name is Taylor."

"OK, thanks."

In an examination room, we go through the usual list of eye questions, and I do my best to read the letters she projects on a screen.

As she types into the computer afterwards, Taylor reports, "You're correct, Meera. Your prescription does seem to have changed just a little bit."

She pushes herself away from the desk and stands up. "Dr. Sill should be in soon." And she leaves.

After a few minutes there is a vigorous knock, and the doctor enters.

"Hi Meera."

He washes his hands at the sink. Dr. Sill seems young, and he's wearing a crisp pink oxford shirt. He has sparkling brown eyes.

He sits down and grins at me. "So, Meera, I just saw you not too long ago?" Still smiling he turns to look at his computer screen. "And you feel like your vision is a bit worse? Is that right?" He continues to stare towards the screen.

"Yeah, I'm having a little trouble with the board again at school," I reply.

"OK, let's take a look."

He turns the lights way down with a dimmer switch on the wall. I worry that he can tell I think he's cute. I'm blushing and glad it's dark. He sits on his wheeled stool and brings the eye machine thingy down close to my eyes. We are face-to-face—just inches away. He smells like fabric softener.

"Meera, take this…"

"Take…?" I ask apologetically, not sure what he means.

"It's to cover your eye…"

I reach out my hand, and I fumble to grasp the plastic eye-covering he's handing me.

"OK Meera, cover your right eye, and tell me what you can see of the letters ahead? Start at the top row."

"E, F, P, T, O, Z...L...P...C?...O?"

"OK, try covering the other eye and repeat. Just read as far as you can go."

"OK," I reply, squinting towards the chart.

We go through many more cycles of checking and reading. Then he pauses and pulls the eye machine away from my face.

"You're a senior, aren't you?" he asks. "Are you headed to college?"

"Yeah...I'm thinking about going to U of MN," I answer out loud. *But will I actually go?* I ask myself.

"Ahh...good choice. I did my undergrad there. Great city, Minneapolis."

He swings the machine to the side. He does a few more tests with me covering my eyes and asking me to tell him how many fingers he is holding up as I stare straight ahead.

"It looks like your prescription is going to need to be a little stronger. It's not a really dramatic change, but it's worth getting the new lenses I think. Now I need to take a look at the back of your eyes...so this light is going to be kind of bright."

He brings the machine towards my eyes and I set my chin on the rest. We are so close...he smells really nice. I hold my coffee breath, worried it might smell bad. I'm also relieved. I'm not crazy...I *do* need new glasses.

"Meera..." His voice sounds lower and slower. He clears his throat and seems different suddenly. "...how well do you see at night...in the dark?"

Before I could answer, there was another knock at the door and the nurse delivers my mom into the darkened room.

"Sorry, I apologize..." she says.

"Have a seat...that's OK," Dr. Sill assures Mom quickly, still focused on my exam. My handsome doctor's voice is now definitely lower and darker. His beast mode, CrossFit confidence seems to have drained from him. He resumes shining a hideously bright light into the back of my eye.

"So, you're Meera's mom?" he inquires, sweeping the light back and forth across my eye.

"Yes, I am," my mom replies warmly.

"So I was just asking Meera how well she sees in the dark," Dr. Sill says as he finishes scanning my right eye and then flips over to the left. Nobody had ever asked me that question before.

"I don't see very well in the dark and it's been getting worse lately," I report, curious why he's asking.

"Well, none of us see as well at night as we do in the day..." my mom interjects without being asked.

Ignoring my mom, he continues questioning me. "Uh huh. Like at night, do you ever have trouble or bump into things?" he says, moving the bright light around and then holding it still.

"*All the time*," I offer. I'm feeling surprised and mildly excited as he seems to understand my situation.

He pulls the machine away from my face and then raises the light in the room with the dimmer.

"So Meera, what I am seeing in the back of your eye is something unusual. I want to put some special drops in to dilate your pupils–that will give me a chance to really see what's going on, OK?

The drops kind of burn for a few seconds and then we have to wait for them to work."

He hands me a tissue and then puts the stinging drops in each eye.

"One more question Meera, before I leave and let those drops work, can you see the stars...when you're outside at night?"

I could remember seeing the stars many times–camping, on 4th of July, and at Park Point as a little kid. But last summer Penn and Jared and I and some of Jared's friends were up at Pike Lake in his backyard, and everybody was talking about how bright the stars were. I couldn't see them. I never said anything.

"I have seen the stars, but there was one night last summer when I couldn't see them, but my friends could. I could see the moon, but not the stars."

My mom interrupts me, with exasperation. "Meera–of course you can see the stars!"

"Mom! *I'm not lying*," I say, simultaneously embarrassed and also trying not to sound rude. I can't believe she's doubting me.

Dr. Sill stands there in the doorway, not seeming to know what to say to us.

"OK...let's give the drops a chance do their work and I'll be back in a few minutes." He seems relieved to be able to exit.

Mom and I sit in silence for a few moments.

"Meera..." my mom starts to try to say something.

"Don't even talk. *Just don't,*" I reply, cutting her off.

It stings that she corrected me...does she think I would lie about that? We sit in silence, and so many emotions are welling up inside of me. I'm tired of everybody doubting me...of doubting myself, and I feel something huge is happening. And I'm a little scared.

My mom sighs, as if she's been thinking, and offers, "Meera, I just want to say–it's not that I don't believe you, but I'm just surprised...you never said you couldn't see the stars before."

WTF. Before I can respond, Dr. Sill returns, closing the door softly behind him.

"OK, let's take another peek," he says.

I wipe my eyes with the crumpled tissue; he dims the lights again and brings the machine between us. I reflexively set my chin back into the plastic rest. The light is even brighter this time. It's hard to not want to squeeze my eyes shut. My eyes ache as the light enters. He looks into both eyes for a really long time in complete silence. He pulls the machine away from my face and slowly turns the room lights back up again.

"So Meera and...I'm sorry Meera's mom–your name?" His whole attitude feels slightly hesitant and more serious now. Where has my handsome champion gone?

"Lorraine, it's Lorraine," my mom says, her voice now more businesslike.

He turns to me. "So Meera, I believe that you have something rare...we will have to do a bit more testing to confirm, but I am fairly certain given your difficulty with darkness and your history...I believe you have Retinitis Pigmentosa. What happens in RP is that the light sensitive part of your eye progressively degenerates. So that is why I asked you about the stars. Not being able to see the stars is a classic history for RP. As your peripheral vision begins to be reduced, you develop tunnel vision. And that's what causes the tripping and bumping into things. I was looking back at your whole chart and saw that a few years back you were evaluated by neurology for clumsiness...that could have been the beginning of this peripheral vision loss."

I'm thrilled he seems to have figured out what is going on with me but "vision loss" and "degenerates" don't sound so good.

He continues on. "When I tested you today, I saw that you have already lost quite a bit of your peripheral vision in both eyes. In RP, for some reason, we don't know why, this disease often accelerates in adolescence....we suspect it's hormonal."

My mom interrupts. "So what are you telling us...I mean what can we do?"

He continues patiently. "I'm going to get to that...what this all means is we now have an explanation for why you've been bumping into walls and..."

He is trying to finish, but my mom nervously interrupts. "She practically got hit by a car the other day!"

He looks at my mom and nods patiently. "Yes, not having peripheral vision can be dangerous–especially when you aren't aware of it. So, Lorraine...here..."

He takes his hands and makes them into open fists as he instructs her. "Take your fists and make them into cylinders, like this, and put them up to your eyes like goggles."

My mom obeys and, as I watch, she begins to move her head side to side.

Dr. Sill continues. "This is the world that Meera is seeing... more or less. And at night her vision is substantially more limited."

My mom continues to pivot her head around testing this new vision simulation.

He adds, "So if someone or something, a car or a bike, approaches from either side..."

He takes his hand and slices the air next to my mom's head.

"...Meera can't see it–unless she actively moves her eyes and scans around. Also, anything immediately beneath her on the ground at her feet or above her head will be out of her field of vision."

Dropping her hands back into her lap helplessly, my mom seems to be thinking. "So...what can we do?" Mom presses him. "And why didn't we catch this earlier? I mean I'm a nurse and I've been taking her to doctors. But..." There's a sharpness in her voice. She's in full-on Hummingbird warrior fierce mode now.

I'm thinking, *Let the man talk!*

He continues, more slowly. "So Meera's history is actually pretty typical. RP often takes a few years before we detect it...and it's because the physical findings are subtle at first. There isn't much on exams until things have progressed. The difficult part of this is that the disease is progressive. It takes, typically, several years to decades for significant vision loss to occur. And, unfortunately, we don't have a cure for this yet. Even if we had caught it earlier, unfortunately, it wouldn't have changed anything...we still wouldn't have much to offer."

"So what's our next step?" my mom asks, sounding only slightly calmer.

"Well, we do know that it's inherited. So, if Meera has other siblings, they should be examined too, to see whether they are having vision troubles or not."

"She's adopted and we don't know of any siblings..." Mom replies quickly.

"OK, well, the good news, Meera..." He turns towards me. "...is that there are lots of assistive technologies that can help make things easier for you. Knowing your vision is limited, you can make choices that will enable you to be safer and feel more comfortable. And there are proactive things you can do too that can help you in the future."

My mom grabs my hand, and even though I don't want her to touch me right now, I let her hold it because I get the sense she needs to hold onto something. I am trying to take this all in. I feel numb.

"Do you have any questions for me, Meera?" Dr. Sill asks me gently.

Slowly, I begin. "So what does this mean? I mean...my vision is going to get worse and...you said it's progressing. I mean I was hoping to go to college next fall?" I am worried that this somehow will stop me from going. I'm suddenly imagining a never-ending curtain of darkness descending between me and the world. I can feel tears coming.

He says, "With RP, there are no rules, but typically it's a slow progression over many years. Often, a decade, but sometimes longer. But there are no guarantees about this. And I think it's likely that, with some accommodations, you'll be able to do just fine at college. We have a really amazing group of resources in town, and the nurses will connect you with them. And in school, you should be able to get some help too. This isn't easy to hear, I know, but there's lots of help."

Slow progression...does he mean blindness?

My mom interrupts again. "And what about research—are there any therapies or trials at all...or at Mayo?"

He answers, "There may be ongoing trials, but I am not the one who can help you there. During your appointment with Dr. Galbraith, the retinal specialist—she's the expert—she'll be able to go over that. I know some of the things that can be helpful in RP are improving the lighting in the environment and large print books.

Let's get your next appointment scheduled and then you can bring all of your questions to the expert, OK?"

We exit out onto the rooftop parking lot of the clinic. The sun is shining so brightly, my eyes tear up and ache. I squint hard as I dig in my coat pocket and unroll the cheesy plastic eye shield they gave me and put it onto my face. I probably look really stupid, but I'm relieved. With it, I can open my eyes again.

Our car is parked facing Lake Superior, which is still ablaze with a wave of shimmering light and, instantly, I realize that at some point in the future, I won't be able to see this gob smacking beauty. How can this be? It feels like all the air has been sucked out of my lungs, and a lump grows in my throat as I draw in a sharp breath.

My mom unlocks the car doors. The natural world seems to glitter and shimmer and, somehow, it's even more beautiful than it was before, from the waiting room window…as if the lake is showering me right now with an extra burst of beauty because at some unknown point in the future it will all be gone.

I open the car door and climb in.

I feel simultaneously devastated, and also grateful. It's insanely freeing to know that I'm not crazy. There's an explanation now: for my clumsiness and my inability to navigate in the dark. I'm also freshly aware of all the insanely beautiful things I've seen in my short life: the amazing fabrics, rooms, trees and flowers. I got to see

Colombia! I'm suddenly acutely grateful that I wasn't born blind. A part of me, an extremely calm part says, *This, too, will be OK.* And I feel Sweetie close by…her cool nose leans in to touch the space between my eyes in the center of my forehead. As I close my eyes, I feel so deeply connected with her…with everything. A dark violet light pulses in the center of my forehead. I've sensed this pulsating sensation before, and it's made me curious. *Is it from Sweetie?* This experience always makes me feel connected to the calmest part of me.

"Meera, you need to buckle your seatbelt," my mom says, and as I do, the car's chiming bell falls silent.

As Mom drives down Superior Street, parallel to the lake, I stare out the window.

My mom opens up hesitantly. "Meera…oh my gosh, I feel just terrible. All those times you were telling me you couldn't see in the dark…I didn't *know*. All the doctors saying there was nothing wrong. I am so sorry…I feel like I've failed you. Like we all have. I hope you can forgive me."

At a stoplight she turns to look at me and I stare straight ahead. Tears are spilling down my cheeks.

She continues talking at the red light. "The pediatrician we saw a few years ago literally took me aside and told me that you were…" She uses her hands to make air quotes. "…*seeking attention* with your behavior, and I believed him? I should have believed you."

I can tell she's feeling horrible.

"You didn't fail me," I say slowly. "But I do wish you would have believed me."

It feels good to speak my truth and to have her acknowledge the mistakes she made. I'm feel strangely calm. A little like that underwater feeling I had after the dream of the white tablets the night before

Lexi died. Something else seems to have taken over, momentarily. *Something that wants to help.*

As I stare out the car window, I'm flooded with memories that I'm newly making sense of. Like that time last winter when I was unable to read a menu in the dimly lit restaurant and my phone (my flashlight) was dead. So I just parroted somebody else's order, rather than asking for help to read it. I'd given up trying to explain to people that I couldn't see in the dark. I quit asking for help because nobody else seemed to be experiencing the world the way I did. All the times I had tried to tell my mom that *I was paying attention.* I just really never saw the wall. Or the shoes on the floor or whatever it was. Now that I had the explanation for all of it, it was a strange relief. I wasn't mad at my mom either. How could she have known?

Finally, settled beneath the comforter in bed with my door closed, the tears come. Sobs. The thought of being helpless and utterly dependent on others makes my chest ache. At some point, I won't be able to see the lake. Or Mom's face. I glance around my room looking at all of the things I love. The graceful cedar trees bend and dance in the wind outside my window. In this moment, they suddenly feel so significant and beautiful. Their curved, soft fronds of green. A canopy of arching branches that shelters my room. The cedars, I notice, seem to have a different opinion of what's happening to me. For them, everything is fine. They just continue to wave and waggle in time with the gusts, casting shadows on my floor. Do they have a song too? If they do, I imagine it sounds like comfort and gentleness.

When my wave of tears subsides, I begin to think more practically about how the future will be…how it will all work. Determined on some level to deal with this new reality, I consider my prospects. My brain begins to fill with thoughts. *Will any guy ever want me…a girl who's going blind? Is it happening because I haven't fully forgiven my mom? Is this a kind of punishment? Why can't I be nice like Penn is to her mom? Does my birth mother or father have Retinitis Pigmentosa too? It's genetic. Is this why she couldn't raise me?* For a moment I imagine my birth mother as a helpless and vulnerable blind woman, and I feel pity for her. *If this is a kind of punishment from God, <u>what do I need to fix it</u>? If I'm a better, kinder Meera, then is it possible to reverse the damage or could the disease progress more slowly?*

Fresh hot tears rise and the pressure in my sinuses is building. My head throbs. I try to imagine myself blind. I get kind of a Stevie Wonder/Meera mash-up. In this image, I'm smiling idiotically, my head is shaking and nodding, my curly hair is frizzy and style-less, and I have a huge zit which I haven't bothered to put cover-up on… because I am fucking BLIND. Or maybe I could be more like the blind girl on the show we used to watch on DVDs at Grandma Max's cabin in the summer. Mary in *Little House on the Prairie.* That's it! I'll be perfect and kind. Better. But how?

At least Stevie Wonder is a musical genius. We still have all of my dad's Stevie records from college. Me? I'm not even a high school graduate yet. Beyond him, I can't think of anybody blind I even know. And when I go completely blind, will it be black as night *all the time* (and terrifying) or will I still see something? Anything?

Blind interior designer…yeah no, *that's not happening.* It feels cruel that the thing I love the most is being taken from me…my love of beauty. Why? It's the one thing I feel like I know how to do. That

I want to do? Isn't that my purpose? My stomach tightens as if I'm defending it against a punch. But also, a weird willingness and determination is growing inside of me: to see what I can do now. A quiet power. I want to live as well and as BIG as I can until I can't see any longer, and then I guess I'll deal with that when it happens.

I suddenly remember my sixth grade book report that I did on Helen Keller (who was not only blind, but also deaf)...the fucking IRONY! I remember skimming the book and watching the movie, instead, to get the main points. My favorite scene is where her teacher is signing the letters for "water" into Helen's hand as water pours into it from a pump, and she finally connects the signing with the meaning of the word. *Will it be that hard? Why did I choose her? Will I find a guide like she had...my own Anne Sullivan?* My worst thought is this: I will end up alone. In a world of darkness, devoid of beauty.

I think back to my waiting room wish...*to be different, nicer.* This Retinitis thing is terrible news, but in a way finding out I have an actual disease also feels like an answer...like a beginning. It also proves to my mom that I am not a liar or a faker. I'm vindicated. Something *was the matter* all along...and strangely, that is reassuring. It's more evidence that I can trust myself to know certain things. My antlers of intuition exist. I knew something was wrong; I just didn't know what it was until now.

All of a sudden, Sweetie is here. I turn onto my side and curl up with her around me. I close my eyes and relax my body. We become one. For a moment, I'm perceiving the world and everything through Sweetie's eyes, and I feel peace. I never have to handle anything alone. I still have no idea what all of this means for my future, but I feel calmer.

What am I gonna do? I ask her.

There's nothing to do now, but when there is…trust yourself. You will know.

I text Penn.

Me: Good news/bad news.

Penn: What's up?

Me: I'm not crazy. The eye doctor says my retinas are screwed up.

Penn: I remember retinas from cow eye dissection? Pigmented part, right? How are they screwed up?

Me: It's called RP (Retinitis Pigmentosa). Bad news…can't fix them…I'm going to go blind.

Penn: Whattt? Oh my God, Meera…I am so sorry!

My phone starts buzzing. Penn wants Facetime.

I decline the call and text back.

Me: I'm too tired to Facetime. Let's talk tomorrow, KK? I just wanted you to know.

Penn: I am so sorry. OK. Love you! Talk tomorrow.

⁓ഝഝ⁓

Saturday morning, my phone begins buzzing early. It's Penn, wanting to Facetime.

"Hey, how's it going…I know it's kind of early," she says softly.

As I hold the phone up, my crazy hair is splayed out on my pillow, and now I can see how puffy my eyelids are. Penn, ever the morning person, is already looking fabulous with her shoulder-length, thick black hair already styled perfectly into beachy waves.

"Oh Meera, I am so sorry…what did they tell you? At the doctor's?" she says with much kindness in her eyes.

Somehow, it feels like old times. Before she met Jared. Ever since she's been dating him, it's felt like our friendship isn't as important, which hurts. I've tried to be understanding, but I honestly don't know what she sees in him. She could do so much better.

"Thanks." I start to cry as I reenter the scene at the doctor's office again in my mind. At the same time, it feels so good to hear her kind voice and words. They make everything temporarily OK.

"Hang on..." I tell her as I set the phone down to grab a tissue and then continue. "They didn't say much...like it might take a while to lose all of my vision...like ten years." My voice is cracking. "But they aren't sure. I'm seeing a specialist soon."

"This just *sucks*," Penn replies, her voice breaking. She brushes a tear away.

"It really does." I nod and blow my nose with the now balled-up tissue.

Penn says carefully, "I hope you don't mind but I stayed up late doing a little research–there is this amazing YouTuber with Retinitis. The same thing you have. She's just a little older than us and she's got a ton of subscribers. A TON. And it's weird, you wouldn't even know she is blind? I really want you to check her out because she talks about a lot of stuff." She ends with a smile as if she thinks everything is going to be fine.

"Promise me one thing," I interrupt her sunny enthusiasm.

"Anything! You got it," she responds eagerly.

"You will not let me look horrible or go around with bad hair and makeup?" I ask with serious concern. "I know it sounds vain, but right now all I can think of is when you're blind you have no fucking idea how you look."

"You could never not be beautiful with those pillowy-pouty Meera lips and your gorgeous almond eyes. I will make it my duty to be your beauty professional. And trust me Meera, when you see this girl on YouTube, you will see what I mean...I mean she is legally blind, but you can't tell...she's so stinkin' cute..." Her voice trails off.

I offer more information. "The doctor said every case is different. So I'm really hoping I can keep my vision for a long time? All I can think of is about all of the beautiful things I love that, at some point, I won't be able to see. Will I even remember them?" I feel weak just thinking about this, and the tears keep silently rolling down my cheeks.

"Oh my gosh—I can't even imagine, Meera...it's horrible," Penn consoles warmly.

"Do you know how he figured it out?" I say, remembering the conversation with Dr. Sill. "He asked me a weird question: *Do you see the stars at night?* Instantly, I thought back to last summer at Pike Lake. Remember when you guys were all talking about the stars? That night we had a fire? I stayed quiet because I honestly couldn't see what you were talking about. I did see the moon but that was it. I remember seeing stars as a kid, but that night—*nothing*. I didn't think much of it because...I figured I needed new glasses or something. I guess that's how he knew exactly what I had...the clumsiness and stars thing." As I finished, I got lost in remembering that night.

"I remember..." Penn tells me.

"Ughhh...and will I ever be able to go out at night alone? When I don't have you around or my mom around? And..." My future worries are snowballing. "Once I am blind...will I never be able to be normal? Do normal stuff? I don't want to be a burden...I just want to be normal?"

I roll on my stomach, shifting the phone and trying to find a more comfortable position.

Penn tries quickly to reassure me. "Meera Townsend, you could never be a burden. You are awesome. I know this probably doesn't help, but I just know that you are going to figure this out and I'm here with you."

Penn sounds so confident. I want to believe her.

"Thanks. This is so weird," I say, feeling better that she's not freaked out like I am.

"And today is a day that you do not have to endure a bad hair day and that's one thing *we can control.*"

Penn always looks at the bright side, but right now that feels terrible. I need to wallow.

"This whole thing absolutely sucks Meer, and if it's OK, I'm coming over soon, so get ready. Beachy waves can help, and I'm hoping you'll let me do your hair? I want to add more pics for my portfolio."

"Sounds good to me—as you can see…" I point to my bed head. "…I'm in need of your services."

Chapter Seven

Lorraine knocks lightly. "Can I come in, Meera?"

"Yeah–it's not locked," I respond softly.

"How are you doing?" she asks.

"OK, Penn is coming over this morning, to hang out," I reply.

"I just wanted to see how you were doing...and to say how sorry I am for not believing you all this time about your vision. I mean I thought that after the doctors kept saying there was nothing wrong that I just needed to be positive–to help you. Oh my gosh, I had no idea! I feel just terrible, Meera. I hope you can forgive me."

My mom looks worried.

"It's OK, Mom," I say in a reassuring tone.

I sigh, as I get up to go to my closet to pick out some clothes to wear.

I don't have the bandwidth right now to take care of her too, but I try. "I'm just glad that it wasn't all in my head. I felt kind of crazy for so long," I offer.

"I'm sure we'll be getting more information when we go back for the retinal specialist appointment in a couple weeks, and there are lots of resources to help." Lorraine is gaining speed as she talks. "And the good thing is that you have lots of time now to prepare. We could get you enrolled to learn Braille...I also know somebody who..."

Cutting her off abruptly, I say, "Can we not talk about this now?" a little too sharply from my closet doorway.

Standing at the foot of my bed, my mom replies, "...Sure. I'm here if you want to talk. There is so much that can help and...I love you so much."

"I know. Thanks. I'm just tired."

I want to be patient with my mom, but I can't resist cutting her off and shutting the door between us. And a part of me wants to punish her: to make her feel the way I had to feel years ago when she lied to me about my birth mother. Alone. Betrayed. Shut out. And another part of me right now just can't deal with all of her. She has this anxious way of dealing with everything–flying into action–and I need time to think. I have to deal with my own feelings and can't handle hers too. Does that make me a bad person?

Penn knocks, then enters my room and tells me, "OK, close your eyes and wait for it..."

I cover both eyes with my hands.

"OK...you can look now," says Penn.

She has on some crazy rainbow party glasses, with the cardboard centers of two toilet-paper rolls attached to them.

"What the...?" I'm puzzled by her weird getup.

"I went all over YouTube last night to figure out more about this horrible Retinitis business, and I realized that I had to know how you were actually seeing. So I built these RP vision simulators...and, oh my God, Meera...I had no idea. They simulate tunnel vision. *It's a Miracle you have been able to go anywhere.* With these on, getting around *is so hard*. I wish I would have known! No wonder you can't see steps!"

She begins stepping towards me unsurely with the crazy goggles on.

"Unless I move my head constantly back and forth–I'd miss so much with these things on. This just sucks so much, Meera, and I am so sorry."

She sits on my bed and pulls the glasses off.

"I'm going to wear sunglasses when it gets dark later today to try to see what it's like for you to experience night blindness. I mean when you would always say, I can't see…I would think, Well, *nobody can see in the dark really–but we can see in the dark. Just not as well?* But according to the YouTube girl I was telling you about, she literally cannot see at all in the dark."

I knew Penn was a good friend, but in this moment I feel it deep in my bones. I feel understood in a way I haven't in a very long time.

Grateful, I offer, "It's OK. Even though I always felt like something was wrong, until now I didn't really know either. It feels really good to know I'm not crazy." I smile at her, grateful.

Penn sets the glasses on a pillow and begins to empty her tote bag onto my bed…out comes a bag of caramel corn and one of dill pickle chips. She rips both bags open, grabs a handful of dill chips, and then scoots the open bag of chips towards me.

"Breakfast? I'm pretty sure this stuff has healing powers," Penn jokes, between crunching on her beloved dill chips.

"Are you sure, Nurse Johansson?" I tease.

Penn is going to make the very best nurse in the world. I'm not even remotely hungry, but I pop a few chips into my mouth to appease her.

I muse darkly, "How will I know if my clothes even match? When I'm blind?"

"I solemnly swear that I, Penn, will never allow you, Meera, to go out in public looking anything less than awesome. And about that *head shaking thing* Stevie Wonder does—*it has a name*. It's called a 'blindism'...last night I watched a YouTube where the RP girl explained it."

"Did you sleep *at all* last night, Penn?" I ask, amazed that she already knows so much.

Penn is amazing with hair and makeup; she's been doing makeup for proms and grad photos since ninth grade. But don't think that because she's into this stuff, she's not smart. She could literally be a rocket scientist; Penn got a 34 on her ACT admissions test. But her true passion is making people beautiful. She wants to do nursing. It will make her mom happy, and it will still allow her the time she wants to learn new things. She's an expert on so many things.

"So blindisms—do you want to learn?" Penn offers. "The way Stevie turns his head the way he does. It's kind of telltale sign that you know somebody is blind, right? It's because when your retinas don't receive the visual input and stimulation, your brain makes up other stimulation to take its place. That's what doctors think anyway. And, according to YouTube girl, you probably wouldn't develop that for a long time. I'm guessing that's why you can't really tell she is blind...she doesn't 'look' blind."

Penn pauses, and I see my opening. "I can't stop thinking about what it would feel like to be blind...to be helpless. I won't ever be able to drive. It freaks me out too, because...what if I had gotten behind the wheel—I could have killed someone! Right now, I don't know if I even want to go away for school. And no school here even has interior design, but that's probably fine because...let's face it, nobody wants a blind interior designer working for them..."

Penn interrupts me gently. "But what did the doctor say? Didn't he say it could take quite a while...*years?*"

I hesitate, then tell her, "I have to go back in to see the specialist. Doctor Sill said each case is different. Some people progress more rapidly, especially around hormonal changes like puberty. So I could be blind sooner rather than later, but for most people it takes a while. Ten years he mentioned was average."

Penn encourages me: "Ten years is a long time, Meera. You could go to college in that time and lots of things can happen."

She's always so confident about everything. I wish I were too.

"I hope you're right. I have to go in for an evaluation where they help you with school...not sure exactly what that is. God, I don't want to be a freak..."

It is overwhelming to think about all this.

Penn grabs her bag and starts pulling out her curling iron. She plugs it in.

"Listen, good hair can change everything," Penn says, now snatching a round brush off my dresser. "Can I curl your hair and give you my newest perfected nude lip? I brought my stuff along. I want to stay longer, but I have to run to drive my mom to pick her car up at the dealership."

"Give me what you got," I reply, surrendering to her styling.

Penn pulls my desk chair out into the light of the window and commands, "Sit here...I need good light."

As Penn begins to run the brush through my hair, I'm lost in my head again. I have so many questions. Like do blind people have kids? Will I ever be a mom?

"I need you to tip your head this way. Good grooming improves most things, Ms. Townsend," Penn tells me, interrupting my worrying.

When she leaves, I crash back into bed, carefully spreading my beachy waves out on my pillow so they don't get totally crushed. I then go straight to the link on YouTube that Penn sent. I begin watching Lizzie the RP vlogger. *Holy shit, she's got 2 million followers?* I discover, from her profile, that she's already legally blind. Her RP was diagnosed when she was eight years old. Penn's right—she doesn't look blind at all. She's got a pretty amazing smoky eye going...*are those fake lashes? How does she do that? Maybe her BFF does makeup too?* In her first video, she tells the whole story of how she was diagnosed. I can relate to her fear of the dark and the frustration that nobody really got it when she said she really couldn't see anything.

Lizzie says that even though she's legally blind now, she can still see shadows and glimmers. So she bedazzles her phone and other stuff with crystals, which at first seems kind of tacky to me, until she explains that she enjoys seeing the sparkles. She seems really normal and that's so reassuring. And she's lucky, in a way, because she practically grew up knowing she was going blind. I just want to skip feeling sad and get to where she is. And I wonder if she has a boyfriend?

I flip over on my stomach and watch a half dozen more of her videos.

Another RP vlogger in her twenties, who looks completely normal too, takes us on a tour of her kitchen. She has "bump dots" on her microwave and her stove so she can "feel" where the temperature controls are, and—get this—she's actually married. We don't see her husband, but OK...at least somebody who has this RP thing seems to have a life. A pretty good one. She seems really nice. She's actually funny and comes across as happy.

So maybe there's hope. But what if having RP takes away the one thing you thought you were going to do with your life...interior design? I wonder what she does for a living. If I can't do design... what will I be when I grow up? I wonder what the bump dot girl does for a living. I google "jobs for blind people" and find: medical transcriptionist (OK, not horrible), piano tuner (OMFG nooooo!), packagers (what is THAT?), computer programmers (no...just no) and lawyers.

A lawyer? My mom would love that. What if I have to do something else...something I hate?

It's two in the afternoon, and my mom comes in my room to say that my aunt and uncle and my grandma are coming for dinner tonight.

"They all want to see you, sweetie," she says with a begging tone.

I sigh and roll away from her.

"Yeah...I get it...OK, and I am getting kind of hungry." A pause. "What are you making?" I add, quickly correcting myself. I try, in my own twisted way, to be good.

"I was just planning on throwing together a salad and ordering Sammy's Pizza?"

"Sounds good. I can make my cookies for dessert," I offer, without turning back towards her.

"That would be perfect—do you have what you need for that? I'm running to the store."

"Yep…I was going to make them yesterday, so I already checked."

Later I walk into the kitchen alone, newly aware that, someday, I will need to be OK with cooking blind. It feels like each cupboard I touch, I'm touching for the first time. I notice the touchpad on the oven. Each measuring cup and spoon and the ingredients. I realize that the way I mostly "know" where they are is by sight. I try half-closing my eyes to see what it would be like to "feel" for and find the tablespoon in the drawer. It takes a bit more time, but I do actually know the environment better than I thought I did. Maybe I'll be able to get the hang of this when the time comes.

I start mixing the microwave-softened butter, instant coffee, cocoa powder, brown sugar, flour, egg and vanilla together, and a sweet smell rises up to my nose. Soon all the ingredients have been added, the chocolate chips last. As I plunk the tablespoons of dough onto the cookie sheet, I put one in my mouth and savor it. I mean, if I had to lose one sense, what would be worst? I remember Penn asking me, "Would you rather be deaf or blind?" I think I said deaf, at the time, because I figured I could learn to read lips and sign, and the idea of being blind seemed so completely awful. What good is the world if you can't see it? A bunch of sounds and smells? But I guess there is taste and touch, which is pretty cool.

My eyes well up again. In the process of losing my eyesight, my heart is weirdly swelling with even MORE love and appreciation for the vision I have…and, for all I have seen, so far, in my life. I put the first batch in the oven. My mocha chip cookies are something I am mildly famous for in the family. I guess life would be pretty horrible without taste? I knew a kid in our school who had a head injury in baseball and never got his sense of smell or taste back. That would suck.

I set the timer and sit at the kitchen table with my phone...I go back to YouTube. I discover a guy who's got RP too. He's a bit older–maybe thirty? He describes his experience of night blindness in childhood. He was totally baffled playing "night games" in his neighborhood when the other kids would take off running and he couldn't understand how they would even know where they were going. I'm smiling now. I feel less alone.

His wife comes on later in the video (he's married too!) to say how being married to a blind person offers her an unusual sense of privacy...how not being "seen" sometimes can be a benefit. Hmmm. It makes me wonder, *Do blind people ever marry blind people?*

The timer buzzes, and I take the first batch of cookies out and set the timer to let them cool for twenty minutes. After cooling, I slide them on the wire rack and reload the cookie sheet. I break off a corner of a smallish one and pop it into my mouth, close my eyes and taste it. It is perfect–chocolatey and sweet with the bitter hint of coffee.

I think about all of the things I have ever worried about: my mom dying, not getting asked to Prom, and other stupid stuff...but blindness? It was never even remotely on my radar. In a weird way, I already have been blind for a while, at night? I mean I know what that feels like. Sometimes I feel truly helpless, hesitant and unsure of myself in the middle of the night when I have to find my way to the bathroom. Even with the nightlight on, it's never easy. Or if Mom and I get home in the dark and I have to go from the car to the house and we didn't leave the porch light on. What would it feel like to be permanently in that darkness though? Will my hesitancy get worse? How could it NOT?

My mom reminded me yesterday that the days are going to get shorter…already it's my least favorite time of year. At least now I know why. And Halloween has always been my least favorite holiday. The whole thing triggers me, and I didn't even celebrate this year. For as long as I can remember, I've hated going out trick-or-treating. It's no wonder. I'm practically blind at night. The past is beginning to make a lot of sense. But thinking of the future is paralyzing.

The doorbell rings. Moments later, my uncle bursts into the kitchen.

"Smells like cookies, Meera! Do I get to sneak one before dinner?"

"Only if you know the secret password," I tease.

He moves his lips to mouth "Open Sesame," a secret joke we have had ever since he read to me and my cousin Lexi from *Arabian Nights* and *Grimm's Fairy Tales*. Uncle Mitch is one of my favorite people. He's been my stand-in dad since my dad died. And since Lexi died, I feel like I've become his stand-in daughter.

The cookies are still warm, but not too hot. Using a spatula, I slide one onto a napkin, and hand it to him with a smile.

After taking a couple bites, Uncle Mitch sets the cookie down on the table and tells me, "We brought you a little something…" Out of one of the tote bags he brought into the kitchen, he pulls a beautiful, long-stemmed, white rose all wrapped in pretty tissue paper and cellophane from Saffron & Grey, my favorite little florist shop.

"It was your Aunt Jill's idea, of course. I take zero credit," he says with a big grin.

He's dressed in his red-and-black checked flannel shirt with his hair all messy. It's his Saturday couch potato look. Mom says that's because he's a Taurus…he's good at relaxing.

"Thank you." I take the rose, smiling.

My uncle hugs me tight in his burly arms, crunching the rose between us, and whispers into my shoulder, "I am so sorry, kiddo."

The tears begin to come again. Sometimes I feel terrible about thinking I am a little bit glad that he has to love me like his daughter…now that Lexi is gone.

Then, as the hug ends, he holds both my arms, squeezing them a little tightly, and asks, "How are you holding up?"

"I'm pretty good," I say, wiping tears away. Which is pretty true and surprising to hear myself say. Just getting a hug from him makes everything seem much more OK.

Aunt Jill enters the kitchen as I'm putting the third tray of cookies into the oven

"Oh Meera–how *are* you?" She grabs me by the shoulders and looks into my eyes, assessing me and then she pulls me in tight. Like my uncle, she's also an excellent hugger. My mom isn't a bad hugger but we just don't hug much since I've put some distance between us. I don't make it easy for her. Something in me cracks again, and I start to cry. It's hard to stay stoic when you're soaking in this much love, I guess.

My Aunt Jill looks a lot like my mom, only she has much more meat on her bones. She also seems much less fragile than my mom. Sturdier. She's definitely more relaxed. Aunt Jill says it's because she is the baby of the family. Mom says it's because her sister is a Sagittarius and she tends to look on the bright side of life.

As we eventually stop hugging, I say, "Thanks." I'm feeling grateful to be loved like I am.

"Well, you look absolutely perfect—is your hair different?" my aunt asks, touching my hair lightly.

"Beachy waves…courtesy of Penn."

"Oh Penn—it's so good to have great friends like her. Well, I love you, and this whole eye thing—well it's just awful. Of all the things?! When your mom told me, I didn't know what to say…but we are here, and we love you. Oh sweetie. You are so smart and so strong and so brilliant, and we are all right here, and I just want you to know how much we love you." She is looking at me, her eyes searching my face.

"I know it—thank you." I'm wiping my eyes again and the timer rings. I'm relieved to have something to do as I head towards the oven.

"Where's your mom, Meer?" my aunt inquires.

"I think she's still in the shower?" I respond.

My Uncle Mitch grabs a phone out of his back pocket and asks me, "Should I just order the pizza in that case, Meera? I'm starving. What do you want…some pepperoni and pineapple?"

"Yes please," I say, lifting the cookies off the pan and onto the cooling rack.

"OK, then that and a veggie with extra green olives."

My uncle heads into the living room with his cell phone to his ear.

"Hello!?" my Grandma Maxine's sing-song voice calls from the front hall.

The rock of the family, she marches into the kitchen, sets down her *New Yorker* bag stuffed with salad makings, and silently opens her arms to me. Without a word, I approach her, and she pulls me into her heart. I melt. I'm crying again. I wish I could do this with my mom too. Why can't I let her in? What is wrong with me? The whole kitchen is silent except for my breathing, the oven's fan whirring and our hearts beating. With my eyes shut, it's dark and little particles of light dance. It's comforting and peaceful. Finally I sigh and let go.

My mom enters the kitchen with a towel on her head. "The gang's all here," she assesses with a smile.

"We wouldn't want to be anywhere else," says Aunt Jill, who just came back into the kitchen. She opens a box of wine and then pulls out glasses from the cabinet.

On one hand, I feel utterly alone in facing this scary thing–this blindness that is somehow going to eventually be completely real. Another video I watched today guaranteed it would be by age forty, for sure. That seems so far away, but what if it's sooner? I have to face it on my own, and yet I feel so grateful for my people...almost like I don't deserve all this love (because I'm a jerk sometimes) but here they are.

Soon we're sitting around the table in the formal dining room and eating, with the cardboard boxes of pizza, Grandma Max's salad in Mom's glass bowl, and a huge platter of cookies within arm's reach on the buffet. My mom brings out the wine-in-a-box and pours herself and Jill each a second glass. Grandma Max and Uncle Mitch both drink beer. My mom is dominating the conversation by talking about how many people with RP are living fulfilling lives with all of today's technology, and there are even trials going on with stem cells to repair the malfunctioning and dying rod cells that cause RP in the first place.

Suddenly, I feel stupid and also irritated…like, *It's my disease.* Shouldn't I know more about it than her? DO I get to have an opinion? She even read something about a bionic eye implant. *I hate her for being so positive right now.* I want her to feel crushed too. I also want to be the kind of person to face this thing head on—it's so confusing. She finally takes a pause and gets up to grab the Parmesan cheese from the kitchen. Thank God.

My aunt jumps in. "Now Meera, I don't know how your mom will feel about me telling you this story. But a long time ago—like over twenty years ago—I got what felt like a terrible diagnosis. Now it's nothing like what you're going through. It's not the same, I know, but it's really been popping into my head ever since your mom called."

"What happened?" I ask, truly curious because I never knew my aunt was ever sick.

My mom reenters the dining room carrying the cheese.

"Oh Lorraine…" Aunt Jill interrupts herself, looking carefully at my mom. "…I was just getting ready to tell Meer about the shaman in Mexico."

"Oh?" my mom replies with her brow furrowed, like she's not sure she'll like this conversation. Mom says she and Jill can be a little oil and water sometimes: Virgo (Mom—perfectionistic and detail-oriented) and Sagittarius (Aunt Jill—friendly and open-minded).

"Well anyway," my Aunt Jill presses on, "your Uncle Mitch and I had been trying to get pregnant for three years, and finally we went to the fertility specialist at U of M in Minneapolis. They did a study that showed both of my fallopian tubes were 100% blocked by scar tissue. They said, without in vitro, I'd never get pregnant. We were crushed because IVF was really expensive, and it had pretty measly success rates. We didn't feel like mortgaging our house."

She stops to sip her wine as if remembering more. My mom is staring down at her plate as if she's distracted.

Jill continues. "A few months later, I was in Oaxaca, for work, researching a few new textile sources, and I shared my story with my favorite translator. She suggested I get a healing from this woman she knew. I don't know what made me do it. It sounded kind of crazy, but I was also desperate. I really wanted to be a mom. A month after seeing the shaman, we got pregnant with our Lexi. *I got my miracle.*"

She looks at my Uncle Mitch with a happy-sad smile, and he puts his arm around her.

Aunt Jill adds, "I know it might sound nuts–but I definitely believe that miracles are possible, and that there is more to healing than medicine…there is spirit too."

My aunt directs a piece of pizza into her mouth as she looks at me.

Mom sighs a little too heavily. She seems riled up and begins, "Now Jill–this is very different…Meera has been given a pretty firm diagnosis here. Infertility is one thing. I mean you hear stories of people being told they can't get pregnant and they still do. But Retinitis Pigmentosa….this is a known *genetically transmitted* disease, and I don't want you giving her the idea that…"

"I know…I know, Lorraine…" Aunt Jill says, waving her hand apologetically. "I probably shouldn't have even brought it up. I know we see medicine in different ways, but it has been on my mind all day. Sorry!" My aunt put her hand up in surrender.

Aunt Jill does see her regular doctor, but she's more apt to go to her naturopathic doctor or her yoga teacher for health advice–which bugs my mom to no end. Lorraine is suspicious of nonscientific approaches–which drives me nuts because she seems so damn sure of astrology. Isn't that a contradiction?

Intrigued by what my aunt shared, I offer, "We met somebody like that...a healer...a medicine man or something? In Colombia, on our trip...Mom, remember? When we were in Villa de Leyva? And we got to have that ceremony done for all of the families with the guy? I really loved that."

I look at my mom.

Grandma Max offers, "Yes, I remember him. He was a shaman, yes. That was a beautiful ceremony. I remember the jaguar pendant he wore. When we were in the Peace Corps in Guatemala, there was a healer like him in one of the villages we worked in."

My Uncle Mitch sheepishly interrupts, "Anybody want the last piece of veggie say something now or it's a goner..."

We all shake our heads as he quickly snags the slice, relieved.

"Yes Meera, I think he was a medicine man, a shaman," my mom admits. Then she continues, "But Meer, there's a lot we can... we haven't even begun to look into the possibilities yet. And shamans, I mean, *that's pretty primitive sort of stuff.*"

"We have come a long way with science and medicine," I counter. "But if it worked for Aunt Jill?"

I watch my mother's face for any signs of openness.

"If that stuff *really* worked, believe me, we would have it here in our clinics and hospitals," Mom responds. "It would be proven..." And then she pauses and appears thoughtful. "*If woo-woo really worked*, we would never have even had to develop modern medicine. So many cancers and even genetic diseases are now being cured, thanks to *evidence-based* medicine" Lorraine shakes her head.

"But, what if, without that shaman, Lexi never would have been born? How can you be so sure?" I say, challenging her.

"Maybe…" Mom's voice trails off noncommittally.

Thinking about Lexi, I see her in my mind's eye, sitting between my aunt and uncle at the table with a huge smile. She would know what to say right now to help.

And before I think, I say, "I miss Lex so much…I can just hear her now. 'Meera, you are going to kick this eye disease's ass!" I half-laugh/half-cry at the thought of her.

I look at the forlorn faces of my aunt and uncle. I wish I could erase their pain.

Uncle Mitch agrees, with sadness in his voice. "She sure would have, Meer…she loved you like a sister. I only wish she would have let *us* champion *her*." He was referring to the way Lexi loved to help others but rarely shared her own worries.

"She was a teacher for all of us for sure, Meera," my Aunt Jill notes as she leans back into my Uncle Mitch. "I miss her so much every day."

We all sit for a moment in silence.

Aunt Jill sighs and begins talking again, in a softer tone. "I don't want to make a huge deal out of it, Lorraine, but I know what it's like to get news that feels like the end of the world. All I can say is…I *do* believe in miracles. *And I got one. We did.* And I am grateful. I just wanted Meera to know that."

"Are you saying that I *don't* want a miracle for Meera?" my mom replies, now defiant and looking straight at her sister.

"Of course not, Lorraine. That's not what I meant at all," my aunt counters. "I just…" She wipes her mouth with her napkin and then sighs.

My mom stands up and says, "Who wants decaf?"
The subject has been closed.

Later that night, I have a strange dream. I'm standing by a closed door and somehow I know I'm in *her* house: *The shaman from Mexico that Aunt Jill was talking about.* I can't move. And it's getting darker in this room I'm in. There is a glowing light radiating from around the doorway, but I'm too scared to open the door. When I wake up, I feel disappointed that I didn't have the courage to peek at what was on the other side.

Chapter Eight

It's Monday again. I sit in Trig class and drop my mechanical pencil. I look down and move my head side to side scanning for it. *Where did it go?* It takes me a while until I spot it and then I lean down to grab it. A few minutes later, Peter—who is sitting next to me—drops his too. In one fluid motion, he simply looks down, grabs it and goes back to writing. I suddenly realize, thinking of Penn's crazy RP glasses, how easily he did this because he's not staring down two tubes of cardboard like I am. Wow. The insights keep coming all day. Everybody else can see everything, but what I see is constricted, through tunnels. No wonder I feel so different from everybody.

My world is so different from theirs right now. So much is up in the air for me. We didn't really learn anything new from Dr. Galbraith, the retinal specialist, except that there are some clinical trials in California. My mom is super excited about that option and making a bunch of phone calls to learn more. Dr. Galbraith sounded extremely cautious about them, so I feel kind of meh. She also said that even if I qualified, there would be many trips required. I'm concerned about the money, which I know is already tight.

The good news…I got the new lenses in my glasses, and I can see the board again in Trig when the lighting is OK. I'm corrected to 20/40 in one eye and 20/60 on the other, which isn't too shabby. The bad news, I still find math insanely boring and frustrating.

Sitting there in Trig class, I'm feeling bone tired. I've been trying to keep it together all day, but somehow seeing a stupid bad quiz grade makes me feel awful all over again. I just want to get out of there.

I text Penn.

Me: I need a break. Can you meet me? During my gym?

Penn: Sure. English is just review today. Meet me at my locker?

Ensconced at Amity Coffee, in the very back, on the couch next to the bathroom door, we sit with our mochas.

"This whole girl-going-blind thing is exhausting, I'm wiped. Also, I didn't do so hot on the Trig quiz." I sigh.

"I heard it was tough. James said he barely got a C," says Penn, ever focused on being positive.

I'm kind of annoyed. "Seriously—math is hard...life is hard, and Lorraine is making me crazy."

"What's up with your mom?" Penn asks.

"She's talking about me going to California to do a research trial thing and, get this, she made me an appointment for the Lighthouse for the Blind to check out stuff that can help. I'm just not ready." I immediately feel guilty for even saying it. I know Mom's just trying to help.

"One weird thing I found out though..." I add impulsively, to change the subject.

"What's that?"

"Well, my Aunt Jill was told by doctors that she would never get pregnant on her own. So she went to this shaman in Mexico for a healing, and one month later...boom, she was pregnant with Lexi. She says it was a miracle."

"That's wild...I mean a shaman, that's like a witch doctor, right? I'm surprised she'd go see somebody like that?" responds Penn, sounding a little judgy.

"Yeah..." I feel a little hesitant because Penn seems weirded out by the whole thing a little.

But I continue. "...I mean, I'm not sure exactly what they do. We met one in Colombia who did a ceremony for all of our families. It was pretty cool. He made this fire and put all these colored candles out, and we each made prayers with the candles for ourselves and our families. Weirdly, it was one of my favorite parts of that whole trip."

I watch Penn to see how she's reacting. She sips her mocha and seems OK, so I continue. "I did a little googling, and I guess a shaman can cure the spiritual part of a disease. It's like they repair things, the stuff we can't see...and they do it so that whatever the disease is, in the material world, can be healed, if that makes sense? It's kind of wild. I'm not sure I get it, but there is something really intriguing about it."

Penn's eyes light up in recognition. "There's a California girl I follow who posts cool makeup from Coachella, and she's always talking about a shaman she works with. She talks a lot about spirit animals and stuff?"

"Yeah exactly. I guess they can see things others can't," I say, lost in thought. Saying this out loud makes me think of Sweetie and my dad. I mean they aren't "here," but I do "feel" them. Is that the same or different?

"So, what are you thinking?" Penn asks.

"Well, maybe I could ask for a miracle too?" I say to Penn, curious how she'll respond.

She sips her mocha and looks at me. "From a shaman? Do you think your mom would ever let you go do something like that?" Penn glances down at her now buzzing phone. "Ooof…it's almost 1:30," she tells me.

We stand up and set our mugs on the counter before heading to Penn's car. I feel a little hurt because Penn seems a bit distracted.

⁓⁓⁓

As we buckle up and she starts up the car, I continue. "I don't know. Lorraine doesn't believe in this stuff. She's pretty much skeptical–you know–if it's not science, it's not legit. Though she loves her horoscopes…go figure."

I decide to try to explain to Penn why I'm even interested in the shaman. I tell her, "I mean–Penn, what if in twenty years I'm blind, and I look back and *I feel bad* that I never asked for a miracle? And it's too late? My retinas are gone." I'm asking a question, but not sure I really want input. I mean there's nothing to lose by trying the shaman.

My question hangs there in the air.

"Facts," says Penn, passively shrugging her shoulders in agreement as she drives.

As we get closer to school, I'm aware that my eyes are throbbing, my head hurts and my throat aches.

"Penn…sorry. Can you just take me home instead of back to school? I think I'm coming down with something. I feel terrible."

"Yeah, of course. I'm still OK for time. And I can be a little late for Psych. She doesn't care."

~ellee~

"Hi sweetie, I'm making your fav—pesto and pea pasta tonight... the one from Ina Garten's cookbook?" says my mom, poking her head into my bedroom's doorway.

"That sounds yummy. Thanks," I reply, trying to sound cheerful. "I'm going to take a bath...I think I'm getting sick. Can you call school and excuse me for fifth and sixth hour? I came home early. Penn drove me."

There is a moment of hesitation, as if Mom's considering it, and then she says warmly, "Will do. Do you want some juice or something? I have Sprite in the basement fridge I can get for you."

Phew. She's not mad.

"No thanks, I'm good. I'm just going to take a bath."

~ellee~

I put a few drops of my mom's essential oil into the hot water tumbling out of the faucet. The oil fills the room with a dense greenhouse scent of crushed geranium leaves...somehow so green, summery, ALIVE and comforting. I've put Coldplay's "O" on repeat on my little speaker. I heard it in a yoga class once and became obsessed with the lyrics. It's a happy/sad vibe and soothes me when I am frazzled. I slip into the hot water. That loving mothering bird I see sometimes in my dreams pops into my head. I'm trying to imagine my aunt in Mexico with the shaman...she's so adventurous. I love that about her. I think about Lexi. She'd be all for going to see a shaman. I miss her. I could never see my mom doing anything like that.

I was reading yesterday on the Internet that the shaman restores balance to a person…or cures what is ailing them by working with helping spirits. They work with animal spirits like bear or eagle, depending on where they live. Sometimes they have to remove the bad spirits from a person. I have so many questions. Could RP be from some bad spirits inside of me? That's kind of creepy to think about and I try not to think it.

I close my eyes and submerge myself completely under the water. Beneath the surface, it's quiet except for my breath, my heart-beat and the muffled melancholy music. Then I float, and my whole body rises and falls in the water as my chest fills and empties of air. After a while of floating like that, my chest begins to feel cold again and I turn the hot water back on using my foot.

Finally, sweaty from the heat, and feeling a lot better, I sit up higher, turn off the water, dry my hands and pick up my phone. I search "shaman" on YouTube. I begin watching an interview of a shaman in Peru with subtitles. He's sitting on a stool near a fire in the jungle. I keep the video playing as I get dressed in my jammies and robe.

Something he says stops me in my tracks: "Sometimes a challenge is there to help the person grow. To mature. We are all here on this earth to grow up…spiritually." If going blind is to help me to grow up, *what the heck am I supposed to be learning?* That I should try to be nicer to my mother? I feel upset by this idea, but also curious if he could be right.

After dinner, I lock my door and go into the closet to call Aunt Jill. I don't want to make my mom feel left out. And I know she isn't supportive of something weird like seeing the shaman.

My aunt answers, "Hey Meera—how are things? Did they connect you with a helper at school yet?"

"No, not yet…I'm dreading that. No, I think that's next week. I was calling to ask you more about that shaman…that woman you went to." I want to get straight to the point.

"Oh yeah—gosh…I was just saying to your Uncle Mitch that maybe I shouldn't have mentioned it. I'm not sure how your mom feels about it but…something in me had to say it. That's me, irrepressible. What do you want to know?"

"Well, do you think she could help me?" I ask, not sure where else to begin.

"I don't know, Meera, and I'm not sure I could even find her. It's been over twenty years. I do have my contacts there still, but…"

This sounds discouraging and suddenly it all feels futile.

"Even if you could find her…I don't know if my mom would be OK with it," I say with a sigh.

"No? You could be right…but I also know she loves you and wants the best for you too," my aunt responds with kindness. "Have you tried talking about it with her?"

"No…but I had a dream about your shaman the other night. In the dream, I was afraid to open a door leading to bright light in her home. What do you think that means?"

I am hoping my aunt might have some idea. She is pretty intuitive and always knows what to say, just like Lexi did.

"Really. Hmm, not sure…but I always think that paying attention to your dreams is very important," Aunt Jill says encouragingly.

"I guess…I'm wondering—what did the shaman do? I mean what was it like?" I ask, curious about her experience.

"Well, truth be told, I don't remember a lot. Actually, I do remember being pretty scared to go through with it." My aunt laughs softly.

"Why would it be scary—if she's trying to help you?" I am even more curious now.

"Well, for me, it was the unknown. I didn't really know her, and I was way out of my element…up there in the mountains. Plus, you had to eat some mushrooms. I didn't mention that part at dinner. Gads! Your mom is *not* going to be happy with me…" Aunt Jill pauses and sighs.

"Eating the mushrooms was part of the healing," she continues. "I guess the 'tripping' part was what made me feel worried. Like *what if they were poisonous* and she didn't know what she was doing, or what if this was all a bad idea. I had my doubts. I had tried magic mushrooms once in college, and it was kind of a weird experience… not bad but weird. So I was scared of that for sure…"

"Mushrooms? Wait…" I feel confused.

"Yeah, this is why…well…umm, I wondered if I should have mentioned it. *Lorraine forgive me!*"

She seems to be asking Mom's permission, though my mom is not there. I can tell this conversation is tough—Aunt Jill wants to help me but is afraid of how her sister will feel about it.

She continues. "Well, in Mexico, in the place I traveled to, the mushrooms are revered. They're actually sacred. It's not like here in the US where kids eat them to go see a concert, see the psychedelic patterns or to have a laugh. For this shaman, the mushrooms are the spirits that heal–if that makes sense? She called them Little Saints? *Santos?* Or something like that?"

"Weird…" I say, thinking this whole thing sounds even more strange than I had imagined.

"Yes, like I said, I was definitely out of my element, but I trusted my friend, my contact from the textile cooperative, very much. I just decided that *if she trusted this woman,* then I was going to trust her too. The experience was really powerful and kind of, I hate to say it, overwhelming? But obviously I was so glad I went through with it. We got Lexi out of the bargain. I actually read somewhere that the mushrooms were a big part of a fertility cult in early history."

I could hear emotion in her voice. I loved my Aunt Jill so much for how far she was willing to go for what she wanted. For how adventurous her whole life was. I wanted to live like that too.

"I really think I'm interested. But my mom…do you think you could talk with her?" I venture.

"I certainly could, Meera," Jill offers. "I don't know what she'll say, but no matter what, she loves you. She just wants the best for you. And I bet if you spoke with her, she would listen."

Lorraine is knocking at my door. I peek at my phone; it's 6 am.

"What do you want?" I half-moan from my bed, annoyed. It's not time for me to wake up yet.

"I'm just leaving for work now and I hate to wake you up. Sorry Meera, but what do you think about taking a last-minute girls' weekend to the cities…we'd leave Saturday morning around eight?

We could do a bit of holiday shopping?" She sounds so positive and cheerful.

One thing my mom and I can always agree on is the love of great shopping. We hit the usual suspects—my favorite Minneapolis junk shop Hunt & Gather, Anthropology on 50th and France, and The Galleria in Edina.

"Meera? I've got to get to work...what do you think?" she presses me. "I need to know because I would try to trade a shift today to make it work..."

"Yeah—sure I'll go." I can't seem to let myself sound happy about it...ughhhh. I know she's trying to be nice.

My alarm is going off, and I can hear English Christmas carols on the kitchen Alexa speaker. It's gotta be Grandma Max? I begin to smell a buttery sweetness and I know it's crepes. A few years ago, when my mom and my grandma took me back to Colombia, we tried a lot of the traditional foods: *ajiaco* soup and *arepas*, these corn cakes. As weird as it sounds, French crepes were the food I fell in love with. We ate them at a little bistro in a fancy Bogota neighborhood that we would walk to from our hotel each afternoon. We had them Parisian style with Nutella, whipped cream and slices of banana, and that's how my grandma makes them now.

I thought visiting Colombia would make me feel somehow more settled, and in a way, I guess it did. As we stepped onto the plane in Miami to go to Bogota, I felt, for a moment, like I fit in even though I didn't know a soul. For once, I looked like almost everyone else. I belonged. It was so cool.

Then my mom interrupted the moment, whispering to me, "Take a look around, Meera...a lot of these people are Colombian!"

"So am I," I whispered back, annoyed. I know I'm different and am reminded of it every day.

We walked around our little hotel's neighborhood in Bogota to visit different local restaurants and shops. Everybody was so incredibly well groomed. The older men wore beautiful tweed suitcoats with hats, and the women...the women of all ages...were super decked out—in dresses and wool coats with scarves carefully arranged. They were so much more elegant than what I was used to seeing at our Minnesota mall: ripped jeans, baseball hats and sweatpants. You could feel the pride in who they were. They had so much style.

We were staying in an upper-class neighborhood. But even the people selling fruit in the market or bundles of roses on the street corners seemed to pay special attention to their appearance. It made me feel like I was part of something elegant. Proud...I guess that sums it up—they seemed proud of who they were and seeing them instilled that feeling in me too. Getting to be there in my birth country helped me to feel pride in myself and the place I was born in.

"Meeraaaah?" my Grandma Max calls to me now.

I slip out from under the covers, put on my fuzzy robe and head for the kitchen.

"Morning Gramma," I say as I hug her.

She hugs me tightly back.

"What are you doing here?" I ask, genuinely confused.

"Your mom had to work early today, and I thought I'd come and make you crepes. Sit. I'll get you one." She smiles warmly.

I think I'm getting special treatment because of the RP.

As I use my fork to dig into the pillowy crepe stuffed with deliciousness, my grandma pours another crepe onto the griddle and says, "I've been thinking about you, and I wanted to tell you about something that happened to me, Meera. Would that be OK?"

"Uh huh," I answer while chewing.

She begins. "After your mom was born, and we brought her home from the hospital, I started having a really hard time. I was having lots of bad thoughts. I was terrified I was going to do something bad to the baby–your mom, who was just a few days old. In those days we didn't know anything about postpartum depression. Anyway, I had a lot of dark thoughts. I tried to tell your grandfather, but he was so busy with work and he didn't really understand. So, in desperation, I left the house one night after your grandpa got home and everybody was asleep. I planned to go to the cabin and swallow a bunch of pills to end my life. It sounds terrible now, but at the time I felt there was no other way. I was so terrified I was going to do something really bad to your mom…I was going to do it to keep her safe. I honestly believed that everyone would be better off without me."

"That sounds awful," I say. I can hardly believe what she's telling me. Grandma Max killing herself? It made absolutely no sense.

"And I'm not telling you this to scare you but to tell you what happened. In the middle of the night, realizing I was gone, your grandpa drove up to the cabin. He had the idea I might have gone there. He brought me to the doctor, I had my stomach pumped, and I was locked up for two weeks on the psych ward. My mom took Lorraine, your mom, home with her. It was the worst two weeks of my life.

"But during that horrible time on the ward, I developed compassion. In my depressed state I could see that all the people there were just like me, but they needed support and understanding. My heart was broken open. With the help of medicine and lots of love, I returned home. And little by little, I recovered and was eventually able to be a mom again.

"The reason I'm telling you this whole story is that, sometimes, a crisis, or something really horrible that happens to you, it has a purpose. It's preparing you for something good. That dark postpartum depression eventually led me to the work I did for forty years as a social worker and therapist. And with these sorts of things, you can only understand it backwards. I had to go through that darkness to be able to discover my biggest gifts. It took me years, but today I am extremely grateful for that terrible time."

I can't imagine my grandma in a psych ward...she is the sanest person I know. So calm and loving. My grandpa must have been so upset. He died the year before my dad did. I was only eight and I didn't feel super close to him. He was pretty reserved, but I remember how sad my mom and grandma were. He died in his sleep, which everybody said was "good." But I remember that idea was scary to me in second grade...the idea that people could go to bed one night and not wake up.

After finishing the last bite of crepe, I share, "Wow...I can't imagine you ever wanting to hurt anybody." I am unsure of what else to say.

"That's the mystery of it all, Meera. We may not know for many years why something had to happen the way it did."

"But Grandma, this RP thing...it just feels like a punishment. I mean you know the one thing I have always wanted to be is a designer—and now what? I'm so confused. I mean, do I try to become that still? Knowing that I am slowly losing my vision and trying to enjoy it for a few years or...if I'm lucky...a decade—but then what?" I am attempting to explain my confusion.

"I don't know, but I do know that you will find your way. So be curious, OK Meera-bear?"

She turns back to the stove.

Curious? I'm so confused. How can I be curious about this? What does that even mean? I feel more confused than ever.

"Is there another crepe for me?" I ask.

Maybe I'll see what she thinks of this whole shaman thing.

"Absolutely."

Grandma expertly pours the batter into the hot cast-iron pan and tilts the pan to cover it with the mixture.

I begin slowly, as my grandma is pretty Catholic and I'm not sure how she'll react. "I'm curious regarding what Aunt Jill was talking about the other night."

"What's that?" Grandma asks, using the spatula to lift up the crepe edge to check for doneness.

"That shaman—the one that helped her get pregnant with Lexi?" I say.

"OH yes...I remember," she replies, with her back to me, sounding neutral.

"Mom thinks it's dangerous and she doesn't believe in that stuff," I continue. "I really don't even know if Aunt Jill can get in touch with this person but, somehow, I wonder if I should go there too? To ask for a miracle."

Grandma Max lifts up the crepe now filled and puts it on my plate with the spatula.

"Well, if you feel drawn to it, then by all means Sugarplum, you need to explore that feeling," she says calmly. "I really liked the fellow who did the ceremony for all of us in Colombia too."

Surprised by her acceptance, I add, "Yeah–I talked to Mom about it and she's really against it." Then I say hopefully, "I wonder if she might listen to you?"

"Well, your mom knows a lot–especially about healing and medicine. But yes, I could talk to her."

Chapter Nine

I'm sitting in Art again with my senior project. I feel stuck. It's about a bird somehow, and I want the design to tell a story, but I just can't seem to figure out what the story is. Across the room, Steph, the girl in class who has tattoos on both arms, is making a huge mess with her papier-mâché sculpture, and Mrs. Griffin is trying to get her to clean up. Steph's being kind of rude to her. I cringe. Maybe this textile design with the bird is about freedom? To say what I need to say. I quickly sketch a bird in a cage on one panel and then a second panel with a bird flying free. The bell rings. I quickly erase the cage before putting my things away.

In bed that night, after I turn off my lamp, I think about what Grandma Max had said about how her biggest nightmare, her suicidal depression, weirdly empowered her...how it helped her become a therapist. But her problem wasn't permanent, and losing my sight sure feels like it will be.

Unsuccessfully, I try, as I had tried a million times before, to imagine my birth mother. How hard was her life that she had to leave me? When she stood in that park that morning–did she do a rosary? Did she hide behind a tree to see who ended up realizing that the box contained a baby...or was she blind maybe from RP and somebody else had dropped me there in the park? That must have taken some courage–and trust–that the right person would find me. And if she hadn't left me there, who knows where I'd be. I never would have had my wonderful Grandma Max or my aunt and uncle. Or my mom.

My mom's lie of omission about my birth story has made one important thing happen. It made me trust myself in a new way. I discovered that my own inner guidance is powerful and *real*. My intuition is legit. All those years that she'd been lying, something had felt off to me. I didn't know it at the time, but it had been my inner knowing....saying to me...*something's not right here*. And it's that same feeling I get now when my mom says I can't go to Mexico...somehow I need to find a way. Somehow it's going to help me. *I must go.*

I sense Sweetie alongside me with her calm stillness and big dark eyes. She doesn't need me to do or be anything, and that's a relief. And I notice something unexpected...her fur seems different. There are less spots on it. *Are you changing?* I ask her, confused and unsure if it's still her. *I'm not changing, you're just seeing me differently.* This catches me off guard and I doubt myself. Even if it is real, what I'm perceiving, I'm not sure that I understand her. I kind of want her to stay the same, because everything else is changing so fast. I decide to let go of my thinking and begin to sense her love filling me, enveloping me.

~eelJlee~

We are on 35W headed to Minneapolis for our weekend. It's cloudy and 12 degrees below zero Fahrenheit....freaking cold. I've been pretending to be asleep in the front passenger seat, so I don't have to talk. It's easier that way. One bright side to Retinitis Pigmentosa: Lorraine has finally stopped bugging me about signing up for Driver's Ed. The thought that I may never have to drive is sort of a relief. I always assumed I'd eventually have to get over my fear and learn to drive. *Will people get sick of having to drive me everywhere?* Tears rise again. I pretend I need to readjust in the seat so I can rub my eyes and not arouse suspicion.

During the last few weeks, Mom has been trying to convince me to enter this trial for RP in California. They stick tiny needles (What fun!) into your eyes to put some retinal cells in there to replace the ones that are quitting on you without your permission. Apparently in the first phase of the trial, people experienced some very mild improvements. Not a cure, but it's something. But I wish she wanted a miracle too like I do.

My mom has NPR on, and there's a story being broadcast about the first deaf and blind person to graduate from Harvard Law School–a modern-day Helen Keller. Haben Girma is her name. *You cannot make this shit up.*

I hear my mom softly say, "Meer?" She wants me to listen.

I deepen my intention to look like I'm in a complete coma. It works, and she stops trying to wake me up. *But I'm at rapt attention.* Haben talks about how hard it was at college to navigate the cafeteria as a visually impaired person...and so she asked the cafeteria to provide menus in a format that she could read. The staff refused, saying they were too busy. Then later, when she posed her request, more convincingly, as a civil right, they began providing her with an emailed menu daily that she could read using an text to speech app. Just the thought of navigating a cafeteria with no vision freaks me out. My biggest fear is that I'm going blind and somehow that will make me unrelatable. Unlovable. The awesome thing about the interview is that this woman sounds like a fun and cool person.

An hour later, we make our first stop of the day at Hunt & Gather. God, I forgot how much I love this little thrift/antique shop. Christmas music is playing, and everything is decked out with greenery and lights. The creative thrill I get is even more intense than usual, almost urgent. I am drinking in the details of every crazy object. It feels more important than ever. Life feels more alive right now. The colors. The visual stories everywhere. I can't get enough. I enter the first room filled with letters and numbers from random vintage sources…spelling word flashcards, 1950s school glee flags and crazy schoolroom accessories. Every room you enter here is a fantastical world.

One of my favorite spaces is a 1950s camp, complete with taxi-dermized chipmunks, old Hudson Bay wool blankets and ancient swimming trophies. Unlike your typical dusty and exhausting antique store, all the raw materials are organized into refined categories and curated into amazing vignettes. It's so uplifting. I feel 25% better already. I linger a bit longer in the French girly bedroom booth filled with gilded china and old faded millinery flowers. I love the velvety emerald leaves and raw silk petals in faded violets and pinks.

I end up spending most of my time in a booth at the back, with a huge bank of windows. It's filled with religious relics—sacred hearts surrounded in barbed wire, and dozens of Virgin Marys. I feel really drawn to a figurine who, on first glance, looks like the Virgin Mary to me. On closer examination she's different. Her face is brown, like mine. It's a heavy resin figure, maybe twenty inches tall. Her gown is emerald, and she's held up, beneath her feet, by an angel's wings and what look like a set of bull's horns. I don't remember Grandma Max's Virgin Mary having horns. Red apples and roses are painted all over the lining of her robe. There is something completely irresistible about her. I pick her up. I'm not religious, but, to me, she feels holy. I carry her around as I complete my rounds of both floors. My mom and I are moving, like always, separately through the store, but we're continuously aware of each other. And sometimes we share what we find. When we finally finish up, back at the front desk, Mom's carrying an old green enamel watering can.

"That's cool. Are you going to get it?" I ask, nodding at her find.

"I think so–do you think Grandma would like it for her sunroom?"

"Yeah, I think it would be beautiful with her stuff," I agree.

"What do you have?" My mom points at my figurine.

"I don't know, it's…I guess it's like a Virgin Mary–but she's different? I kind of feel like she wants to come home with me."

There's a lady sitting behind the cash register, with oversized thick and stylish black frames and blond pigtails. She offers, "That's from my booth…she's Our Lady of Guadeloupe."

"Oh…I really like her." I turn the statuette over in my hands, looking at her again.

"I lived in Mexico for a few years, and I collected them," the pigtailed lady explains, while pushing her oversized tortoise glasses up onto the top of her head. "In Mexico, she's a really important symbol of protection and compassion. If you need a miracle of any kind, she's the one you pray to."

I look right at my mom, eyebrows raised, and we both shrug, half-smiling.

"That's kind of weird because I could really use a miracle right now," I say.

"Guadeloupe is definitely your girl then! Shall I wrap her up for you?" The clerk gives me a warm smile.

I look at my mom.

"Grandma would love that you love her...how much is she?" Mom asks.

"Forty-two..." I say, peeking at the label at the base.

So weird because four plus two is six, and in numerology, according to Aunt Jill, that's my life path number. Another funny synchronicity. Somehow this makes me feel even better, that something wanting to help is with me. Maybe.

"What if part of this can be paid with your birthday money? You still have some from earlier this year. I haven't cashed that check."

"Perfect, I can pay you back for the rest," I say, happily.

As she begins wrapping Our Lady up carefully in paper, the clerk adds, "I'm so glad she's found such a good home! In Oaxaca, during her feast days, they cover the churches in pink and red roses—it's so beautiful. You should go sometime."

As she says that, I'm getting goosebumps.

I turn to my mom and ask with curiosity, "Oaxaca? Isn't that near where Jill was for her healing?" If that's true, then maybe it really is something I need to pursue.

"I think so...yes," my mom says absentmindedly as she's signing the credit card receipt. She clearly doesn't think it means anything.

I don't let her lack of response get to me. I'm just so happy with my find, and it feels extra lucky now. It's going to be a great day!

I don't let her lack of response get to me. I'm just so happy with my find, and it feels extra lucky now. It's going to be a great day!

As I follow my mom out the exit, somehow I miss the step down. I land on the sidewalk, catching myself with my hands. The bag with my new purchase, Our Lady, slips out of my grasp and drops too.

My knee stings and aches. My palm burns. I stand up to survey the damage. My jeans are ripped and my knee is scraped. Pinpricks of blood are rising on my right palm. My bubble of lightness from finding Our Lady and her connection to Oaxaca is suddenly deflated, and here I am again—the klutzy, soon-to-be-blind girl.

"Oh no, Meera! Are you OK?" my mom cries out.

"My knee just really hurts. I'm OK," I say, feeling defeated all over again as I look at my leg.

My mom gets a tissue out of her bag and hands it to me. I dab carefully at the scrape.

Back in the car, I slowly unwrap Our Lady and find that, despite her collision with the concrete, she survived unscathed. *Miraculous.*

"I'm so sorry, Meera—if I had noticed the step down, I wouldn't have let you…" Lorraine starts.

"Can we *not talk* now?" I interrupt her with an edge in my voice.

I pull down the visor mirror and wipe my now smudged mascara with a tissue.

Mom seems to be waiting.

"I'm ready…can we just go now?" I say, frustrated.

Lorraine looks at her watch and hesitates before telling me, "I thought we should have lunch at Edina Grill next?"

She turns out of the parking lot.

"I'm hungry...I could eat," I agree.

At the restaurant, I get my knee cleaned up a bit with a napkin and some water. The patty melt tastes good, and I'm feeling ready to continue our holiday shopping extravaganza again. As we finish lunch, Mom keeps looking at her phone (and she tells me I'm obsessed). The waitress comes to clear our plates, and my mom orders a latte, which surprises me.

"I thought we were headed to Galleria? You could just get a coffee there," I suggest, feeling anxious to move on.

"I really need a boost, if that's OK. I'll ask for a to-go cup," my mom says, acting a little distracted and looking towards the door.

"Sure. OK," I reply, accepting.

I decide to go the bathroom, and once in the stall, I text Penn.

Me: I wiped out again today.

Penn: R u OK? How was Hunt and Gather?

Me: Yeah I'm OK. It was amazing.

Penn: Jared and I are fighting again—hate this drama. See u Sun?

Me: Yes. Hope it gets better w/you 2.

Penn: It will.

Chapter Ten

As the waitress returns to deliver the latte, I am walking through dining area. I see that Lorraine has left our table and she is standing at the entrance. There's a tall woman with a wavy silver-streaked bob, and Mom's hugging a guy who looks like her son. He's brought their dog in with him. *Weird.* After plopping down in my chair, I go back to sipping water and checking my phone. Then they all start heading my way. *Damn.* I'm not really in the mood to be social.

"Meera—I want you to meet my old friend Leslie. We were in a mom's group together when you were a baby, and now she lives in Minneapolis."

Leslie smiles warmly at me.

I shake her hand perfunctorily and smile. "Hello—nice to meet you."

Mom continues. "And this is her son, Trevor. You guys actually slept on the same picnic blanket, as little ones. Trevor was a toddler, and you were just a few weeks old. How old are you now, Trevor?"

My mom looks towards the boy.

"Just turned twenty-one," the guy offers with a shy smile.

He's got wavy, sandy blond, hockey hair that's ends just above his shoulders—the guy has major "flow," worthy of the State Tournament

Annual Hockey Hair video. Hockey boys aren't my type. Too cocky and cliquish for me.

"So anyway," my mom continues, looking carefully at me, "I was talking to Leslie on the phone last week about you, Meera. I knew that Trevor was visually impaired, and after we talked–we thought it would be great to connect you two."

Wait. What! Did she just say visually impaired? Oh my God. I can't believe this is happening.

Trevor's mom chimes in, "Hey, Lorraine…next door, the shop has some things I think you'll love. Should we go browse a bit and let these two talk a while without us?"

My mom hesitates and then nods agreeably, looking nervously at me as they continue conversing.

Unbelievable. Before I can glare back at Mom, Trevor steps forward.

"Hey Meera, good to meet you. This is Eleanor," he says, gesturing towards his dog, a sweet-looking yellow lab wearing a bright orange harness.

He continues, "And I'm not too great with handshakes, but I'm working on it. My high-five game isn't too good either."

His warm, friendly voice is decidedly un-hockey boyish. Trevor offers his hand out toward me, a little high. I reach up and shake it. It's steady and friendly. I look into his eyes, but he isn't looking at me. Or is he? It's hard to tell. He doesn't really "look" visually impaired. *Is he really blind? Like, blind, blind?* I wonder.

"Hey Meera and Trev," Leslie calls out in a bright voice. "Don't want to interrupt, but Lorraine and I decided to slip next door. I want to show the shop to your mom, Meera…it's one of my favorites! That will give you guys a chance to talk."

As Leslie turns towards the door, I glance at my mom and raise my eyebrows at her. *WTF?* She smiles nervously and then follows Leslie out.

"Oh hey–hi, I'm Meera," I clumsily offer.

I notice that under his charcoal North Face puffer, Trevor's got on a Hippo Campus band T-shirt.

"OK if I sit down?" he asks.

"Oh, sure…absolutely," I reply, feeling irritated and mildly panicked.

He puts his hands on the back of a chair that his mom had out for him, follows them down to the seat, and then sits down. I can't believe my mom put me up to this. I'm mad about the ambush, and feeling like she's hiding things from me all over again.

What am I supposed to do with this guy? What if he needs help? It's so awkward. On the other hand, I AM curious. There's something about him…and I don't have time to ruminate on all this because Trevor doesn't seem bothered at all. And he's looking towards me but not exactly at me…and it's weird.

"So…your mom said you've been having some vision problems?" he says and seems matter of fact and calm.

His dog is sitting up at attention.

"Yeah, ummmmm…I was just diagnosed with Retinitis Pigmentosa," I start in, realizing I really don't know that much about my own disease, which is suddenly embarrassing.

I continue. "I have tunnel vision, though I can see pretty well now except at night. They told me that eventually I will become blind, but it's going to take a while…maybe years. They aren't really sure." I feel numb.

"That sucks. I'm really sorry." His voice is so kind.

Now I feel like crying all of a sudden. *Ugh.* I take a deep breath in and push down the tears. "Thanks. Yeah, it's all kind of new right now." My voice is cracking. *God.*

"How about you?" I ask, honestly curious about his story and anxious to get the focus off me.

"Well, about three years ago, I was having some trouble skating. My balance was off. Before this, I played hockey."

I knew that was hockey hair.

"Actually, I still play now, but it's different." He smiles.

"Anyway, we found out I had a brain tumor. The tumor was benign…harmless, like no problem. But when the surgeon went to take it out…we knew it was a risk…it was really close to my optic nerves. So, when I woke up from surgery, I was blind. I guess they had told me it was a possibility but, I don't know, I was still completely caught off guard."

I suddenly feel for him; how awful to think you'll be OK and then wake up blind.

Hoping it comes out alright, I offer, "Oh my gosh, that must have felt horrible. I mean what was that like? I'm so sorry."

I suddenly feel more open to him. He's not like most of the guys at my school. He seems much more mature, somehow.

"Yeah at first it was pretty rough. I'm not gonna lie. They told me it was a possibility…you know before the surgery…but you never think something like that will happen to you? You always think that ten percent, or whatever it is, will be somebody else. Not you. So I was pretty down about it at first. My mom would say I was depressed. But after a while, I realized that I had a choice…I could either make the best of it or I could be miserable. I've had a lot of help adapting and I'm realizing that I'm pretty lucky."

145

He pauses and pulls his jacket off, letting it rest on the back of his chair.

Trevor continues. "It hasn't kept me from living and–it's taught me a lot–like how to ask for help." He chuckles. "That's something I wasn't too good at before now. I think it's made me more multidimensional too. I always liked English class a lot, but I'm not sure I would have pursued writing because before this…I was pretty sport-centric. So…that's me, but what about you–how are you doing?"

Being with him is easy. He's so normal.

He adds, "I don't know much about RP. I have made a few friends at the U; I call them my BBs, my 'Blind bros.'" He chuckles again. "One of them has RP too, like you, but he's had it since he was a little kid, I think." He pulls one of his feet up onto his knee and rests it there.

I begin my story slowly. "For me, it was actually kind of a relief to find out. But yeah, I feel like the future is super uncertain. I applied to go to the U for design school this fall, but now–that's not going to work. Interior design has always been my thing, and I'm not sure what I'd do if I can't do that."

I can't believe I'm opening up to him, but it's kind of a relief. He's the only person I've met who is my age that has lost their vision.

Silence falls.

Trevor starts in gently. "Not that I would wish it on anybody, and not that I don't wish every day that I could have my sight back… but I will say that it sort of opened me up to my life. This might sound crazy, but in a way, losing my vision has been a good thing. Before it, I was just kind of asleep at the wheel and now…I don't know…I guess maybe I'm just more grateful for everything I have. I was kind of an asshole before. It definitely humbled me."

"I'm not there yet," I confess, shaking my head.

Suddenly, it sinks in that he can't see me or anything I'm doing. And that's kind of freeing and I feel less self-conscious. At least I don't think he can?

"But…" I begin cautiously, "…I do know what you mean about being grateful. I had never thought about the things I have seen and that feels somehow more precious to me. Can I ask you something?" Feeling bolder, I've decided to ask a more personal question.

"Sure, anything," he says smiling. He's got a great smile.

"What *can* you see? I mean is your world just completely dark, or…?" I hope I'm not being weird.

"No–I actually see quite a bit of light and shadow. And the doctors say I may continue to gain a bit more vision over time. I use that light a lot–to see cars coming–to avoid obstacles. Like, as I'm looking towards you, I can see your outline like a shadow, and I can see the bright lights behind you. But details are extremely fuzzy."

I try to explain myself. "Ahhh, I was just wondering…because when I hear that I'm going *blind*, it feels like everything is just going to go dark. Hmmm…maybe I'll see light too when I'm 'blind'?"

"Most people, that I know, who are blind see *something*…light, shadow…something," Trevor tells me as Eleanor settles down to the ground and makes a low groan.

I have *so* many questions, I dive right back in. "OK–another question–how do you get around the U?" I ask. "I mean that campus is so huge! That's probably what scares me the most–I mean right now I can see during the day. But getting around at night in a strange place is terrifying for me. How do you do it…were you ever scared?"

"Well OK, the U…I know this isn't what you asked, but the big bonus is that my tuition is free. I get a waiver because I'm legally blind. So, that's a big deal, because it means I won't have loans."

"Seriously?" I say, surprised. "Could that help me?"

"Yeah—it depends on your vision loss, but you might qualify too. They hook you up with extra services. They got me oriented to help me figure out the best routes to my classes. I have an app that basically reads all of my screens to me—whatever is on my laptop screen. It's still much faster to read Braille or sometimes I listen to lectures on audio recorded at 1.5x speed. I have another program that converts the notes that I voice-record into Braille."

There's that Braille again, damn. I had forgotten about that…and my appointment's coming up. Ugh.

"Braille is kind of huge in my world," he tells me. "It's good to have audio for books and lectures, but Braille is much more efficient. I went to this intensive training in Louisiana. I took a year off between high school and college to do it, and that really helped me. I'm still learning. I'm trying to reread all of my favorite books in Braille this year. I'm working on *Charlotte's Web* at the moment. I'm big on E.B. White. I'm really glad I don't have to lose reading. And Eleanor here—she really helps me out—I'm never alone."

Eleanor sits up again and looks straight at him, as if she is ready to go wherever he wants to go.

"When I got her, it was a huge game-changer," he says. "I got my independence back. The place that trains these dogs is just incredible. That experience was amazing. Plus, I got to be around a bunch of people who were blind like me. I also realized that there are a lot of pretty angry blind people, and I don't want that to be me. So

I kind of decided then and there that I was going to make lemonade, you know?"

Eleanor sits up again at attention as if she knows he is talking about her.

I can't help but wonder what the hardest part is for him. "Do you ever miss seeing faces or beautiful things?" I blurt out, immediately wishing I hadn't.

He looks thoughtful. "Yeah, there are definitely times when it's hard. Like this summer, we were all at a friend's cabin sitting down by the lake, and people were oohing and awing at the beauty of lake and the sunset. I couldn't really join in…stuff like that or sporting events too…I don't go to those much now, but I realize what I've gained too. It's…I don't know how to say it…but I'm also really lucky to have a great family and so much support."

I'm not sure but I think I detect emotion in his voice as if he is almost tearful.

"Yeah, totally, I feel like that too," I agree. "My family has been so great."

"Also, another hard thing is…" He pauses as if he's deciding whether to share this or not. "I thought I'd remember everything I'd seen, like faces and things…but some of those memories have already started to fade for me. They get replaced by different memories, voices, smells…but that kind of bums me out. Like I don't want to forget my friend's face, my sister's face? My little niece's and nephew's? My mom's…"

I jump in agreeing. "I have a similar thing with my dad. He died when I was nine, and I get scared when I can't fully *remember* him. I mean we have photos…but…it's weird…I still remember him, but *how I remember him changes*. It's not the same."

"I'm sorry you lost your dad," he offers kindly. "Wow and so young, that must have been tough."

I keep looking at his face and then remember once more that he can't "see me back." *Weird.*

Again, I feel more open with him somehow. I continue, "Thanks, yeah I'm OK now." I pause, then say, "I already feel like I'm starting to forget how stars look in the night sky. I haven't seen them, probably, for years." I ask, curious, "Is it true, what they say, that your other senses get stronger?"

Trevor rubs the back of his head, thinking. "I don't know–I think that's kind of an urban myth, but I guess I'd say I rely more on my other senses for sure. For me, the best thing I did was to try some of the things they offered–like the cane. It took me a while–like to admit that using a cane would be a good idea. I've got the scars to prove it." He laughs and shakes his head.

"But the cane became a way to feel my way through an environment. The cane is another way to see, kind of? Eventually I got Eleanor, and she makes it so that I don't need the cane. She's a huge deal."

He smiles down towards her.

I change the subject. "Hey–I see your shirt. I love *Hippo Campus* too!" I share and then worry I sound too enthusiastic.

"Ha! Forgot I was wearing it." He rubs his chest as if remembering. "Yeah. Just went to their concert last summer." He pauses as if thinking and then begins again. "OK, since you asked, one of the hardest things for me has been giving up the driving thing. Kind of an ego thing for a guy, I guess. I've got a few good friends who take me everywhere." He pauses and leans forward. "Hey! I've been talking way too much...what about you? How did you realize you had RP?" He sounds genuinely curious.

Realizing that my whole life story has been rewritten, I share, "Looking back, it's been going on for years...probably since I was ten or maybe even eight? Maybe longer. A few weeks ago, I almost got hit by a car."

"Oh wow," he says with gravity, as if he could really sense how hard it was.

Tears spring up in my eyes. It's kind of nice to know that he probably can't see them.

I clear my throat and add, "So now, next week, I'm supposed to go to the Lighthouse for the Blind or whatever, and I don't feel like I really need that yet." I sigh and confess, "But honestly, I don't know what I need."

"Yeah, there's a lot of good stuff out there; you're going to figure it out," he assures me. "You said you love Hippo Campus. Have you heard their new album?"

"Yeah–I love it," I say, thinking I can't believe we share this; nobody I know at school is into them.

"I've been listening to a cool live recording of it...I can send you," he offers.

"Sure!"

"If you ever want to come visit the U too. I can take you around and introduce you to the people who helped me out," he says.

"Yeah–thanks...I might take you up on that," I reply, noncommittal.

I don't want to tell him that I'm not really needing all that support stuff. *Yet.* The thought of even visiting the U right now feels like too much. Suddenly, with Trevor, I feel guilty that my vision is still pretty great. I rub my knee, which continues to throb.

Just then, my mom and Leslie appear, and they are approaching the table. *Perfect timing.*

"Hey you two! Hope we weren't gone too long?" Leslie says, breathlessly, as they arrive.

Trevor tilts his head up, now aware our moms are back.

"Hey, wow that went fast!" he comments. Trevor smiles up towards them.

Then he turns back to me. "Meera, do you want to exchange numbers–in case you have more questions?"

"Sure, that sounds good," I reply, feeling weird now that we're not alone.

He's so different than the guys I know at school...is it the three years that make the difference? I'm never going to see him again, but it's easier just to exchange the numbers.

"How 'bout you text me your number. That's probably easiest," he says.

"Sure," I tell him, grabbing my phone out of a coat pocket. "What's your number?"

I enter the digits and send him a text.

"Great! And if I don't text you back right away, sometimes it's because I'm in class," he explains. "I use Siri text, and I have to listen to it before I can respond. So it's a little slow."

"Gotcha," I say, suddenly feeling so awkward.

A part of me just wants to leave. I'm mad all over again at my mom for setting this thing up, and I feel embarrassed that it seems like I've enjoyed it.

"It was great to meet you, Meera." Trevor pulls his coat on and rises from his chair.

Eleanor gets back up too.

"Yeah–you too, Trevor," I reply, feeling shy now.

Our moms say their good-byes close to the door, and Trevor, Leslie and Eleanor leave as Mom walks to the front to pay.

"Wasn't Trevor great?" my mom asks, with way too much enthusiasm, as we get back into the car. "His mom Leslie is such a sweetie. She and I…"

I cut her off sharply and say tightly, "*Why did you do that?*"

I'm buckling myself into the car and staring straight ahead. "Why do you think you can just do stuff like that and not ask me?"

Though I enjoyed my time with Trevor, a twist of anger is now rising in my belly and up into my chest. I should have been asked.

"I'm sorry, sweetie, but I thought if I told you about it you might not…" she says, trying to defend her logic.

"*Exactly.* I might not want to meet him? Can we just go to the hotel?" I give her no room for further explanation.

"But it's only two o'clock? Don't you want to go to Anthro and Galleria?" she pleads. "Our hotel is all the way back at the Mall of America."

"Not anymore," I tell her in a low voice.

A part of me desperately wants to go enjoy the rest of the day, but the part of me that wants to punish my mom is stronger. I can't let this go.

Mom reluctantly starts the car.

As we enter the freeway, my mom begins regrouping. "I guess I could just check us in, and you can stay the hotel while I shop?" she says, defeated.

"Sounds good to me," I snap back.

After a long hot bath at the hotel, I binge-watch *Love It or List It* on HGTV, which is horribly uninspiring, and then fall asleep. I wake up starving. It's dark. I feel around for my phone, which I had set on the nightstand. It's completely dead. *Ugh, why didn't I think to ask Mom for my charger?* I had put it in her purse before we left home.

The room is pitch black; I had turned off the TV and lights before crawling back into bed. I feel for the remote on the side table and then I remember that I had set it on the dresser. I have to pee. Across the bed, as I scan, I see a dim green which must be the bedside phone? I wish I never would have pulled the curtains...this place is an abyss. My heart starts to pound. What's it going to be like when I lose all of my vision—will it be like this? An eternal darkness. It feels so daunting...an empty scary nothingness. Once I'm blind, will I remember where things are and how to get around? Will I have to call out to strangers, "HELP?! I can't see." I'm back at the rear door of our house fumbling with the key in the dark, the night our neighbor came to help me.

What if next time it isn't a neighbor, but somebody who isn't so nice? I'd heard of a girl being roofied at U of MN—somebody slipped a pill in her drink at a party. She woke up in some random suburb crackhouse, aware that she had been gang-raped. *Jesus.* I tell myself, *Stop scaring yourself and breathe.* I inhale, pleading with the air to go deep into my belly. Exhale. *OK, I can do this. I don't know what's wrong with me. I shouldn't be panicking.*

I swing my legs over the side of the bed and stand up, feeling forward into space for the wall, and as my fingers touch it finally, I start to follow it along towards the bathroom. *I've got this.* As I move in the dark, I'm thinking about college. I'll need to be more careful, and be sure my phone is always charged. This was all Lorraine's fault. If she hadn't made the stupid setup with her friend, we'd be having fun right now.

I know the bathroom is just on the other side of the wall. I turn, but instead of entering the bathroom I run smack into something hard. I misjudged the turn in the dark, and I have hit the frame of the doorway. I grab my nose, which is now stinging. I can feel a warm trickle, it's starting to bleed. I touch my tongue to my upper lip and taste the metallic saltiness. I hear the card in the door and the lock clicking. The door swings open, and light floods the room from the hall. Lorraine is back.

She looks at me and suddenly drops her bags as the door slams behind her. "Meera! Oh my gosh! What happened?" she says, sounding alarmed.

She rushes towards me.

"It's just a nosebleed," I explain, still irritated with her.

I rub my nose with the back of a hand and see that it's then covered in blood.

"But it's all over," she tells me, concerned.

I look down and see that my shirt has a few big splashes of bright red and some drops have landed on the carpet.

"Hold still…pinch your nose and I'll grab you a washcloth." Mom is now in full-on nurse mode.

She finds tissues first and hands the box to me, and then she begins soaking a washcloth in the sink. As I pinch my nose hard, out of nowhere I start to sob and choke. I sputter and swallow some of the blood, which instantly makes me feel nauseous. Since the diagnosis, I haven't wanted her to see me like this—to protect her so she doesn't worry—but it's coming out.

I spit blood into the toilet and then lean my head forward while applying pressure to my nose with a Kleenex like I have done dozens of times.

Mom heads my way with the wet washcloth from the sink.

"Oh Meera, I am so sorry," my mom says, her voice tired as she dabs all of the blood off my face. "I shouldn't have left you here alone."

I continue to pinch my nose with one hand and I lean into her, letting her hug me, and she strokes my hair. It's been a long time since I've been open to her affection. Or since she's hugged me this tight. The part of me that wants to be hugged temporarily wins over the angry part of me.

For a few minutes, I just stand there with my head on Mom's chest while holding pressure on my nose and breathing heavily through my mouth. My breathing slows down and I can hear her heartbeat too.

Mom squeezes me even a little tighter.

"It's OK, Mom. It's nothing you did," I finally say as she relaxes her arms.

"Well, if it makes you feel any better, I brought some dinner. You must be starving?" She releases me and places a kiss on my shoulder.

"Yeah I'm pretty hungry," I tell her, relieved that everything is shifted.

I change my T-shirt and then head over to the bed.

Mom stands by the bathroom door. "Let me try to clean up the carpet quick, and then I have all the supplies for a bed picnic in my bag."

When we were in Colombia, sometimes we were too tired to go out for dinner. So we would get takeout and make what Grandma calls a "bed picnic" instead.

After her rescue of the carpet, Mom swings opens the minibar and offers me a Sprite and grabs a miniature bottle of wine for herself. We sit cross-legged on the bed and dig into the edamame and California rolls she picked up. I delicately dab each roll with a little wasabi–not too much.

"Thanks Mom," I say quietly, feeling grateful.

"You're welcome, sweetie. And for dessert!"

She leans across the bed, picks up a small bag from Nordstrom and drops it into my lap. I peek in: Vosges chocolate–three big bars.

"Whoa!! Which one should we open first?" I ask.

"You choose," she says.

I unwrap the Barcelona bar–milk chocolate with sea salt and roasted almonds–and break off a piece. Then I push the bar and wrapper towards her.

I decide to try to talk about how I was feeling earlier. Avoiding eye contact, I tell her, "Trevor and his mom are super sweet but…I feel like I need to figure this out alone? His situation is soooo different. And he already has it all figured out. I'd also just prefer that you tell me stuff…that you ASK me first?"

I look down at the bar of chocolate now between us on the bed, and I break off another piece.

"I'm sorry. As I said before, I thought you'd say no if I asked."

I feel myself getting stubborn all over again, but something in me stops and I soften. "You're right…I would have." I shake my head.

"He *is* kind of cute." My mom smiles, looking at me with her eyebrows raised.

"Yeah…I guess…for a blind dude," I reply, smiling too and breaking off another piece of chocolate.

"Meera Luz!" My mom lightly bounces her hand on my knee, scolding me.

"I'm just saying…I mean I'm the RP girl, I can have my opinions."

We continue savoring the chocolate in silence.

Soon I begin again. "He's nice, Mom—it's not that. It's just the whole thing made me feel like I can't trust you all over again…like I have to worry that there will be another bad surprise."

I don't want to reveal that I was surprised about how cute he was. It all seems so stupid and superficial now…what does it matter? Eventually I'll be blind and have no fucking idea how I look or how anyone else looks either. Once again, I'm the asshole.

Lying in bed that night with my eyes closed, I can't sleep. I'm not tired because of my earlier nap. As I relax more, pinprick dancing lights appear against the pure screen of darkness behind my lids. They remind me a little of stars, but instead of twinkling in place they're in constant buzzing motion. "We love you," say the dancing lights, silently. *Who are you?* I ask. As soon as I ask, they're gone.

I bring Sweetie to mind and, quickly, I sense her soft body curled up next to mine. I remember the beautiful clearing in that stand of white pines where the deer dream. I picture Sweetie and me there. She's lit from above by silvery moonlight, sort of like when we first met so long ago. Now, alongside me, she blinks a few times, settles her head on her rump, and looks at me sideways. *How am I going to do this blindness thing? What's it going to be like?* I ask her. She leans closer to me and closes her eyes, and I know she's right. Sleep will improve everything. I curl up with her body now around me, my breathing slows and I relax and drift softly to sleep, marinating in the peacefulness of Sweetie's presence.

Chapter Eleven

I'm completely blind and alone in a room. My mom is dead; she's united with Dad and long gone from the earth. *Those are the facts.* Even though I'm blind, somehow I know the room is all black. Nobody remembers me or can locate me. I'm stuck here, and I can't find my way out. I keep yelling for help, but nobody comes.

I wake up feeling utterly alone and hopeless, but so glad to be no longer dreaming. I'm still in the hotel, and the bathroom light is on, casting a soft glow in the room. I lie there in bed for a while, realizing how horrible *being forgotten* would be. I suddenly realize that being remembered by another person is really the only way I exist. Suddenly, I'm more grateful than ever for Mom, Penn and my aunt and uncle. They know who I am, which is really how I "exist." I think of my dad and Lexi. I never want to forget them. I loved that Disney movie *Coco*, about the little boy and his guitar, and my dream helps the movie make sense. It showed how we only exist, in a way, when people "know" or remember us. When they speak our name. So, even if I lose my vision, as long as I am "known"…my dream seems to be suggesting…maybe I'll be OK.

I sit up in bed, and I'm suddenly aware of my throbbing skinned knee. A scab has formed overnight, making it painful to bend. I check my phone, it's 8:30 am. I get up and find a note from my mom at the sink:

WHERE THE DEER DREAM

I'm at breakfast.
Come down to the hotel cafe when you wake up.
Mom

I feel irritated, remembering the ambush with Trevor and his mom. I wish my mom would ask me what I think…or what I need… instead of keeping me in the dark. I try to be positive and push it out of my mind. I just want to get along with my mom. I wish we could be more normal together. I wish it wasn't so fucking hard.

I find her reading the paper in a booth by the window.

"Morning! How'd you sleep?" Mom calls out as I approach. She's chipper as usual.

I feel even more like a jerk.

"Fine," I say, yawning.

"It's a buffet–you can go get what you like," Mom explains.

After I sit down with my plate of eggs, fruit and toast, my mom leans forward while sipping her coffee. She begins to look at me intensely. "Now I know you don't want to go on Monday, but I really think this Lighthouse for the Blind meeting will be good. We can find out all kinds…"

I cut her off mid-sentence. "I'm not going," I say resolutely.

She presses back. "Remember, the doctor said it's good to get connected to those resources, early rather than later."

I continue my rebuttal. "I already told you *I need to deal with this on my own*…in my own way. I'll do what I need to do when I need to do it. I'm eighteen…I'll be on my own soon." As I say this, a voice inside me asks, *Will I?*

"You're eighteen, Meera, but you're also my daughter. I love you and want the best for you."

I see an opportunity now.

"If you love me…" I begin slowly.

"Yes?" she says, with her eyes searching my face.

This could work, I think to myself.

I tell her, "I've been thinking a lot about what Aunt Jill said of that healer…the shaman. I even had a dream about her."

"What about it?" my mom asks, picking her newspaper back up, signaling her desire to leave this topic alone.

I have to go slowly here, I warn myself.

"I'd like to go see the shaman…I mean if there was a way to go," I say cautiously, hoping Lorraine will stay open long enough to consider it.

With a certain finality, Mom tells me, "Listen Meera—the doctors right at the clinic can give you everything you need. Your retinal doctor trained at the Mayo Clinic."

"I know the doctors are good," I reply. "I know all that, but there is something about what Aunt Jill said. I'm curious and I wonder…if I don't go now, will I regret not asking for a miracle in twenty years? Put yourself in my shoes. Wouldn't you be wanting to ask?"

I search her face.

Mom sets down her paper and looks at me with a pained expression. "I pray every day for a miracle for you, sweetie. Grandma is praying too. We all are."

My mom reaches across the table to touch my arm.

I press on, trying to get her to hear me. "When we went to that fire ceremony in Colombia…looking back, it was my *favorite part* of our whole trip. I can't stop thinking about it, and I'd really like to give something like that a try."

"Meera, the thing is…this shaman stuff can be dangerous. I spoke a bit more with Jill about it, and the shaman she saw used *psychedelics*. Now I knew of a girl in college who never was the same after taking some LSD…do you understand? She *never recovered*. She's not OK. We have more modern ways now–better ways that don't involve people taking drugs *like that*. So…I know you are eighteen but I'm not supporting a trip like that because it also comes with risks."

Ignoring her, I continue impulsively. "I have some money saved from working last summer still. I could probably pay for most of a ticket. I have like six hundred dollars." I offer this, trying to show her that I'm willing to contribute.

"It's not about the money; it's about being safe, Meera. I don't see any value in you going to Mexico. And I don't share Jill's sense of adventure."

"So you'd keep me from doing *the one thing* I believe might be able to help me?" I say, feeling helpless with a lump growing my throat. I wish my mom was more like her sister sometimes, at least Aunt Jill understands me.

"Yes, I would, because I have life experience which you don't yet have. When you're older and have kids of your own Meera, you might understand. But until then…" She shakes her head and pours herself more coffee from the carafe.

Silence falls. I wonder if she's thinking what I'm thinking. *Do blind people even have kids? Is that even OK to do?* Just thinking about possibly not becoming a mother, another thing I assumed I would have to look forward to, brings up a wave of awfulness.

I stand up and push my chair back in.

"I need your room key. I'm going upstairs."

During the drive home, Mom and I are mostly silent. I try to sleep but can't.

My mom turns the radio off and sits up a bit straighter, adjusting her grip on the steering wheel. I look up and notice we're in a dense fog. This sometimes happens on our way from Minneapolis back up to Duluth. I stare ahead. You can barely see ten feet ahead. The car in front of us has slowed to a crawl on the freeway.

This fog is sort of what it feels like when I'm navigating the dark. There is an inner need to slow down because what's on the other side of that fog, or darkness, is completely unknown. Maybe a jackknifed semi is lying up ahead, hidden behind the opaque curtain of vapor. Or maybe there's absolutely nothing? There's no way of knowing...you just have to slow down and hope there isn't something dangerous ahead. It's a vulnerable feeling. Unnerving.

Then my phone buzzes. Trevor texts me a photo of Eleanor.

Trevor: I'm sending you a pic of Eleanor...but in case it's not Eleanor and something more embarrassing...forgive me. Once I texted what I thought was a selfie to my mom, but it was one of my roommates in his boxers instead. I hope the rest of your trip with your mom was good. It was great to meet you. (At the bottom of his text it says, *This message powered by Illumina App.*)

Me: It's just a pic of Eleanor...you're good.

(A few minutes pass.)

Trev: Phew.

(Smiling at this, I decide to text back.)

Me: I can't tell you how many times I've knocked over chairs or run into things…but texting half-naked people…you got me there.

Trevor: If you don't laugh, you'll cry. We have a saying around here…#BPHMF.

Me: What's #BPHMF?

Trev: Blind people have more fun—it's a little joke I have with one of my BBs here.

Me: Ahhh.

Trev: Like…talking to yourself when you thought somebody was there. Or…once I tried to drop my empty Gatorade bottle into a guy's lap at the airport—to me, he had the absolute perfect outline to be a garbage can.

Me: Shoot!

Trevor: I hope your Lighthouse trip goes well next week.

Me: Thanks.

(I don't have the heart to tell him that I'm not going.)

Trevor: I'm here if you want to talk.

Me: It's been a relief to meet you…it makes me feel less alone. Thank you.

Trevor: OK, until next time! I have to run…today is hockey day for me.

Me: Have a great game.

I want so badly for the fog to lift…to be able to go fast again. To not hesitate. To figure this whole vision thing out. To figure out where and who I'll end up being. To know where I'm going and how to get there. I close my eyes again and silently make a prayer. *If you are there God, please help me out of this nightmare. Heal my eyes. I promise to use all the gifts and talents you've given me to help others. I promise to be kind to my mother, even when she makes me batshit crazy.*

I open my phone and add to my list of beautiful things I've been cataloging:

Eleanor, Trevor's lab

The moss-covered rocks and swaths of princess pine at Hawk Ridge

The booth filled with Madonnas and sacred stuff at Hunt & Gather

The lupine blooming in June in the ditches on the way to Two Harbors

Magenta-edged white peonies on my grandma's kitchen table with the light catching the blooms

I pause. Maybe I can also add other sensory memories, not just things that I "see," to this list.

Sammy's Pizza with extra green olives

The lavender-scented candles that fill Jess's design studio office with the smell of possibility

The sun-warmed sand beneath me on my beach towel at Park Point

Trevor's strong hand

Sweetie's dark eyes

I think about Sweetie and her graceful body, her curved and pointed ears, like elegant satellite dishes that swivel and twitch. Her perfect black nose. It's funny, because Sweetie is somebody that nobody else can see but me. Sometimes I forget how weird it might be that I have this connection with a deer nobody can see. And I feel a bit of relief too, because RP can't take away Sweetie. I don't need my retinas to know her. Last night in my dreams I saw her, and all her fawn spots were gone. She was wearing a grand floral crown, ala artist Frida Kahlo, made with wild roses, lupine and daisies. Her legs felt stronger and longer. She seemed determined, with a slight grin on her doe lips.

On Monday, Penn picks me up for school. It's brutally cold, minus 20 degrees Fahrenheit. Even with my UGG boots, a hat and the polar fleece quarter-zip under my coat, I'm shivering to stay warm in the not-yet-heated car. As she drives down the hill towards the lake, the sun's light is beginning to paint the horizon. The steam and clouds hovering over the lake are a juicy orange-red beneath the violet sky. It was going to be one of those magical sunrises.

"Penn, can you be five minutes late?" I ask, hoping the answer is yes.

"Yeah, I can be a little late for English—why?" says Penn.

"Can we just quick run down to Brighton Beach? It's just so beautiful!" I'm excited by the possibility.

"Sure...but I may not get out—it's too cold." Penn is laughing.

She pulls into the beach lot. Only one other car is there.

"I'll just be a minute," I tell her.

"You go, Nature Girl!" Penn laughs again as she puts the car in park and picks up her phone.

I walk onto the beach, rigid now with ice and snow, and move quickly towards the water's edge. I'm surprised to see dozens of frying-pan-sized disks of ice spinning in circles. In the still morning, they gently bump and spin around atop the steam-covered lake, polishing each other beneath the open sky. The perfect disks of ice seem so improbable and add to the sense of wonder I'm feeling.

I remember our Mr. Simon, in physics class, talking about this phenomenon, but I'd never seen it before. I grab a quick video of the spinning ice pancakes, lit up by coral tinged light. I remember him saying that they were created by rotational shearing forces. As the ice fragments are rotated by the current, each was ground into a perfect circle. I understand, now, why he'd been so excited. It was *amazing to see.*

Beyond them lies endless open water that's bleeding slow trickles of steam into the bitterly cold air. Up towards Stony Point, the sun is now beginning to grow…an expanding pinprick of intense light. Perfect timing. A few minutes pass and the blaze grows so bright, so quickly, that I finally have to look away. The sun infuses the vapor over the water with an opalescent fire.

The beach is buried under snow, so—without access to any exposed stones—I quickly pluck a wedge-like piece of snow and ice instead. I hold it in my hands and whisper into it, "Dear Universe, thank you for all of this amazingness and please heal my eyes?" I set it gently into the open water and it bobbed happily. Suddenly, I feel Sweetie standing beside me as we watch my little ice wish slowly drift east towards the sun. As I turn towards her, Sweetie is rolling in the snow on her back, like a big puppy. All the while, I've been being so serious with my prayer, she seems to now be saying, *Hey, let's PLAY!* I smile back at her and realize it would feel good to let go.

As I stride quickly toward the car, I turn back once more. The sun is fully up now, shining through the steam, and the sky has turned pale blue. *And Sweetie is leaping around like a maniac on the frozen ground, having a ball. Message received.*

She's wearing black tights, a denim dress and a down vest, and she speaks slowly and kindly to me, like I'm a little kid, which is annoying. The disability lady travels all over the district to help kids like me find what they need. Right now she's sitting at a desk in the Guidance Counselor's office at my school. I've just walked in for my appointment.

"Good morning, Meera—I'm Gudrun. I'll be helping you with accommodations for school."

I take a seat by the desk and take in Gudrun's "look." Her short hair is silvery blonde and spiked into stiff tufts with gel. The frames of her glasses are thick and fire-engine red.

"Yeah hi," I say, trying to be friendly though I'm doubting this is going to be helpful.

"I understand, from your mom, that you're all set up to go to Lighthouse tomorrow. Yes? We had a nice talk the other day."

She pushes her glasses up higher on her nose and presses her lips together as she squints towards the laptop screen.

I mumble, "Uh huh." I'm not going to argue with her.

"How are you doing? I know that receiving a diagnosis like this isn't easy." She glances up at me with kind eyes.

"Doing OK. Thanks," I say, while feeling tears well up that I wish wouldn't.

"Judy–the person who will probably tour you around at Lightbouse–is wonderful. Please tell her I say hello."

Gudrun turns towards a large black bag behind her and hauls out one huge book, setting it on the table between us. Then she grabs a second one and places it on top of the first. They're each as big as the crazy Victorian dictionaries from Hunt & Gather–so thick and huge they're clownish.

"So, I've gathered large print copies of the textbooks you're using in Math and English. These are all I have so far..." And she points at the two books.

All I can think is: *Am I supposed to drag these things around?*

She lowers her laptop screen a little and looks at me. "Meera, tell me where things are challenging for you? When I looked at your file, I saw that you are corrected to 20/60 and 20/40–so I'm a little confused as your vision doesn't seem as affected as I thought it would be?" She looks at me and blinks.

Great...she thinks I'm faking too.

I attempt to explain. "Well, I have pretty bad tunnel vision. My peripheral vision is mostly gone so sometimes I trip on things I can't see...stuff that is directly underneath me...and walk into walls when I turn too. But I do still have trouble with the board and with textbooks too...like if it's not bright enough in the room, I have trouble reading." I was hoping she understood.

"Ah, OK. I might not be able to help with the tunnel vision, but why don't you see how you do with these books? Large print should help. The best way for me to help you is if you tell me where things aren't working. I can also get you a portable reading light to bring with you to class—I'm thinking that it might be a contrast issue?"

She scans her screen once more and then looks up at me again.

"This is going to take some time...why don't you at least take these books...and then I will get in touch in the next few days, OK?"

I realize that she has just wrapped up our conversation. I feel rushed and frustrated.

"Uh...OK...these books are kind of big," I say in a massive understatement. "Can I just take the Trig one for now?"

"Oh sure. I can leave the other one at the office with the attendance secretary. I'll put your name on it," she tells me absentmindedly.

Great.

My next class is Trig, and I set the huge new book on my desk, hoping nobody will notice. *Fat chance.*

"Nice book, Guacamole...ha!" says Fred, the kid who sits in front of me. His nickname for me refers to my South American roots.

When I asked my mom if that was racism, she said, "Anything that makes you feel put down for who you are is racism."

I didn't want to make a huge deal about it, and even though I couldn't stand Fred, it was still demoralizing.

"What IS that thing?" Fred asks and smirks.

"I need it to read," I respond dully and quietly, hoping he'll lose interest.

I flip open the book to find the chapter we're on.

"Yeah right... what are you blind?" He laughs.

I ignore him. I wish he would fuck right off.

Ms. Fisher walks in and comes right up to me to say in a low voice (which anybody nearby can hear), "I understand you are needing some visual aids, Meera? I wish you would have told me this was a problem earlier?"

She sounds irritated like I've done something to make *her* look bad.

"We will work to get you what you need...I'll be working on it with the district's Special Needs contact person."

She's looking at me curiously as if she doesn't really believe I have a legitimate problem.

Great, she thinks I am faking too.

As she walks to her desk, Fred turns back towards me, raising his eyebrows and mouthing the word "Ha!" as if this is all just hilarious to him.

Hot tears rise. *WTF.* I just want to disappear. To be done with all of this. Somehow, I make it through the hour. The book actually helps, but I can't deal with it. I put the book in the bottom of my locker.

Mom is there in the living room when I come in. She's paying bills on the couch with her laptop on the coffee table.

She pushes computer glasses on top of her head and looks up. "How was school?"

"Horrible," I say, as I keep walking.

She sets her laptop aside and sits up taller. "What happened, Meer?" she asks.

Not stopping, I move towards the kitchen and my room, talking as I walk past her. "I hate school and I'm not going back."

I enter my room without shutting the door.

She follows me to my room and stands in the doorway. "How was the meeting with the lady...the district specialist," she asks. "Can't remember her name...".

I throw my backpack on the floor in the corner.

"Meer...?" she says softly enough that something in me cracks.

I spill. "First, that stupid lady gives me this book that's like the size of our toaster oven—its HUGE. And then she acts surprised that with my..." I make exaggerated air quotes with my hands. "...'vision,' I'm having trouble? Like I'm making it up! Then in Math, the teacher acts like I'm lying too."

My face is hot, and I don't dare blink or the tears will spill. They flow anyway, and I wipe the tears away quickly with my sleeve.

"I'm not going back," I say again.

My mom's face crumples. "I'm so sorry. Oh Meer, I think the Lighthouse is going to help because they have so much more experience with this—what you have is pretty rare, so it's not entirely their fault. I'm sure the teacher didn't mean to be unkind, she just..."

Great, my own mother is on their *side.*

I argue, "She just what? *Thinks I'm making this up?* Thinks I'm pretending to be going blind for giggles? Are you going to make excuses for her?" I'm not sad anymore, just pissed.

"No, I'm sorry, Meera—that isn't what I meant."

There's a long pause. I just want her to leave.

"Do you want to go out for dinner...? We haven't had..." she says, backpedaling.

"No, I don't want to go anywhere. Please just go."

I put a hand on my door, indicating I intend to close it.

She steps back and I shut the door.

I flop onto the bed, phone in hand, and text Trevor.

Me: Horrible day. Did anybody ever think you were faking it when you went blind?

About five minutes pass, in which I think I am going to die.

Maybe he's not there...or maybe he doesn't want anything to do with me.

I go into the bathroom and start running the hot water into the tub. *Gah, what I said was so stupid. He went blind after a surgical procedure. His blindness was legit!*

Ping! My phone vibrates on the tile counter. I turn off the water, grab my phone and return to my room, shutting the door behind me.

Trevor: Yeah, sometimes people ask me why I have my dog, Eleanor. It's like people think that blind people have a look or whatever. Want to just call me? It's easier?

"So, what happened. Tell me everything," says Trevor after answering my call.

"Ughhh, it's so complicated...but at school I got this large print textbook, you know to help me. It's huge, and this super douchey kid in Math laughed and basically said I'm faking. Even my teacher seems to think I'm making it up. Who would fake this?"

"I know the type. Can't give a guy like that too much of your space. He's probably crushing on you," says Trevor, laughing softly.

"What?! No way." I'm feeling embarrassed and surprised, knowing that Trevor thinks I'm crush-worthy. But he's blind?

"Sure–that's how guys are," Trevor tells me with a laugh and a sigh. "We tease and harass the ones we really like....awkward but true."

"Well, he did ask me to be his lab partner in seventh grade and I turned him down," I confess, remembering.

"I rest my case," Trevor replies with a chuckle. "He's brokenhearted."

"OK, I have a question for you," I say slowly and more seriously.

"OK..." he responds calmly.

"Do you ever feel sorry for yourself and if you do—how do you get over it?" I ask, hoping it's not too weird of a question.

"Oh yeah—ask my mom. I got into some pretty pissy, sad sack moods and still do sometimes...it comes with the territory," he confesses. "But I try really hard to not stay there too long."

I hear him sigh.

"To get out of it," he continues, "sometimes I think about this kid I saw once in a documentary about Mr. Rogers. He was basically quadriplegic...I think from a brain tumor also? Not sure?"

"My mom and I saw that movie at a theater," I tell him, remembering that I'd never heard so many people crying so openly in public. Like, several adults actually sobbing.

Trevor says, "It was before my surgery, and I don't know exactly why that guy stuck with me but...it's like *if he can do life, I can do life*. I mean, I can walk, I can still move. I can be relatively independent. Thinking of him makes me realize how lucky I am. There was something too about him...he was just honest and good. Eventually, like as an adult, he got some big award. So...despite all the things going against him, he did great things."

"That makes sense," I respond, trying to remember that character and how I felt about him.

"Yeah...don't get me wrong—I still get upset. It sucks sometimes being the one who can't see. The world is built for people who see...

my world has gotten smaller in so many ways. But also it's bigger. That's why I want to do sports psychology...to help other people find *whatever they need* to perform at a higher level...to live their dream. I'd like to write too...maybe one day I'll tell my story. I mean if that guy can change people's lives, maybe I can too."

"What do you mean...about your world being smaller?" I ask, curious.

"Well, like having to get rides everywhere–relying on other people and asking for help sucks," he explains. "Sometimes I worry I'm a burden even though everyone says I'm not. Or I feel left out or more isolated, because I can't share certain things with sighted people."

"Yeah, I get that totally," I say. "Because I wasn't able to see at night very well...everybody thought I was weird, a scaredy cat, and so, I just learned to keep to myself and avoid situations unless I had Penn or my mom with me. So I guess my world is already small like that."

After I share this, I worry that maybe I've said too much. I'm not dealing with what he is...yet.

To my relief, he seems OK with what I said and continues. "Friends are really what helps me through. Your friends will help you through this too. Also, don't forget to laugh. There are so many things that happen to me now that could bring me down but laughing is much better."

Trevor laughs to himself and then, as if remembering something, he adds, "So, last year, I was with my mom. She was near campus, so took me to lunch, and afterwards we went to buy a few groceries. We're checking out at Target, and I'm helping put stuff on the belt from the cart and I'm going to grab some Tic Tacs, which I know are on the little racks above the belt. So, I'm feeling around the different shelves of gum feeling for the hard little plastic boxes, and then I feel something silky—and my brain is like *what is THAT?* I'm curious. Then all of a sudden I hear this woman's voice go, 'Excuse me?' My mom looks over, and apparently I had the sleeve of a woman's blouse in my hand, and my hand was headed straight towards her chest." He laughs out loud again, reliving the embarrassment.

"Mom grabbed my arm just before it was too late, and she said the lady just gave us both the stink eye. She had no idea..."

"Oh my God!" I laugh too, imagining the whole crazy scene.

"I know—and the thing is, I could have been embarrassed or upset—and, at first, I was a little—wondering how it must have looked. How rude and how pervy I must have seemed. But it was so much better when I decided to laugh about it. The poor lady. Hopefully she figured it out."

"You seem to have such a good attitude," I say, admiring his response to what happened.

"Thanks—it's definitely a choice. I've met people too, I knew a few at my Braille school, who were still really angry about being blind. And it's like, what the use? I can't change what happened to me, but I can change how I react. I try to remember that. And I think about that Mr. Roger's guy."

"Hey Trevor, my mom is calling me for dinner. Talking to you helps. Sometimes I feel bad because I'm asking you so many questions. I hope it's OK."

"Nah...you're good," he responds in his warm voice.

"Thanks for understanding," I say, relieved again.

"Any time, Meera. OK, you better go eat!" Trevor concludes.

"OK! Bye." I hang up feeling lighter and brighter.

Chapter Twelve

"Mmmm hmmm?" my mom responds.

"Honestly, I hate school so much," I say as I help clean up the kitchen after dinner. "I don't want to go back. I know a girl, Amber, who does online school, and I think I'd like to enroll there."

"It's going to get better...it just will. Bad days happen," she tells me, like it's not a big deal as she rinses plates to be loaded into the dishwasher.

"But how? What's going to change? I still have RP. You don't know what it's like having the teacher not believe you, and dealing with boys who are assholes. Have you given any thought to the shaman thing?" I'm hoping this might be a good moment to ask about that.

"Meera..." Mom's annoyed by this topic coming up again.

"You don't understand what it's like for me...I really want to have a chance to see if there's something that can help me."

"Well, the specialist did connect me with the clinic doing that research protocol with stem cells in San Francisco," Mom notes with a take charge sound to her voice. "We're waiting to hear back from the retinal doctor to see if you might qualify."

I remember that the doctor didn't seem that optimistic when she talked to us.

Frustrated that she's hopeful about this when the doctor clearly wasn't, I tell Mom, "Well, Dr. Galbraith didn't seem super excited about it. She said she was pretty sure I wouldn't qualify because they want patients with advanced disease, which I don't have yet. And even if by some miracle I do qualify, we'd have to practically live in California."

"I know but it's something," my mom responds.

"Yeah...but I have this feeling that *I am supposed to go to Mexico...to that shaman*," I tell her honestly.

"Oh Meera..." Mom is shaking her head as if I'm ridiculous.

I try to stay calm to convince her, and share, "I can't stop thinking about it. It feels *right* to me."

"I know this is really hard on you. I wish I could make it go away...I really do," Mom replies.

"It's just really annoying when you say things like that, but you aren't willing to try something I think might help." I see that she clearly doesn't get it.

"I'm sorry...it's just how I feel," she confesses.

"Maybe just stop sharing how you feel," I toss back, my voice raised and full of emotion.

I leave the kitchen. We don't speak the rest of the night.

⚬⚭⚭⚬

The next morning, I hear knocking at my bedroom door.

"Meera? Meera? It's late...you need to get to the bus," she says urgently through the door.

"I'm not going," I tell her, feeling my stomach tighten as I remember yesterday at school.

"You have to go to school..."

"I can't." I dig in my heels.

"Listen Meera..." I notice that my mom's voice is softening. "I'll talk to Aunt Jill tonight after work about this Mexico thing, but I need you to go to school."

Surprised that she's willing to talk to Aunt Jill, I offer an olive branch with a request. "OK, I'll go. But can you write me a pass to excuse me from fourth hour gym so I can go to lunch with Penn?"

Silence.

"At least I can eat lunch in peace and have something to look forward to?"

Mom sighs and then says, "OK. I need to run...I'll leave the note next to the toaster."

"Could you also leave me a little cash for lunch?" I ask, pushing my luck.

"Yes—I'll put it with the note," she replies without complaint.

"Thank youuuuu!" I sing out with a little sweetness in my voice.

"And don't forget...I'm picking you up after school for the Lighthouse for the Blind orientation visit," she reminds me before heading for the kitchen.

"Wait... that's TODAY?" I sit up in bed and yell, "But I'm not ready!"

A moment later, Mom pops back by my door, and says flatly, "I'm leaving Meera—I'll see you at three in front of the school."

As she leaves, I hear the front door close behind her.

I make it through third hour without knocking anything over or falling flat on my face, and I meet Penn at the front entrance. Seniors can leave the grounds for lunch, which is about the only thing good about school right now.

"How are you?" asks Penn with sincerity.

"I've been better…yesterday was *no bueno*. The special needs lady gave me these stupid, large-print textbooks, and horrible Fred was an asshole in Trig."

"Ughhh, he's awful. Forget him. The kid's not worth your time."

"I did my best in dealing with him," I say flatly.

"Well, your hair looks amazing!" Penn tells me, smiling and leaning over to touch my curls.

I grin back. At least something is working.

"Thanks. I used that curly hair stuff and did what you told me. I didn't touch it after combing the conditioner through." I'm happy she thinks it looks good.

"I give you an A+ from the Penn School of Beauty." Penn smiles at me as she starts the car.

She drives towards Amity Coffee. She fills me in on her weekend visit to the beauty supply store and the cool new stuff she got. Penn seems genuinely happy and I'm happy for her.

As we walk into the café, I blurt, "Did I tell you about Trevor?"

I realize I haven't really talked to her since Sunday.

"No…?" she says with a mischievous look in her eye.

We order our chicken wraps and sit down.

"So…who's Trevor?" she asks, leaning towards me with her chin in her hands.

"OK…so, while we were in Minneapolis, my mom ambushed me with this blind dude who goes to the U…long story. His mom is an old friend of hers. He's actually a bit cute–blondish."

I smile now, thinking about him and then continue. "Hair-wise, you'd be impressed. He's got hockey flow for days. Not my usual type, but–hey–I'm going blind so…eventually I won't have a type anyway."

I laugh darkly.

"And he's really nice," I add.

"So, how did he go blind? Or has he been blind his whole life?" Penn asks, while squeezing a lemon into her hot tea.

"Trevor said it happened when he had surgery to remove a brain tumor a few years ago. The tumor was no big deal, but removing it… the surgery itself…left him blind. He told me that most blind people aren't seeing 'nothing'…it's not just blackness. He actually sees some light and shadow, and they told him his vision may actually improve over time."

"Wow." She blows on her tea and then looks at me intently.

It feels so good to be there with her.

"Yeah–it happened like three years ago, and he's a sophomore now. He's doing a major where he can become a sports coach…sort of? He wants to help athletes with performance. If you saw him, you wouldn't immediately know he is blind." I am surprised by my own enthusiasm for him.

"Meera…it sounds like you're crushing on this guy. A little bit?" Penn looks at me with raised eyebrows as she smiles.

She cautiously sips her tea.

"Nah…it's just been really good to know another person close to our age who's going through this." I suddenly find it funny that she thinks I would like him like that.

I rush to continue. "I mean, compared to him, *I am lucky*. I can still see most stuff–just not at night–and eventually it's going to all go away unless…"

"Unless?" she prods, curious.

"I've been thinking about that shaman thing my aunt mentioned," I explain.

"And your mom–what's Lorraine saying?" Penn asks.

"She's actually thinking about it," I say, surprised to hear the hope in my voice.

Our names are called, and I go up and grab both of our sandwiches.

"So…what's up with you and Jared?" I inquire.

"Eh, we had fun Friday but then, like I said, he was so drama on Saturday," Penn shared. "He got jealous of Steve Erickson. Because I was talking to him after the game. Nothing could convince him that it meant nothing. He doesn't get it."

"Well, you already know that I think he should treat you like a queen!" I offer, secretly wishing she'd just break up with him already.

"Yeah, my mom kind of hinted at that too…but I really like him sometimes." Penn's eyes roll. "Can I help it, he's so cute?"

Penn looks at her phone. "Oh God, it's already 12:50. We need to get going." She places the teacup on her plate and then stands.

As we get back in her car, I grumble, "After school I have to do the horrible Lighthouse visit thing."

"I could come with, if you want?" says Penn brightly.

"Really? You would? That would be great…Lorraine is coming at three to the front lot."

"I'll be there!" she tells me, and we high-five.

Having Penn there will be good. I'll have a witness and it won't feel so terrible.

At the Lighthouse parking lot, my mom gets out of the car first.

"Here we are…" she announces cheerily with a nervous edge.

I'm taking my time getting out of the car, but it's not because it is a dark wintry November day. Mom stands on the sidewalk near the car door raising her eyebrows at me through the windshield as if to say, *Let's GO.*

"Are you ready for this?" asks Penn.

"How about you pretend to be the girl who's going blind, and I'll follow you around," I say.

"I don't think Lorraine would be cool with that," Penn replies in a low voice, followed by a smile.

She climbs out, opens my car door and beckons at me.

Once we're inside the building, my mom begins talking to the receptionist. She's in gushy, nursey mode, which I'm hating right now.

The receptionist stands up and reaches her hand out to me. "Great to meet you, Meera. I'm Judy. I'm glad you're here…we have so many different things to help you. Let me take you folks around and introduce Meera to some people."

Out of the corner of my eye, I see an older man using a white tipped cane. He's making his way across the reception area towards the hallway, and it hits me...*this is my future*. Suddenly I just want to get out of there. My face is getting hot. My heart is beating hard. Judy is trying to be so nice, and maybe that is what gets me. I hate how nice she is being. It feels like pity. And everybody else there too.

Next, Judy introduces me to the Braille teacher.

She's an older woman with short white hair cut into an extremely unfortunate bowl shape. Plus she's wearing a groutfit with some kind of black shoes that look like they came from a bowling alley. To top it off, she's got huge ugly plastic sunglasses that block all light from all sides.

Her voice is warm and a little breathy, and she addresses me without turning in my direction. "Meera, I think it would be a great idea for you to come to one of our introductory classes. Knowing Braille is something that can really give you a lot of freedom later... as your vision loss progresses. How are you doing with things at this point?"

Penn and my mom seem to be holding their breath, awaiting my answer.

I can't bear to stand there any longer. I blurt out, "I'm sorry, I, I'm..."

I want to tell her it's horrible that this stupid thing is happening to my eyes. That my whole world is crashing down around me. I'm supposed to be an Interior Designer...not a fucking white cane toting blind shut-in with no future prospects. I can't breathe. I can't speak.

I run out to the car which is, thank God, unlocked. Crying, I grab some crumpled old Subway napkins out of the console, blow my nose and wipe my face. I want nothing to do with this place or

185

these people. A part of me is shouting at myself: *You're being horrible*. Another part hates this place for making me feel this way.

Pretty soon, I see my mom emerging from the building with Penn. They both get in the car.

"What happened?" my mom asks as she starts the engine.

I just turn away and shake my head. I don't want to talk right now.

"Maybe we can try again," Mom says. "I'm sorry this is so hard, Meera...the people are so kind."

Soon she's driving down the freeway. Penn is sitting silently behind me. It's so awkward.

My mom tries again. "Meera, I just wish I knew how to support you better."

"The way you can support me is to believe in me, and let me do *what I feel* is truly going to help me," I fire back, staring pointedly out the window.

I wish Penn were not there to see us like this.

"What's that? I am happy to support you," she says, confused.

"The *shaman*–in Mexico," I tell her flatly. I can't believe I have to remind her.

"Oh...that," she replies, with weariness in her voice.

"Yes that," I parrot, irritated.

She hesitates, then says, "I will give it more thought, Meera. But it's also my job to keep you safe and to be sure that you get all the help you need. Lighthouse has so much to offer you."

Later that night, my mom sets out several bars of chocolate from the co-op and wine glasses on the coffee table. Her lady friends, The Brain Trust, come over, and it's good to hear laugher and shrieking coming from the living room. I stay in my room, but at points in the evening it gets quiet and the voices are soft, and I wonder if my mom is talking about me. I don't care. I know my mom will be in a better mood after this; she's always better after they come over.

In the kitchen later when they're gone, I approach her as she's rinsing the glasses in the sink.

"If I take their introductory Braille class or whatever–then would you let me go to Mexico with Aunt Jill?" I offer.

My mom hesitates, then says, "I'm not saying yes, but I will talk more with Jill about it."

My mom found a Braille class that starts this week, so I went back to Lighthouse again. This time she just drops me off. Judy is there, and seeing her reminds me what a horrible person I am all over again. She shows me the media resources room, and with her help, I find a place where I can access textbooks on my iPad through their online portal. I won't need to lug around those ridiculously huge books at school.

My instructor is not the one I was introduced to the previous week. She's young, with long red hair and wears bright pink lip gloss. Her name is Emily. She tells us she's got two kids. I guess I imagined if you're blind, you'd never have kids…it wouldn't be safe. Her black lab's name is Coco, and she follows Emily around the room. The teacher sings in a band too.

In my first class with her, I learn that Braille was invented by a fifteen-year-old kid. I also learn a mnemonic to help remember each of the A-J letters, and I pick it up pretty quick. Our class is a weird mixture of people: one boy who looks about twelve, several adults and another girl about my age.

After class is over, I approach Emily. She told us to call her by her first name.

After I introduce myself, I begin, "Can I ask you something, Emily?

"Glad to meet you, Meera. Of course," she responds.

Her eyes are a beautiful hazel color, and other than the fact that she's not really looking at me, it's hard to "tell" that she's blind.

"Can I ask you when did you lose your vision?" I inquire.

"I began to lose mine at seventeen. It probably actually started before then, but that's when I first noticed it. I still see some light and shadow that I use for getting around. I have something called Retinitis Pigmentosa. It's a genetic condition."

"That's what I have too." I am surprised.

"Well, welcome to the club!" she says with a wry smile. "I'm really glad you're here!"

Without thinking, I say, "You seem so happy. I don't mean to sound rude, but I thought maybe…" I'm stumbling over my words.

"That all blind people are sad?" she asks.

"Well..." I sputter. "I don't know...you seem so normal, and I'm afraid of what it's going to be like for me. When I can't see..." I hope I haven't offended her.

"Well, I'm pretty happy. I mean Justin Timberlake tickets just went on sale in Minneapolis and, as we speak, my husband is buying a pair for us...so I'm pretty excited. Being blind is just something I have learned to work with, and you will too, Meera," she tells me, warmly. "I have my ups and downs like everybody. You're getting a great start by learning Braille now."

"Yes–they told me that they don't know how long it will be before I lose my ability to read," I share, feeling a little sheepish. "So my mom thought it would be good to get started."

"You're not going to wait around, Meera. You're not like that...I can already tell you're a take charge kind of person! Listen, Coco and I need to go because I'm getting picked up here soon, but please let's talk more again, yes?"

"I'd like that," I say, smiling.

As Emily grabs her bag from behind the teacher's desk, she adds, "Meera, something that helped me a lot was somebody told me to feel my grief about losing my vision, but not to get stuck there. If you do that, you'll learn that being visually impaired doesn't keep you from having fun and doing lots of things that feel good to you. So don't forget that–it's a big key to finding your way."

Waiting to get picked up, I think, *Hmmm, at least Emily sees something in me...that I'm a take charge person? Am I?* I don't feel like it right now, but I know that the designer Jess said that too...that I was really good at what I did. I know I need to think of things that feel good to me.

"How was it, Meera?" Mom asks as soon as I get in the car.

"It was actually OK," I tell her, surprised at my own answer.

My mom smiles at me. "Good," she says, then starts up the car.

"Did you speak to Jill yet? That was our deal," I remind her with my eyebrows raised.

"I did, and she's going to see if she can connect with this woman from over twenty years ago," she tells me. "Actually, a couple nights later I had quite a good conversation with Steve, the hospital doc I've known for years. I really trust him, and he's pretty knowledgeable about alternative therapies. After I told him Jill's story about the shaman, he said that Johns Hopkins is currently doing research with mushrooms, and they're opening a clinical center. They're finding them to be very therapeutic for hospice patients and for PTSD. But it seems that these trials are just for psychological and emotional stuff, not physical illnesses like you have. Anyway, I thought that was kind of interesting."

I can hardly believe my ears. *Maybe this is an opening?*

She turns onto our street and continues. "Even so, I still have big time concerns, Meer. I've seen patients that have come from the ER sometimes...after taking mushrooms or LSD or other stuff...and it really messes them up?"

Mom turns my way and looks at me quickly.

Pulling into the driveway, she adds, "The whole thing still sounds kind of crazy to me, Meera...and I really don't think it's what you think it is."

My mom is smart, and I trust her about a lot of things—especially medical stuff. Maybe she's got a point. Suddenly, even though what I wanted was having my mom be a little more open to this, I begin to worry. What if she's right and it's a bad idea?

As we walk toward the front door, my mom says, as if she's reconsidering, "And sometimes I forget that you're a Gemini, and Gemini are born to be adventurous…always learning new things. Me…I'm a Virgo…and we can be so fact-oriented and perfectionist…I dread making a mistake. I just want to always improve everything and make things better. I want things to be better for you, Meera."

"I know you do," I reply and I truly believe that she does. Then I add hopefully, "And I'm still really curious about what might be possible."

Mom sighs. "Why don't you ask Jill to tell you more about her experience? I feel like if you know more about it that might be good."

Chapter Thirteen

"OK, so let me tell you what I can remember—it's been more than twenty years...so I've forgotten a lot," begins my Aunt Jill.

My mom is still at work, and my aunt is sitting on our couch with a cup of tea.

"Alicia, the healer, lives way out in the country," Aunt Jill shares. "So my friend Ines, the woman at the weaving cooperative, she hired a driver to take us to the healer's house. It took several hours...we went up winding dirt roads...some parts of it were washed out from rain. Where she lives—it's really basic, Meera...like no indoor plumbing kind of basic—and also really beautiful. On the way I remember somebody's truck had gotten stuck in the river that crossed the road, and we stopped to help him. Anyway—it's nothing like here. We had to stay there for three or maybe four days?"

She stops to take the teabag out of her mug and put it onto the saucer.

"As for the ceremonies—I believe there were two. I remember her asking me to write my intention on a piece of paper. Mine was simple: *I just want to be pregnant.* The room was very dark, I remember that. Really dark and really quiet, and you could hear dogs barking and the wind in the trees outside. Then she started singing. The first night was confusing. I remember it being beautiful, but I didn't understand a lot. The other night was different. Once I ate the mushrooms, I remember the music sort of showed me different things. It sounds strange, but it was like her voice made visions come alive in my head. It became really clear that the reason I hadn't gotten pregnant was because I had been receiving the message of 'don't get pregnant' so much. Which seemed funny, but I realized how true it was. It was something Grandma Max drilled into me beginning in childhood. My mom's sister, my Aunt Lydia, had been sent away to a home for unmarried mothers, so Grandma Max passed that fear of pregnancy on to me. It was like I had been preventing pregnancy out of an old ancestral fear–if that makes sense? So, I'd created all of these unconscious barriers to pregnancy, and once I let them go, I got pregnant."

"I guess I understand, kind of…?" I say with growing confusion.

"All I can say is that the experience made me a believer. I mean you know–your mom and I were raised strict Catholic, but I'd never been religious–or maybe I was just never sure of God or the divine? But in those ceremonies, I encountered something powerful. Something very loving. When I went home later, I just began to be a lot easier on myself and not so self-critical. I was kinder to others too. A month later I was pregnant. Now, was it, like your mom suspects–just a matter of timing? I don't know, but that experience was extremely valuable to me. I've never forgotten it."

Aunt Jill digs into her purse, pulls out an envelope and hands it to me. "I brought a little photo of her that you can see."

Inside the envelope is a bent and faded photo. In the picture my aunt looks so young in her funky floral embroidered dress. She has her arm around this tiny woman with sun-weathered skin and a pink dress with embroidered birds on it. They're both smiling. The birds on the shaman's dress feel like another nod from the Universe. *Yes, I am supposed to go.*

"Do you think she could help me?" I ask as I stare intently at the photo.

"I don't know, Meera. I just don't know–but I'm willing to help you try to meet with her if it's something you want…and your mom and you decide it's OK."

"Yeah, I'm working on my mom," I say.

My head is full of so many questions. It all sounds so weird. Maybe Mom's right, and it's not what I think it is?

Aunt Jill offers, "After talking to that doctor, the one she really trusts…Steve, I think? She's opening up to it, Meera…she's just nervous. Her world is science and medicine. So this is scary territory for her. She wants to keep you safe."

I nod and then say, "I know. I just have a feeling about this. It's something I really want to try."

What if I never try? It's all so unknown. It would be easier not to go. I feel Lexi with me, smiling and encouraging me.

"Well, I can send an email to my friend who will know how to find her," Aunt Jill tells me. "The friend and I haven't connected in a few years, and I can let you know as soon as I hear anything."

After my aunt leaves, I text Penn.

Me: Do u know anything about magic mushrooms?

Penn: No but I'm sure Jared's friend Mike does, he's done a lot of different drugs and stuff. Why?

Me: I guess that's what the shaman in Mexico uses to heal people.

Penn: Seriously?

Me: I know, weird? On one hand, that terrifies me–I mean, you know me. But what if it could cure me...it would be worth it, right?"

Penn: Hmmmm.

Me: Yeah...I just don't know.

Penn: The only people I really know who do that stuff are stoners. I'm also pretty sure it's against the law?

Penn could be pretty conservative sometimes. Her mom was like that too. I realize that I don't want to share any more about it with her. She doesn't get it.

I had tried weed once with my cousin Lexi. It did nothing for me and it smelled horrible. She said I should try it again, the second time might be better, but I hated the burning sensation in my throat and the smell. Penn has always refused to try anything like that, saying she didn't want to do anything illegal. She could be kind of a prude sometimes.

Me: Yeah I know. OK, gotta go.

Penn: KK see you tomorrow.

I feel hurt that Penn isn't supportive. So I go onto Reddit thinking that at least I can read about some other people's experiences, people who've actually taken these mushrooms. As I surf through dozens of pages of entries, some of the "trip reports" are funny (involving roller-skating cats and cosmic disco balls) and others sound amazing (like the person who felt connected to every single being on the planet). My favorite is from a girl who felt what it was like to become snow: to suddenly assume the form of an utterly unique and stunningly beautiful intricate snowflake among billions of others and fall slowly to the earth. The girl said she felt like pure love as she fell as that snow. Wow. But, strangely, none of these people seem to have a serious physical illness like me. It comes across like they were kind of just experimenting. Or seeking a generic sort of psychological healing? There are no shamans described. These are no ceremonies.

Then I run into one guy's story that creeps me out. After eating the mushrooms, he perceived something so evil, that he believed he had encountered the Devil himself. He had never experienced terror like that before. *Whoa.* He said he'd never, *as long as he lived,* touch mushrooms again. Curiously, he also shared that, two weeks after the experience, he quit smoking weed, got a proper haircut, found a job and got a girlfriend. Maybe the bad trip was more therapeutic than he thought?

A miracle would be nice, but Trevor, the blind YouTubers, and my Braille teacher do all seem to be managing amazingly well. Their lives aren't perfect, of course. And, in a tiny way, I remind myself, I already know what it is like to be blind…because I'm already blind whenever it's dark. It's scary and unknown but, with help and a little planning, I'll manage. If I lost my mind and went crazy with a nightmarish psychedelic trip, as my mom suggests could happen, it would defeat the whole purpose of seeking a miracle.

Today I bring my iPad instead of my textbook to classes. It's been making a huge difference in Trig. The quiz went better this week. Knowing I have tunnel vision, I've been making a habit of scanning around more carefully before I move. Knock on wood, I haven't stumbled yet today. Plus, horrible Fred is absent from school. What a fucking gift.

After school, I'm making myself some toast in our kitchen when my phone buzzes. It's Aunt Jill.

"Meera, I've got bad news," she tells me. "My friend Ines got back to me right away, but nobody seems to know how to connect with Alicia, the shaman. It's like she's disappeared. Nobody knows how to contact her. The old number Ines had for her isn't working."

"Weird. Can't they just look her up?" I ask.

"A lot of people don't have phones in those little villages, so communication can be kind of hard," my aunt explains. "I'm so sorry. I feel just terrible that I said anything."

"It's OK. Does your friend know any other shamans? I mean, she can't be the only one, or is she?" I ask, feeling desperate. Though I ask this, in my heart I'm feeling defeated. It feels like *if Alicia is not there, then I am not supposed to go*. It felt like she was *the one* in my dream.

"Hmmm. I didn't think to ask Ines that, but I certainly can send her a message to inquire. Ugh. I'm just so sorry I don't have better news for you, Meer. How are things otherwise?"

"They're OK. I got some help...I put these large print textbooks on my iPad which is nice," I report. "Nothing has really changed, but everything has changed. If that makes sense. Oh...and I've started to learn a little Braille? So, there's that." I realize how many things have shifted.

"That is awesome! I'm so proud of you, Meera–like everything you do. You're going to do amazing things."

Later that night in bed, I add to the list in my phone of things I love, and I begin making a separate list of things I haven't seen yet that I want to see.

> The old growth forest in West Duluth. It's private property but is supposed to be amazing.

> The Kips Bay Decorator Show House in New York City that made Mario Buatta famous

> The Peony Farm up near Brimson that Grandma Max told me about

> To get permission to go on the Aerial Bridge at night and ride the lift to the top on a full moon to see the moon river on Lake Superior (maybe play the "girl going blind" card to pull some strings?)

I'm feeling strangely relieved that the shaman can't be found. Like…maybe I won't have to go through with this thing. I act like I'm pretty courageous, but really I'm full of fears. Maybe it's all just a sign that, like Mom said, this whole thing isn't a good idea.

I hear the front door open, and my mom's footsteps coming towards the kitchen and then to my room.

"Meera?" She knocks softly at the door.

"Are you asleep?" she persists.

"Yeah," I respond faintly. I feign like I've gone to sleep already for the night.

I'm not wanting to engage; I am feeling so confused. She cracks the door open slowly and moves into the doorway.

"Er…sorry to wake you up, but I just wanted you to know that I got a call from the nurse coordinator for research in California yesterday Meer…and this is really disappointing, but there are absolutely no trials that you qualify for anywhere in the country at the moment. They are keeping you in mind and will keep looking though. She said one could pop up at any time…six months from now…a year? I wish there was something for you now, but most researchers are currently seeking subjects with more advanced disease than you. Ughhh. I am so sorry to tell you this, and I can't believe medicine has absolutely nothing new to offer you that might be curative." She pauses and sighs as if she's deeply defeated.

Finally, she sees the truth. Medicine can't really help me here. But it doesn't matter anyway. I couldn't qualify for any of those trials.

"I did speak with Aunt Jill and Grandma Max and The Brain Trust and, I hope I don't regret this decision, but if you want to go ahead and go see her…the shaman…I don't want to be the one to stop you."

She pauses as if waiting for me to respond.

I roll over on my side, pull the covers around me.

She continues warmly. "In your birth chart, you've got Jupiter in the ninth house, which is foreign travel, and your sun is in the sixth, which is all about healing and health. When I looked at all of that, it kind of felt like a sign too? You can have an airline ticket for your Christmas gift."

Now she's on my side because of the flipping astrology, I think to myself. None of it makes any sense. *Ugh. She must not have heard from Jill yet that she can't find the shaman.*

"It doesn't matter anyway," I half-mumble. "She can't find the shaman."

I pull the covers over my head.

"What?" my mom asks, confused.

"It's a long story, Mom…can we talk another time?" I say.

"Sure…see you in the morning. Sweet dreams," my mom replies.

Coming out from under the covers, I flip my pillow over to the cool side to try to find my happy place. Which is impossible now. I can't get back to sleep.

My phone buzzes…it's Trevor. He sends me a photo of Eleanor decked out with angel wings and a halo.

Trevor: What's up? Thought I would send you a pic of Eleanor in her holiday best. Some friends dressed her up.

Me: So cute. What are you doing for Christmas?

Trevor: Hanging at home with the family—you?

Me: Yeah same. Looking forward to chilling out on break for a bit.

Trevor: Will you be in Minneapolis at all?

Me: I don't know. Probably not…

Trevor: If you are, it would be great to hang.

Me: Yeah I'd like that. (*Was he asking me to hang?*)

Trevor: OK, keep me posted. Night.

I want to tell Trevor about the shaman, but I feel guilty for wanting a miracle for myself when he seems so accepting of his own blindness. I don't want him to think that I'm NOT OK with going blind. Plus, maybe he would think I'm nuts or judge the whole shaman mushroom ceremony…or think I'm a druggie. I hate keeping secrets...concealing and hiding. I just want to be open with him. Maybe I'll tell him next time we talk.

The holidays are always something I look forward to and this year, weirdly, I feel it more than ever. Maybe because I want to drink in all the beauty of things I can see. My room is already decked out with lights, and I also put up my grandma's 1950s pink tinsel table-top tree with the faded vintage glass ornaments. I love their sweet, sun-weathered colors. The string lights for my room are fuchsia and white, and they make me happy and a little sad too as I think about the future and not being able to see Christmas.

Only two long days left of school before the weekend and the holiday break. God, I had wished my mom would write me a pass to get out of school today–Thursday. All we're doing is watching movies or working on independent projects in every single one of my classes...it's so pointless. But by some act of holy mercy it starts snowing, and by afternoon they send us home early because of the snowstorm.

Nearly six inches of new snow is already on the ground when I step off the bus. The woods are calling to me.

I drop my backpack off inside the house, throw on my boots, and enter the trail behind our home. It used to be part of a private estate, but now I like to think of it as a secret park just for our neighborhood. I rarely see anybody there. The creek that runs in our backyard goes through it. The land is filled with graceful cedars and enormous old willows that lunge dramatically over the water. Everything is muffled and quiet today in the fresh blanket of snow.

I stop near the bend in the creek to plunk down and sit on my favorite old fallen willow tree, to watch the stream. The tree feels like a very old friend. She's always calm and makes me feel welcome, no matter what state I'm in. Parts of the creek are frozen now. On my mittened hand, I catch snowflakes and study them as they land momentarily and quickly melt. Each one is so intricate and so different from the next. *What could issue this beauty so quickly and in such abundance?* I remember the girl on Reddit who said that as she experienced falling as a snowflake, on her mushroom trip, she was pure love. As I lift my head to see the hundreds of thousands…perhaps millions of snowflakes gracefully and silently falling to earth, I am momentarily staggered. *How could this not be love?* My eyes well with gratefulness and grief too.

As I blot my tears with my mittens, I suddenly see a family of deer across the stream. They are moving through the forest and stop to look at me. A feeling of knowing washes over me. I feel their kindness. Their love for each other and for this place. Like me, they're vulnerable too. Fragile bodies subject to fast moving vehicles. I feel Sweetie standing beside me now and, without words, she leans into me and I *know* that everything is going to be OK. Somehow.

My aunt texts me as I'm walking in the door at home the next day after school.

Aunt: Good news, Meera.

Me: About?

Aunt Jill: I'll call you…is now OK?

Me: Yes.

"So…they were able to track down Alicia after all," Aunt Jill reports. "Her contact's cell number had changed, and Alicia doesn't have a phone. But she can see us whenever we are ready–my friend Ines just needs to arrange it. Now that your mom is OK with it too? They aren't too far from Oaxaca–but we could have a driver take us there. I have some time after Christmas and into the new year. I know that's coming up really fast, but I just thought maybe it could work? I could look into airfares today, and see if there's anything decent that we could consider?"

"Um…OK," I say, trying to sound enthusiastic.

I'm feeling this discomfort in my gut. *Is this the right thing?* I feel my stomach tighten. This is so fast, I'm not sure it is even what I want anymore. I think about the Reddit thread and the devil story.

My aunt adds, "OK, I'll check into the fare situation, and maybe I can swing by tonight after your mom gets home so we can consider the trip together?"

"OK, sounds good. Thank you so much."

Temporarily numb, I set my phone down on the kitchen counter. I'm so grateful that my aunt is trying to help. But maybe my mom is right, and I should just stay here and *not* put myself into a situation that could be bad for me?

I grab my phone and Google "blindness" and "miracle cure." A story pops up about an Arizona mother of three who was blind and visited some museum's relics, basically old holy statues, taken from a church and had a miraculous healing. The doctor chimed into say, in the article, that they could not explain the return of her 20/20 vision medically. *Maybe I should go there?* It's so fucking hard not knowing which way to go. It feels like it's all on me to figure it out.

In my room, I stare at the Our Lady of Guadeloupe figurine on the dresser from under my covers. I close my eyes, my breathing slows down, and I enter the darkness. I relax and let out a sigh. My heart slows. My breathing gets deeper and more even. The tiny friendly bobbing pinpoints of light are there now. Despite the darkness, there is this glimmering. I need to stay relaxed. *God…Dear Universe?… Dear shimmering lights…Our Lady? If you're there, I need your help… guide me. Let me know which way to turn. I want to heal my eyes. I have this passion to help people with design…I feel like it's why I am here. I am so confused–just tell me what to do?* Nothing seems to happen.

There's knocking at my door. I must have fallen asleep. My mom is gently talking to me through the open doorway. "Dinner is ready…"

Mom has made Greek salads with grilled chicken and garlic bread. I spoon some more feta cheese on top of my salad. I'm grateful she's home tonight.

"The salad looks really good," I offer.

"Oh good…glad you like it," she says brightly.

"So…" I begin slowly, "…Aunt Jill texted, and I guess that now she was able to contact the shaman…" I'm sounding more hesitant than I'd like to.

"How are you feeling about it?" my mom asks. Her tone is almost neutral, which somehow makes me feel even worse.

I decide to open up to her instead of holding back. "I don't know…I mean what you were saying about tripping–or having a bad trip–kind of scares me. But then there is a part of me that feels like it's also the right thing?" I hope I'm striking a balance between being transparent with my mom but also not showing too much of my doubt either.

"I want to keep you safe from *everything*, Meera, and honestly I don't really know how this shaman thing could help you." Then she pauses and adds almost reluctantly, "But I was reminded by Jill and Grandma Max that I want to encourage you to trust yourself too. We've each really regretted the times we've ignored our inner knowing…"

"What do you mean?" I ask, genuinely curious.

"Sometimes a feeling is there to point you towards something that's right for you," my mom explained. "Like, after your dad died, every time I'd drive by St. Mary's I'd get this weird feeling *I should work there*. It made no sense to me. At that point, all I knew was painting…art. It was what I went to school for."

Mom takes a sip of her herbal tea.

She continues. "Then I started seeing all these ads for an RN training program. None of it made much sense. Your Grandma Max told me that maybe it was a synchronicity…a sign that I was supposed to explore it more. I'm so glad I did because I absolutely love what I do. Truly it was a godsend. We've been OK all these years. It's been a wonderful way for me to make a living."

I'm confused and say, "But what if that *inner knowing* keeps changing…like, how do you trust which feeling is right?" I am simultaneously relieved she's letting me choose my direction and worried I'll screw it up.

"When I get alone and quiet…like when I'm driving with the radio off, or on a walk by myself…that's when I can hear it best, I guess?" Mom shares. "*You'll know when you know* is the best way I can put it."

My mom pauses and then, as if remembering something important, she launches into a new topic. "We're going to go to Jill's

205

for Christmas Eve dinner and then a holiday church service, and they're all coming here Christmas Day. How does that sound?"

"That sounds good, Mom," I agree, then add, my voice a little wobbly, "I was sort of hoping we could go to a movie Christmas night?"

It's weird but I feel like I want to do all of the things that someday I won't be able to do…and Christmas movies are a thing for me.

Mom stands up, and as if she knows how I'm feeling, she walks behind my chair, leans over and wraps her arms around me.

"Oh Meera, you're so easy sometimes…I can forget what you're going through. For sure we can do a movie. You pick which one."

It feels good to have her arms around me. *Why do I resist her so much?* A tear streams down my cheek. Weirdly, this is going to sound crazy, but without RP…maybe my mom and I wouldn't be hugging right now? Maybe my going blind is helping us grow closer?

Her phone rings. "Hi Mom. Mmmm uh huh, she's right here. Should I put her on speaker?"

My mom looks over at me a little uncertain. "Meera…Grandma has something to share with you…OK? It's about the shaman? I'm going to put her on speaker. The shaman? I'm so confused. How could she know anything about the shaman?"

Mom sets her phone on the center of the kitchen table in speaker mode.

"Meera? Are you there?" my grandma says.

"I'm right here, Grandma!" I answer, speaking toward the phone on the table.

"Oh good. Well, I was just telling your mom, I know you're thinking about going to this shaman that Jill saw. I wanted to share a little story because I feel like I'm supposed to. I got a nudge you might say."

She begins. "So, when I was in the Peace Corps in Guatemala, there was a shaman in the little town we were based out of who did his healings right inside the Catholic church in Chichicastenango. It was a very old and simple church...I just loved it there. Well, I saw this shaman inside the church often when I went to pray, and it bothered me a lot. Being Catholic, I thought it was absolutely wrong that he was allowed to do his work there. I saw what he was doing as primitive and also against my religion. I was raised to believe that only the priest should connect with God or the spirits directly, like he was supposedly doing. I had been taught this was wrong. And dangerous too. But the local community had always let shamans work there for as long as anybody could remember. Well, I wasn't very nice to him because of what I thought of his practices.

"Anyway, time went on, and one of the men from a village that we worked in lost his youngest daughter in an accident...she drowned. I think she was four or five years old...very young. He was so heartbroken, we all were. It was more than he could bear, and he couldn't stop grieving. This terrible grief possessed him for months. He was unable to farm, abandoned his family, and just drifted through the villages and on the roads weeping and calling out to God. I guess it was a sort of nervous breakdown, now that I think of it. We all felt terrible and nobody knew what to do.

"Well, one morning as I went to pray at the church, this man was brought in by several of the neighbors. The men had to carry him in, he was so exhausted from his grief. It was heartbreaking to see but also wonderful how much this community cared about him. The shaman, the guy I really disliked, placed him onto a blanket there in the back of the church, and he began to light candles and sing and rattle around the man. As I sat in my pew, I found myself unable to leave, though I worried what I was seeing could be dangerous. But I was so curious. The shaman sang and prayed over this desolate father for a long time…at least two hours I'd guess. When it was finished, the man stood up and hugged the shaman and then he hugged each of his neighbors, and then he even hugged me. And then, he walked out of the church on his own two feet."

She laughed softly, and then continued. "In that moment, I could see that the man was different. He was better, lighter or something. It wasn't totally an instant cure…but in the months that followed, he recovered. He was able to get back to his fields and to feed his family once more. So, I'm just telling you all this to say that although I haven't said much this whole time about shamans, I believe this kind of work, these healers, are somehow working with God too…and so somehow I wanted to tell you."

Over the phone we could hear Grandma Max sigh.

"Thank you, Grandma, for telling me," I respond.

"That must have been really something, Mom," Lorraine acknowledges.

"Oh, it was, I felt something…a really beautiful power in that space as the shaman worked. It was beyond words, and it truly challenged everything that I believed. Life is, of course, a mystery, and I'm not telling you what to do, Meera…but I am sharing this because I felt like I was supposed to."

My phone buzzes.

Trevor: Happy Christmas Eve Eve. I'm watching *Elf*. You?

Meera:. I'm just hanging…should I call you? Easier?"

My phone almost immediately begins to ring, and I pick up.

"Hey," says Trevor.

It's good to hear his warm voice. It's weirdly comforting like a Disney movie narrator or something. So funny too as I was just thinking about movies.

"OK...so how do you watch movies, I am so curious?" I ask.

"Well, it's kind of cheating because I saw *Elf* so many times before...so as I listen, I can remember the scenes, and my imagination fills in the rest. Kind of like reading, I guess? There's also this new thing called 'audio description.' It's out there for a lot of big films and TV shows–in a theatre, they tell you on a headset what's happening on screen. I haven't used it, but my buddy tells me it's pretty cool and I'd like to try it. They have it at the big theatres in Minneapolis. It's available for some titles on Netflix too."

"That sounds amazing. And it's nice to know because I was just feeling sad. Movies are a big part of what I love about the holidays, and I assumed that movies would go away as I lose my vision. Cool to know. So, what else do you guys do for Christmas?"

"We usually go to my sister's house–and eat crab legs. I've got a little niece and nephew who are pretty fun. So, I get to play uncle to them. You?"

"It changes but my aunt and uncle are coming over here this year Christmas Day. We play a good game of Scrabble. Nothing too crazy," I tell him, laughing.

"Now that's another game we still play at our house," he says. "My mom got the Braille version when I started learning."

"That's awesome...and you'd be proud of me, Trevor. I finally did start Braille–I was surprised that the alphabet was pretty quick to learn. Not sure if I'm ready for Braille Scrabble yet. Maybe Santa will bring it."

"Just keep at it, little by little…you'll be amazed," encourages Trevor.

Worried I might freak Trevor out, but also not being able to stop the impulse, I ask, "OK…this might sound weird, but did you ever pray or ask for a miracle after your surgery when you realized you were blind? I don't even know if you believe in God…"

"I guess I did have a few conversations with God," Trevor confesses. "Mostly I was mad, as in, WHAT THE HECK…WHY ME? I think I told you before…I was pretty mad at first. I don't remember much praying. It was more raging! I'm not super religious but I do believe in something. How about you?"

"Well, this might sound bad, but I've just been thinking–if not now…when? Like shouldn't I ask for a miracle now, before it's too late?"

I try to explain more. "But I'm not sure if it's possible or even if it's OK to ask for such a thing? Like, maybe I should just accept it?" I'm worried I've said too much.

"Yeah, I guess. I mean…I'm not sure what you mean?" says Trevor, sounding confused.

"OK…I wasn't going to say anything to you…I'm kind of embarrassed–because you seem so OK with everything, with losing your vision. So I'm hoping you won't think I'm weird…but I just kind of want to ask for a miracle now. So I don't regret not asking for one later. Does that make sense?"

"I won't judge, Meera, and, absolutely, I see why you would ask," he responds. "For me, it all happened so fast. I don't know that I ever even thought about the *possibility* of it going away–if that makes sense?"

His words make me feel safe to continue. "So OK...my aunt had a kind of miracle happen for her after going to this healer in Mexico. It was like over twenty years ago–she got pregnant with my cousin even though the doctors told her that she wouldn't be able to..."

Trevor responds quickly, "Ah...well, I guess I should say, *I have seen crazy impossible things happen.* That kid from the Mr. Roger's documentary? He seems like a miracle...that he could do so many things, despite everything he had against him? And my cousin...he has autism, and they said he wouldn't ever speak. But they worked with him and worked with him and at eight he suddenly began to talk...and not just like 'Ma-ma' or something like that–it was in full sentences. Seemed like a magic to me. How can you explain *that*?" There is a note of awe in his voice as Trevor finishes.

"Whoa..." I respond, marveling at how it must have felt to witness that.

Trevor continues excitedly, "He was on the local news. His doctors were shocked because they didn't think it was possible. So yeah...I definitely believe in miracles. The doctors said it's possible I could regain some sight, and I have had some light come back–nothing detailed yet. I'm not counting on it...I guess? But, believe me, I wouldn't turn it down."

"I worried maybe you'd think I was pathetic that I told you about the miracle," I confess.

"What? Why?" says Trevor, sounding a bit wounded.

"Well, I found out that I can go and see this shaman if I want to with my Aunt Jill. My mom is OK with it, more or less. But now I'm scared."

"Because…?" Trevor wants me to fill in the blank.

"Well, I found out that she works with magic mushrooms…" I say, hesitantly, testing the waters.

"Hmmm? How does *that* work?" he replies, softly laughing, but also sounding genuinely curious.

"Not really sure—I guess it's in a sacred ceremony so it's a whole different thing. My aunt said it's definitely not tripping," I quickly explain.

"Hmmm. No experience there…but I guess I like reality a lot," Trevor says kindly with another laugh.

I'm wondering if he thinks it's a bad idea. *Oof.*

"Yeah I know, me either…that stuff scares me," I confess, revealing my own worries.

"Sounds like you have a tough decision," Trevor observes warmly.

"Yeah. Hoping it will come to me," I say, relieved to have it out in the open.

"My mom always says—when you're not sure, sleep on it," Trevor offers.

"Sounds like my mom." I laugh.

This is so much easier than talking with Penn about it.

"Keep me posted, Meera…you'll figure it out. Hey, my family here is wanting to put the movie back on—they paused it for me. So I should go, but let's talk soon. My mom says hello."

"Tell your mom hello from me and thanks for listening. Merry Christmas." I smile at the thought that he wants to keep our conversation going.

"Merry Christmas to you too, Meera."

Just hearing Trevor say my name makes me smile deep down inside. Then the doubts come. *What am I thinking? This was not my plan, to have a crush on a blind dude. This cannot work. We would be hopeless and hapless together. I mean how could we do things for ourselves?* These horrible thoughts swim in my head and then Trevor texts me one last time.

Trevor: Eleanor believes in you!

He texts a photo of his dog with a Santa hat on her.

OK, maybe just, for now, I can enjoy having a little crush.

Chapter Fourteen

I'm standing in a clearing in a dark forest at night, and, one by one, deer are entering the open space and kneeling down before me. They all peer at me curiously with their kind eyes. Soon, I'm completely surrounded by dozens more, and though it's dark, somehow I can see the stars again…they're glittering perfectly above, and I feel incredibly calm and peaceful. The deer are waiting for me to tell them something important. They have complete trust in whatever it is I'm about to tell them. My whole body tingles. I wake up before I discover what it is I was going to tell them.

Now awake, I wonder, *What is it that I knew?* I feel so good. I don't want this feeling to go away.

We pile into a pew at the back of church on Christmas Eve. Me, Mom, Aunt Jill and Uncle Mitch are all snuggled in tightly. The church is packed. It makes Grandma Max happy when we all go together.

Back in the pew, after receiving communion, waiting for the final hymn, my grandma leans over and whispers, "Do you want to get prayed over tonight?"

I look at her like "huh?"

She tilts my way again and says in a half-whisper, "My friends Anne and Jean will be up in front after the service is over, and they lay hands on people who need prayers. I would like it if you'd go? After telling you about the shaman in Guatemala, I realized that we could do something right here too for you…in this church."

She smells like spearmint Lifesavers and White Shoulders perfume.

"Sure…" I say, feeling surprised at myself. I'm looking for a miracle, after all. Maybe this is where it's supposed to happen?

As the service ends, and the congregation begins to pick up their coats and head for the exits, Grandma Max grabs my hand and tells Mom what we're up to. The two of us go to the front as the organist is blasting the final send-off hymn. I'm relieved everybody seems to be leaving. Nobody seems to be watching us.

There are two grandmotherly ladies at the front. One is wearing a down vest and long skirt and looks slightly frail, and the other is rounder and has a sequined-covered Christmas sweater on and Pac boots.

Grandma Max introduces me, "Anne and Jean, this is my granddaughter, Meera…" She is speaking loudly because the organ is still going strong.

"Hi sweetie, what would you like us to pray for?" Anne, the one with the sequined sweater, grabs both of my hands in hers, and her huge eyes feel like they are drilling into my soul.

I feel exposed. Her stare feels intense. Suddenly, tears come.

The organ abruptly stops blasting, and the church goes still with just a few quiet voices echoing. I look at my grandma. She nods, encouraging me to speak.

I tell Anne, "Well, I recently found out that I'm losing my vision, and I'd like to ask for my eyesight to be healed. Is that what you mean? I hope that's OK…" I feel unsure in this new territory.

"Of course, Meera. We put it all in the hands of the Lord." She squeezes my hands gently and smiles.

I feel relieved.

Then Anne lets go of one of my hands, picks up my grandma's hand, and directs us to form a tight little circle together, leaning in and lightly touching our heads together. We are off in a corner, hidden from the rest of the church, and I'm grateful for this privacy.

Next, stepping over to our circle, Jean puts her hand on my head and begins to pray. "Lord, we ask that you take good care of Meera and restore her vision so that she might see clearly once again. We ask that she…" and Jean keeps praying for a good long while. I lose track of all of her words.

As she is speaking, I feel this weird tingling in my body, and it's as if the outer world has disappeared. There is no floor beneath our feet and no roof on the church above us…we've opened up a space between heaven and earth where things can move freely. Now something opens in me and I'm sobbing. I can see Grandma Max is crying too.

Jean finishes. "…And Lord, we thank you for Maxine and for her strength, that she and Meera's whole family will be lifted up too. In Jesus' name we pray, amen."

Then Anne and Jean both hug me, and Jean whispers into my ear, "You're going to be fine, Meera."

"Thank you," I say, trying to convey gratefulness with my eyes.

Grandma hugs them both and then we walk arm in arm to the back of the church.

"How was it?" my mom asks as we approach.

"I'm glad we went up. Aren't you, Meer?" Grandma Max says, looking at me.

"Me too...it was really nice," I reply, taking a tissue from Grandma Max's outstretched hand.

As we step out into the freezing darkness, I stop and blink my eyes several times...checking my vision. Nothing seems to be different. *No miracle. Yet.*

"Meera? Are you OK?" my grandmas asks, confused at my sudden stop. I still have my grandma's arm.

"Oh sorry...I was just letting my eyes adjust."

I grip her arm tighter as we make our way to the car.

In the back of the car, on the way home, I think about Jean's words, "You're going to be fine, Meera." How could she know this and did she really know? It is confusing. Nothing seems different. But it did feel really good to be there. I feel lighter.

We pull slowly into the driveway and Mom says in an excited half-whisper, "Ooooo look!! All the beautiful deer bedded down? I don't think I have ever seen so many and that buck—wow—he must be a ten pointer!?"

"Oh, they are so lovely," says Grandma Max with wonder in her voice.

I swivel my head back and forth and squint my eyes, but I can't see what they're seeing. It's too dark. I remember my dream deer and wonder, *Is there a connection?*

Wanting to be part of it, I blurt out, "I saw deer in my dreams the other night."

Aunt Jill asks with curiosity, "Really? What was your dream?"

"There was a clearing filled with deer, and it was so peaceful...I can't even describe it—it was just beautiful. And I felt really good there." I didn't want to share the part about me knowing something.

Mom turns off the engine, and we all sit in the stillness until Jill says, "Hmmm, that's pretty interesting...did you know that Oaxaca—in that area—where the shaman Alicia is? The people there are called 'Mazateca' which means 'People of the Deer.' Deer are featured in a lot of their art and textiles."

Later in bed, I google "Oaxaca and textiles"—dozens of fabrics with leaping deer pop up, and there's a dress like the one Alicia was wearing in the photo with Aunt Jill. The fabrics and the dress feature beautifully embroidered birds, which seems funny because of my senior project. Could this be a sign saying that I should go to Mexico after all?

We've opened all of our gifts on Christmas Day, and I'm lying on the couch as my aunt and Mom are chatting over coffee near the heavily decorated tree in the living room. Grandma is off making brunch for us in the kitchen. My uncle drove to the gas station to look for his beloved eggnog, which Mom forgot.

I wait for a lull in the conversation and then plunge in. "I think I *do* want to go to Mexico?" I say, feeling this growing calmness inside me. It feels right. "What are the fares like?" I add.

Aunt Jill and my mom look over towards me.

My aunt says, "Oh yes! I meant to come over the other night to discuss flights, but work got the best of me! All I have to do is send a message to my friend, and we'd have to see what the flights are like now but–yes, we can see if we can get it together? I am still free to go if we go soonish?"

"Mom?" I look at her.

"What about school? Are you OK to miss?" she asks.

"Yeah, we still have a week and a half off. And even if it's a few days into January, I'd be fine," I tell her. "I can catch up and Penn can pick up assignments for me."

"Well, I guess it's settled," my mom says. She gives me a serious look, and adds, "You know I'll need to stay here and work, Meer..."

"I know Mom. I never expected that you'd be coming with us and it's OK," I say, trying to be reassuring. I don't want her to have one more thing to feel guilty about. And, to be honest, having her there would be hella hard. I feel like I need to do this on my own.

Mom walks over to me, smiles warmly and rubs my back.

"OK!" says Aunt Jill. "I'll send an email to my travel agent right now to see what's available...she'll probably get back to us first thing tomorrow. "

My aunt picks up her phone and begins to type.

Mom gets up from her chair and begins cleaning up wrapping paper. She says, "Well, I hope you'll find the answers that you need..." She sounds a tiny bit exasperated suddenly.

Her words sting. She just doesn't get it. I'm not looking for an answer, I'm asking for a miracle. I wish she could understand what it's like to be me.

I decide to share this with her. "Mom—I'm not looking for answers, I'm asking for my eyesight to be healed. You don't get it, and you should just *not talk* because you're making it worse."

The tears come again. *Fuck! Why is this so hard?* I leave the room and go to my bedroom, closing the door behind me.

"You're going to be just fine, Meera"…those words from the woman in Grandma's church echo in my head. How does she know? Could she know? And what if I'm not? Is a miracle possible? Maybe I'm supposed to simply be happy and grateful and stay home?

We found out last week that the last-minute flights this time of year are outrageous. Luckily, Aunt Jill is diamond platinum titanium, or whatever, from all her work trips, and she offered to buy our tickets with her miles.

She told me, "Meera, Uncle Mitch and I want to do this for you and, to tell you the truth, I'm excited to ask for some healing for myself. This is coming at a good time for me too."

It's Lexi's birthday in January, which is always a hard time for my aunt and uncle. I'm glad to hear that this trip isn't all about me. Maybe my aunt will get what she needs too.

The day of our departure, I drag my suitcase into the hall at home and pause.

My mom hugs me briskly and presses two twenties into my hand. "Always keep your passport case tucked under your shirt—there are pickpockets. Jill has the money I've given her for the shaman, plus hotel and food expenses when you're not staying at the shaman's retreat. This cash is so you can buy yourself something beautiful to remember the trip."

"Thanks Mom, will do."

Last night Penn gave me a good luck faux rabbit foot, which I attached to my backpack zipper. I looked up rabbit in *The Book of Beasties* last night, and it made me smile.

Rabbit leaps confidently into your life to urge you to explore the rabbit holes you find before you. What may seem like an unnecessary or illogical detour can lead to the most peculiar kind of magic. Can you imagine a world in which Alice had not followed the white rabbit into Wonderland? Rabbit counsels that you must be willing to entertain chaos and confusion before you receive the treasure or the understanding. Hidden all around you are beautiful clues and hints, but to see them you must be willing to let yourself wander off the prescribed path.

The rabbit's message felt reassuring. To find magic, maybe I need to take this trip that feels a lot like a strange detour.

Uncle Mitch's pickup truck is in the driveway. I hug my mom again. He puts my luggage in the back as I slide in next to Aunt Jill.

"Are you ready for this, Meera?" She grabs my arm and gently squeezes it.

I smile back at her. I hope so.

❧

We land in Oaxaca on New Year's Eve just as it's getting dark. The air is warmer and softer, and at the same time altered...like somebody put a perfumed dryer sheet into the ventilation system. The shiny tile floors of the airport complex sparkle under the fluorescent lights, and we find our gray-haired driver, Juan Carlos, in the luggage area. My aunt and he are old friends from twenty years back.

After they banter in Spanish, he hugs me hard and then grabs me by the shoulders. Carlos smiles as he examines me more closely, then looks at my aunt and grins.

"*Tan lindo*, eh!" he says.

I know that this means "so pretty!"

He smells really nice, like lemon and flowers and baking spices.

"*Vamanos!*" he tells us.

My aunt nods.

His car feels warm and steady like his hug. It's super clean, smells like baby powder and has a mini nativity scene affixed to the dashboard.

He hands my aunt a bottle of water, and then offers one to me.

"*Agua?*" he asks.

"*Si, gracias,*" I reply in my high school Spanish.

On the way to the hotel, Aunt Jill suggests we stop off at a church. Carlos waits outside for us. He has a call he needs to make.

"I hope you don't mind, Meera? But I will feel better if we stop here."

I shrug. "You're the tour guide..."

We enter the church, and my aunt whispers to me, "Let's light a candle before we leave."

I nod in agreement.

It's beautiful, very cool and quiet inside. Dozens of candles are burning at the little table along the wall. I'm glad we came.

As we step farther in, I see an enormous and intricate gilded altar inset at the front. It shines in contrast to all the heavy stone. Soaring columns rise everywhere into an impossibly grand ceiling, joining all the parts of the enormous space into a whole. I'm not religious, but I can feel something here. The quiet feels so full of calmness.

The church's great quietness is similar to what I felt in that place where the deer were sleeping on Hawk Ridge. My aunt goes up to one of the cushions and kneels down. I slide into a polished wooden pew a few rows behind my aunt and stare up at the ceiling for a minute. I'm not sure how to pray but then I remember what Grandma Max said…"I just talk to God like he's my friend."

God, if you're here, please…all I am asking is that I'm able to be normal. Is that too much to ask? I don't want to be a burden to my mom. She's already struggled enough. I also really don't want to be a freaking Stevie Wonder spinster. I promise I'll design beautiful spaces for people, and I'll be nice to my mom. (I cringe at that last promise a bit as I'm not sure I am humanly capable.) *If you could just help? Please heal my eyes. Thank you. Amen.*

The cathedral is silent. No holy angels descend. My aunt stands up, and I follow her to the table at the back. We take turns lighting candles. She drops coins into the metal lockbox. I light one for my mom and one for Grandma Max and one for Lexi.

As we leave the church and emerge outside again, you can hear lively guitar music coming from a speaker in the distance, and there's a woman sitting on the stairs who's selling little figurines on a cloth laid out on the ground. There are many different animals and Jesus in the manger sets. I spy a small resting deer that's covered in hundreds of tiny colorful glass beads. It has a set of graceful, arching antlers.

I pick it up, and look at Aunt Jill. "I have money–but it's not changed yet. Can you ask her how much?"

"No worries, we can do that at the hotel. I've got it," says my aunt.

She talks with the woman, takes out some pesos and pays her.

I tuck the beaded deer, wrapped in newspaper, into my back-pack. He feels like my good-luck charm for this adventure.

In the morning, we stand and wait in the hotel lobby for our driver Carlos, who will take us from Oaxaca to where Alicia lives. There's another guy and a woman sitting in there on a bench, and they look like they are from the US too. She has a scarf over her head and no eyebrows. They are maybe in their thirties or forties? I look away and suddenly feel guilty. She's very thin and doesn't look well, and he looks so nervous. At least I am not dying. Maybe I have no business asking for a miracle when other people are really sick.

Juan Carlos arrives with a huge smile. Our driver is dressed in a freshly pressed, white button-down and a straw cowboy hat, which he removes while approaching us. He greets Aunt Jill and me with big warm hugs. I feel shy and also comforted that we are so welcome here.

"Momento por favor…" Carlos says to us, then strides towards the couple. They both stand up after talking with our driver for a moment and follow him.

"Listos? Are we all ready?" he asks.

After helping Juan Carlos bring the bags out one-by-one, we pile into the car. Jeff rides up next to Carlos, and the three of us women are in the back with our smaller carry-on bags in our laps. The slender woman joining us is pale, and her eyes are an icy blue, like a fragile china doll's. While Carlos drives, I look out the window, and my aunt introduces herself and me to the other Americans.

Jeff, who's a warm and graying version of Ross from *Friends,* looks our way and shares, "Amanda got sick; I mean we found out last summer."

He glances over at Amanda. Looking a little tired, she nods, as if to say, "Go ahead and tell the story."

With her approval, Jeff continues. "So we were thinking about starting a family. We'd been married for seven years, and it just felt right. Amanda got a positive pregnancy test and we were so excited. But when she went to her doctor to confirm her pregnancy, the ultrasound showed masses on both her ovaries. First it was the ultrasound and then a biopsy and then–this was such a shock–they told us it was cancer. No idea where it started exactly, but they narrowed it down to probable breast cancer. We weren't even remotely prepared. And then she miscarried, which was probably for the best..." As Jeff finishes, his voice trails off. He's clearly distraught.

"Oh gosh you guys, I'm so sorry." my aunt murmurs, and she puts her hand on Amanda's knee.

Amanda smiles at her.

Jeff says, "Thank you. We've been through…I mean, *Amanda* has been through…a lot."

His eyes anxiously search Amanda's face.

"You have been too..." Amanda notes, and then she turns to stare out the window beside her.

I'm relieved to hear her warm voice. Amanda's not an alien after all, but she does seem distant.

Jeff tells us, "Anyway, Amanda has done all of the different chemos. They have helped a little, but none of them seems to be stopping the progression. She wanted to seek out a different type of healing. So, with her oncologist's blessing, here we are."

Amanda suddenly joins the conversation. "I'm accepting that I'm not going to be cured, but I just feel like there are parts of me that are missing…I really wanted to see a shaman."

She reaches through the seats and squeezes her husband's hand as his eyes tear up.

"I'm just here to support her," Jeff says as his eyes fill up.

"So, Jeff, how did you and Amanda find out about Alicia?" Aunt Jill asks with her face full of compassion.

"We learned about her from a friend of my parents who were here a few years ago," replies Amanda. "And I studied Native American Spirituality in college and was fascinated by the story of Maria Sabina. She was a well-known healer and poet from this area made famous in the seventies. My father's friend was born around here and made some calls and helped us find Alicia."

"Well, Alicia is how I conceived my daughter about twenty-two years ago," Aunt Jill shares. "She really helped me a lot."

"Wow," says Amanda softly.

"She's a really special person," explains my aunt.

"So you've gone through this type of healing ceremony before. Maybe you can tell us more?" Amanda asks, now turning towards my aunt.

"Yes please," says Jeff, enthusiastically, from the front seat.

I am wondering how his wife Amanda can be so calm, even though she knows she's dying. She kind of glows in a beautiful way. It seems impossible she could die. I want Amanda to ask for a miracle too. Doesn't she hope to be cured also?

My aunt responds, "Well…it's been a long, long time, but I can tell you that the ceremonies begin at night, by candlelight, and part of it is in the pitch dark. I'm no expert, but, you know, Carlos knows this work much better than I do..."

My aunt puts her hand on the back of Carlos' seat.

"Maybe, Carlos, you can tell us a little more about Alicia and this medicine?" Aunt Jill asks Carlos in Spanish.

"*Claro que si!*" Carlos agrees.

As he speaks, my aunt begins to translate for Carlos. He rambles for a bit and then pauses, and that's when she translates for us. I can catch a few words here and there with my Spanish too.

Aunt Jill tells us, "He says that the people here believe *the mushrooms are divine.* They call them the "sacred children"–*Niños divinos.* They...umm...also sometimes call them the 'spit of God.'"

My aunt and Carlos both laugh when she translates this.

"Spit...because they get us to talk and think and maybe work things out for ourselves. They are very playful, he says."

I am having a hard time imagining playful mushrooms...a Disney-cartoon-like mushroom dances in my head.

Carlos talks some more, then my aunt adds: "Many people have come here from America or even farther away, and they are confused...and he says, *They think they are here for a party with the mushrooms*–or that you eat them to have fun or to see crazy things. Hippies!" My aunt pauses and laughs. "But that is not what the mushrooms are for; they are only for healing and they are very sacred. They have a lot of respect for them here."

Our driver seems to get serious as my aunt translates this last bit. He shakes his head back and forth in disapproval at the Hippie part. I catch his expression in the rearview mirror.

Carlos continues talking, and my aunt translates. "During the conquest, long ago when the Spanish came here to colonize the place, the mushrooms warned the people what was going to be happening. The people who worked with the mushrooms…they retreated high up into the mountains where the Spanish soldiers would not find them. Of course the Spanish sought to destroy these methods of healing and to convert all people to Catholicism. So the people and the *curanderos*, or healers, took this knowledge with them into the high mountains and kept it secret." As Aunt Jill translates this bit, Carlos waves his left hand towards the mountains which are beginning to get larger.

"They hid this knowledge and kept it safe. But now, the shamans, the *curanderos*, are able to practice more openly again. And they have returned. But people here are very suspicious of outsiders coming for these ceremonies, because of the hippies that came in the 70s." Carlos rubs his chin as my mom shares this last bit, as if considering a problem.

"You will also see something that often confuses people," Aunt Jill translates. "Alicia, and other *curanderos* like her, have Jesus, Mother Mary and other Christian symbols on their altars. That also came about as a way to hide this knowledge. You see, the people here were wise; some tricked the Spanish into thinking they were Christians to protect these traditions. But those symbols have different meanings to us."

My aunt remembers something, and adds, "Yes, I recall some of this from my last visit. For example, Mary would be representing Mother Earth–not simply the mother of Jesus. And Jesus…I believe represents the Sun." My aunt pauses, then asks the driver in Spanish, "Is that right, Carlos?"

"Si, Doña Jill," he affirms, and then goes on with the backgrounding.

My aunt translates. "The sacred children, these mushrooms, are here to help us...to heal us. So it makes us very happy when earnest people like you come to seek healing–not just hippies looking for a party."

Carlos seems to be done with his "class" for now and we fall into silence.

I try to imagine people fleeing the Spanish and living in caves with their beloved mushrooms. It must have been hard, to be forced to leave home just to keep your way of life.

Carlos continues to drive up and up along narrow roads into the mountains, and we pass through tiny towns with tire shops and cafés and stray dogs and little kids on bikes.

Carlos says that the mushrooms get you to talk, but I don't really want to talk. I just want to have my eyes healed. I want to be a designer and make places beautiful. My eyes fill with tears, and I get that horrible "why me" feeling all over again. I try to look for something beautiful to change my mood. I open my phone and begin creating a new list of beauty from the trip to distract myself:

Roadside cross with bright wildflowers surrounding it

A colorful wall mural of a family

The huge white clouds dotting the bright blue sky

We stop briefly in a village, where Carlos parks and runs over to a roadside stand as we stretch our legs. He returns with four small Styrofoam cups of hot chocolate and a bag of warm tamales. The hot chocolate is like nothing I have ever tasted before…spicy and creamy and gritty and earthy. It's good, but really different. My aunt and I share two tamales between us. One is sweet almost like a yam in flavor, and the other has spicy mole sauce.

"Fast food Mazatecan!" jokes Carlos in English. "No McDonald's here!" he scolds, shaking his head and smiling.

A few hours later, we arrive and Carlos kills the engine. It's pitch dark. His car lights are shining on a low crumbling mud wall. *Maybe I made a mistake coming here. It feels like we are in the middle of nowhere. Maybe Mom was right? Our medical system is the only thing worth trusting.*

Carlos gets out and jogs quickly behind the wall. I feel uneasy and I'm glad Aunt Jill is here. What if something happened to her? He quickly returns and says we can all get out; they are ready for us.

My aunt takes me by the hand, warning me of obstacles as we follow Carlos. We enter a small courtyard where a fire is blazing with a grate over it. Aunt Jill greets a slender young woman with long wavy black hair to her waist who wears jeans and a sweatshirt, and they speak Spanish for a few minutes as we all stand by the fire.

The woman then turns to me, and in perfect English, she says, "Hello! Nice to meet you, Meera! I'm Lillian. I am so glad you are here!"

Then she opens her arms wide, and I move towards her for a hug. She's so warm and welcoming. I'm relieved.

"I'm Doña Alicia's helper," she explains. "Usually, I attend the university in Mexico City, but I am taking some time to be here. My next program doesn't begin until the fall. Let's get you to your room, you must be so tired."

Amanda and Jeff will be sleeping in a little house next door, and Aunt Jill and I sleep in a storage room, which also has a double bed in it. There's a small fluorescent light fixture above, and the room is tiny, but clean. An old armoire with peeling veneer stands against the wall. Aunt Jill and I brush our teeth quickly in the small bathroom down the hall using bottled water as Lillian instructs us and then we crash into a deep sleep.

Chapter Fifteen

There is a rooster crowing so loud right now, it sounds like he's in our room. I grab my phone but it's dead. I never did get a chance to ask if there was an outlet. My aunt is still asleep. I slip carefully out of our bed, go to the window, and lift up the thin curtain. In the dirt courtyard the fire is burning, and there's an older woman in a dress and a shawl who's adjusting the wood. The birds' sounds are absolutely incredible, like nothing I've heard before. The woman is using her hands, and she is arranging the slender logs in a very special way. Suddenly, she seems happy with the arrangement. She blows on the fire and sprinkles a little substance into it. I wonder if this woman is Alicia.

"Morning…" my aunt whispers as she groggily awakens

"Morning," I say, still watching the woman through the window.

"What time is it?" Aunt Jill inquires as she yawns loudly.

"Not sure, my phone is dead…is that Alicia out there?"

My aunt joins me at the window in her pj's.

"Yes, that's her! Oh my gosh, her hair is getting silver now—ha! Like mine."

We dress and enter the kitchen, which is partially open to the outdoors. It's chilly, and I have on my light down coat over my sweatshirt and jeans. Lillian makes us a breakfast of tortillas, strong coffee with sugar in it and some scrambled eggs with tomato and onion, and we eat at a small table in the tiled kitchen. The heavily worn Formica table has tubular chrome legs like something out of the 1950s. Lillian has to shoo the chickens who linger outside the open kitchen to keep them from entering. I sip the sweetened coffee. I like it. Lillian says that after breakfast, we'll have our first consultation with Alicia.

Aunt Jill and I follow Lillian into the shaman's cement block home. It has a corrugated metal roof. This is an extension of the place we slept in last night, and there are a few windows with small panes. The floor is tiled in a mix-up of different patterns as if it had all been scavenged from different building projects. Against one wall is a cloth-covered dresser above which hang dozens and dozens of images of angels, Jesus and Mother Mary, in addition to unrecogniz-able holy figures. Some of the pictures are protected by plastic sleeves and others are in frames. Several holy figurines and statues sit atop the dresser/altar.

My aunt goes to hug Alicia and they converse for a few minutes. Lillian translates for Alicia. Alicia does speak some Spanish, but her primary language is Mazatec. She has long black braids with streaks of silver and shining dark eyes that penetrate you.

Soon it's apparently my turn to talk with Alicia, and she turns to me.

"So 'good morning' Alicia is saying to you—why have you come to see her, Meera?" translates Lillian.

My aunt looks at me. She wants me to explain why I'm here.

I hesitate, then reply, "Ummm…well, my eyes are…umm, I'm losing my vision. Right now, I can see pretty well, but in a few years—we don't know exactly how long—the doctors say I will lose my vision. I'm wondering if you can help me."

After Lillian translates my words, Alicia nods.

"Are you in school, she wants to know?" Lillian asks me.

"Yes I am," I tell them, "and I was hoping to go to university in the fall to study interior design—to make spaces beautiful. But without my vision, I'm worried I'll need to find something else…but it's all I ever wanted to do."

I pause, then add, "And I worry about my mom too…that I'll be a burden for her. She's already had a lot of trouble…"

Aunt Jill puts her hand on my back, and tears begin to come to me as Lillian translates what I've said for Alicia. I didn't realize that I was so worried about my mom and how this would also affect her.

"I don't want to be a burden…" I say, even though Lillian isn't quite done speaking with Alicia. She nods at me and continues translating.

Doña Alicia nods and then explains though Lillian. "She's really glad you are in school, and that is very good. You're going to need to ask the mushrooms to help you. And also, you will need to ask the Virgin Mary for her help…she will be praying with you too. Do you understand? And also, you need to pray to the Virgin Mary to ask for her to remove your worries about your mom. Those worries are making you sick."

I nod.

I mean I don't really know—I have never really prayed before to something like a mushroom or the Virgin Mary. I usually do my "Dear God" thing, and I don't even know if I'm doing that right. I don't think I've been that worried about my mom…? Is she right? That's what's making me sick?

Alicia turns to my aunt and asks her what she is hoping for. My aunt explains, and Lillian translates that mostly she is there to pray with me. Also, she would like some guidance about healing her grief.

My aunt explains her situation. "I lost my daughter Lexi three years ago, and I still don't feel like myself…"

With the help of Lillian, she and Alicia continue to talk. After a while, it looks like we are finished, and Alicia is getting up to leave.

I say to Lillian, "Can I ask another question—is that OK?"

"Yes, yes, sure!" Lillian tells me, and she motions for Alicia to stay.

The shaman sits back down and listens.

"Is prayer…I mean, how do I pray? I'm not sure I know how to pray…to the Virgin Mary?" I confess.

I suddenly feel stupid like any human already knows how to pray.

Lillian translates my question. Doña Alicia responds with a slight chuckle and a warm smile.

The shaman then grabs both of my hands and looks into my eyes as Lillian translates. "She says you just have to think upon the Virgin—see her with all your heart and ask. You will know how tomorrow night. She will be helping you…do not worry."

Alicia's warm, gnarled hands feel so solid. She then rises and returns outside to her fire.

Afterwards, Lillian explains to us that on the day of the ceremony, tomorrow, we will be eating a light breakfast and that will be our only food for the day. "Fasting helps you to prepare to receive the healing and to be open to the medicine of the *Niños Santos*. The mushrooms. You can drink tea all day, but no food. We will eat in the morning again once it is over."

By the time we are done clearing the table and helping with breakfast dishes, it's starting to rain outside. I can hear the fat drops striking the dry packed dirt courtyard and the metal roof.

There isn't much to do after breakfast. I rest, flip through some new design magazines, and finish reading a novel I brought along. Aunt Jill and I talk and reminisce about Lexi.

We're served a late lunch/early supper of tortillas and beans with some fresh mango and it's all delicious. I have lots of dreams all night, and I can't remember any of them in the morning.

The next day seems to last forever after our only meal, breakfast. The tea they offer us isn't really like a tea I'm used to; it's just herbs in boiled water. It doesn't taste too bad, but I'm starving. It rains most of the day. I try to nap unsuccessfully, and I write in my notebook that I brought along. Aunt Jill reads magazines she packed. We talk some more. I wonder what Amanda and Jeff are doing today. We haven't seen them at all.

Darkness begins to fall, and Lillian comes to our room to bring us to the ceremony. As we enter the room where we met with Alicia the day before, the space is dark except for the many candles blazing on the dresser. Alicia is wearing a colorful dress with satin ribbons and red birds and flowers all over on it. It looks a lot like the one she wore in the photo from twenty-two years ago. Lillian is also wearing a dress with beautiful embroidery on it but less ornate.

I worry that maybe we are underdressed, but Lillian assures me warmly, "You're OK...this is just the tradition, and we don't expect foreigners to dress like this."

The candles illuminate the golden-framed images of Jesus and Mother Mary and other holy figures. Their light creates a crazy flickering sort of sacred collage above the table, the altar. A huge vase of white lilies from the garden is also on the dresser. The smell is so sweet, almost too strong. Alicia is burning something that's creating a lot of smoke.

Lillian explains in a very soft voice, "The smoke is Copal...it's a resin from a tree...it's an incense. It helps to purify us before the ceremony and also to cleanse the space and the mushrooms that have been collected."

The room began to fill with the smoke, and it makes me cough a little which I try to suppress because I don't want to seem rude.

Aunt Jill and I are shown to a spot on the tiled floor that is covered with a few thick folded blankets. Jeff and Amanda enter, brought in by another woman we haven't met yet, and they sit down on blankets near us. Jeff looks nervous and Amanda is smiling.

Alicia stands at her altar examining something carefully. She seems to be sorting things.

Lillian explains in a low voice, as if to speak in a normal volume might disturb Alicia, "In this tradition, we eat the mushrooms in pairs." Then she asks us, "Do you all have your candles?"

My aunt nods and pulls the candles that she'd shown me earlier out of her bag. We purchased them at a little shop in town on the morning we drove up here. They're carefully wrapped in tissue paper. She hands me my pair. They're pure beeswax and smell delicious and reassuring. My stomach is tense, and my heart has started pounding. I guess I'm more nervous than I thought. Jeff and Amanda are each holding their pair of candles, looking anxious, too, while waiting for our next instruction.

Lillian says, "Once she gives you your mushrooms, you'll light your candles from there." She indicates the large candle on the altar. "Then, using a bit of wax, you will affix them to that board." She points towards a long polished plank lying on the ground in the front of the folded blankets.

Alicia indicates to Lillian that she is ready, and one-by-one, Lillian directs us to approach the shaman. At my turn, I step forward into the flickering light and heat of all those candles and vibe of the holy images at her altar. Alicia takes a chalky wet paste and applies it on my forearms with her fingers in a crisscrossing motion as she speaks some incantations.

She begins with: "San Pedro, San Paulo, San..." It's a sort of prayer in Spanish...she seems to be calling upon Christian saints.

Then she begins sorting through the mushrooms and hands me a small pile of them on a "plate" made of a sturdy leaf. I thank her and then return to my blanket and place my leaf plate with mushrooms nearby on the tile floor. Next I light both of my candles using the altar candle. It takes some doing, but finally I get both of my candles to be "glued" to the board with wax. I return to my seat on the blanket on the floor. I push the mushrooms around in my hands; there are eight dry shriveled pairs. Each one is maybe a half an inch or so wide and one or two inches long. I put the first two in my mouth. They taste really earthy.

As I chew them, I peek around. Everybody else is doing the same. I wouldn't serve these mushrooms at a party, but they're not too terrible. The room is being filled with fresh clouds of the Copal incense smoke as everyone quietly noshes on their mushrooms.

My aunt looks at me, puts her hand on my knee and whispers, "How are you doing?"

My heart is still hammering away, and I've finished eating my mushrooms.

In a whisper, I offer, "Fine I guess...nervous...but I'm not feeling anything yet?"

"It takes a while," my aunt advises, and she squeezes my knee and smiles.

I'm so grateful to have Aunt Jill with me. I couldn't imagine being here with my mom. Somehow this is easier. I don't have her to worry about.

A few minutes later, the shaman Alicia walks towards the board where our candles flicker and sputter, dripping considerable wax.

And the shaman speaks to Lillian, as she points at the board.

"Who are these candles belonging to? Doña Alicia is asking?" says Lillian gently.

"I think they're yours. Meera–yes?" Lillian asks.

I suddenly notice that one of my candles is tipping cattywampus onto the other and dripping wax all over. *Uh oh.* They are both in danger of falling over.

"Oh yes–those are mine," I confirm nervously. "What should I do?"

"Please fix them..." Lillian directs.

As I try to get the rogue candles to behave themselves, I wonder why Alicia's so concerned about my messy candles. It somehow feels extremely important to get them "righted." After much remelting of wax and affixing and holding the candles, I loosen my grip on them for the final time and the two candles seem to say, "We are in place now." I sit back down.

Alicia admonishes us one last time–via Lillian, "Remember your intention...to pray for what you are asking for. Without this, Doña Alicia says, the ceremony will not be effective. She will be praying too. And, of course, remember to relax and breathe."

With that, Alicia blows out all of our candles and every other candle on the altar. The darkness is absolute. I'm scared, and in the moment I conjure up Sweetie in my mind's eye. I feel her settle in next to me, sharing my blanket. My shoulders drop, and I feel more at ease, but not entirely. And I wait to feel something. I move my hand towards Sweetie to steady myself. I'm so grateful for her presence.

Chapter Sixteen

For a long time, we sit in silence which feels really weird. I can hear people's breathing around me and dogs barking in the distance. It's eerie, and it seems as if nothing is happening. After a while…maybe twenty minutes, maybe an hour…it's hard to know, Alicia begins singing in a clear voice. It's in her language, which makes absolutely no sense to me, but hearing her voice feels like such a relief compared to the silence, which was feeling more and more ominous. I felt intensely grateful for her voice. The melody gives my mind something to hang on to in all the nothingness.

As she sings, it's like the curtains of a stage are pulled back inside my mind, and a dark screen of the purest, emptiest darkness emerges. In my body, I begin feeling this strange blossoming—this surge of…I don't know exactly what it is? There is a strong new aliveness or lightness plunging upward through my body, beginning at the base of my seat and working its way to my head. At first, I feel like I can manage it, but then it quickly becomes overpowering. It's very uncomfortable. Like a dizziness, but I'm not moving.

On the pure stage of my mind, a scene suddenly emerges. In it, my mom is devastated…crying and depressed. It's horrible to see her like this…I want it to stop, but it continues and there seems to be nobody who can console her. I reach out for Sweetie with my thoughts, but she's vanished. I can't perceive her at all. That scares me. I seem to have no influence here, and I can't do anything for my mother. There's nothing to be done and I'm utterly stuck. It feels like forever is passing…an eternity….and I wish I had not come to this place. I have a sudden realization that the sun will not rise today despite the fact that it has risen every single day before this. I did not see it coming but this is the end. Of life? Oh my God, my mother was right. Coming here was a terrible idea. I am feeling extreme regret, if only I had listened to her? Why didn't I? The song suddenly ends and there is silence. In the silence another vision unfurls and it's no better.

I'm sitting and watching myself weeping, and I realize that it's because *now* the Retinitis Pigmentosa has taken all of my vision and I'm completely blind. I've become depressed and so stuck. I'm feeling so sorry for myself. There's no escape. I'm utterly alone. No way out. I'm experiencing a crushing feeling of loneliness. I feel hopeless and terrified of the unknown. And there is nothing. It's darkness upon darkness. Next, in my mind's eye, I see these messed up, burn-out kids that I see downtown sometimes when I'm near Jess's design studio. They're drunk or high, and they are fighting. A guy is pushing his girlfriend around. I want to ask for help for them, for all of us, we're all so stuck, but I feel completely separate from everybody. Nobody can hear me, see me or even perceive me. I'm gone. I'm nothing.

In the ceremony room, when I open my senses, it feels like nobody cares about me. I don't matter. Amanda, the woman with breast cancer, begins to weep and say, in a loud, bordering on yelling, voice, "I want to leave…I have to get out of here!" After a few minutes of this, the shaman stops singing and it feels even more chaotic. Frightening. Like anything could happen. Maybe something really awful…I try to breath and calm myself. I feel simultaneously like I should feel bad for Amanda, but I also want her to stop speaking. It's too much.

I open my eyes slightly, and I can see nothing. I can hear Alicia and Lillian trying to calm Amanda down–they're whispering that prayer over and over again: "San Pablo, San Pedro...San..." It sounds scary like an exorcism or something. Could something evil be here in this room? Am I safe here? It doesn't feel like it. Yet I'm unable to ask for help. I can't decide if I am unable to speak up or is it unwilling? It's like an argument inside my brain that goes on and on for eons... back and forth. I must face this alone. I never should have come here. I am permanently messed up. Will I ever get out of here? Even if I do, I won't be able to be with other people because I am not normal anymore. My mind is gone.

Fuck. Why didn't I listen to my mom?

Amanda quiets down, and Alicia begins to sing again and it's unbearable. A new scene is unleashed in my mind, and I'm reliving a time when I was being awful to my mom and lashing out at her. I can truly see just how insensitive I am, and how much I am hurting her with my words and it feels terrible. Yes, *she lied to me about my birthmother*, but I can see now that she lied only to protect me from the truth. She lied *because she loved me*. How could I be so cruel...she is just a human being. Like me. I put my head in my hands and I'm crying. I'm sobbing now. I can't take any of it back. The damage has all been done. Why am I like this? What is wrong with me? Please, please, please...God? Whoever you are...make me a better person.

Suddenly Lillian and Alicia are close to me now and blowing some kind of fragrant smoke on me. Then Doña Alicia comes right up against my chest and blows something that smells horrible, like strong cigarettes, and she whispers those same prayers right into my chest. As she does this, I immediately feel relief. Lighter. Self-forgiveness floods my being, and I feel this enormous sense of love—both for and from Alicia. *I'm not bad, I'm just learning.* Alicia feels like a mother to me. I love her. Eventually, Alicia leaves me and she begins singing again. My relief is temporary. Her new song brings with it a new scene. I wish it would stop.

I'm at the bus stop near our house where I see a blind woman from our neighborhood. I feel so sorry for her. The woman seems so sad and pitiful as she hesitantly walks with her cane and her ridiculous purple Minnesota Vikings hat pulled over her hair. There is nothing to be done; she is stuck being like this and I'm stuck here forever with her. *I am her. I'll never be returning to my nice life as I know it.* I should have been grateful for it when I had the chance. It's too late. How can I get out of this place? I'm trying to find a way out, but there is none? I screwed up. I reach a hand out for my aunt, and I feel something, but I am not even sure it is human. It feels weird, not like my aunt, so I pull my hand back. Terrrifying. Where am I? Why did I need to come here? I'm scared. Where did my aunt go? I start to panic.

Suddenly I remember my intention and, in my mind, I return to it. *I want to have my vision restored...I want to be able to see.* That calms me down a bit, to think a singular thought. Then I hear Amanda across the circle laughing softly and then giggling. How can this be funny to her? She's dying? What the fuck is wrong with her? None of this is funny. I don't trust her or the shaman or my aunt. *Why the hell would you bring anybody to this place to do this?*

I must have lain down at some point because I wake up to hearing the rooster crowing away to announce the new day. I have been covered in a blanket. I hear somebody walking slowly around the room and Lillian's voice. She's speaking softly to Amanda. I'm so relieved. I somehow realize that I am back. Back in this room! From those terrible visions. I don't know where I was, but I never want to go there again. It's over. This floor, I have a strange desire to want to kiss it—thank you, Jesus! I am so relieved to be back to myself. To this world. I was so afraid that I wasn't coming back. I was terrified that I had literally lost my mind. For good.

Lillian softly whispers as she leans down over me, "Can I get you anything, Meera?" Her words feel like the most tender and kindest question anyone has asked in my entire life. It is as if nobody has ever been so kind to me before, ever.

I manage to muster, "No thank you, but thank you," which feels incredibly stupid and insufficient to the sort of intense kindness that she's offering me.

I pull the wool blanket closer up around me and try to unravel everything that has happened. What an awful night. *I have never been so happy to be alive.*

I blink my eyes a few times in the dim early morning light, trying to discern if anything feels different. I extend my hand out of the blanket and reach to touch the cold tile floor, and it feels so solid, so insanely comforting. It's as if I have never felt the ground beneath me before. I have a strange desire to remove all the barriers between myself and the earth. I'm also exhausted. I exhale softly and sink back into the blankets.

Lillian returns with a glass of water, and I slowly sit up halfway and sip a little. It is the most delicious thing I've ever tasted. So quenching and sweet.

I return the glass to her, and whisper, "Thank you so much." Looking into her eyes, I hope that she can see how grateful I am. I slip back to sleep and awake with the sun shining in my eyes. I am still deeply grateful to be back, but now I see Doña Alicia standing at her altar and a part of me is irritated. *Why didn't she help me last night? What did all that stuff happen to me?* I did feel her love at that one point–but the rest of it was a nightmare. I thought this was supposed to be *healing*. I'm so confused.

Alicia and Lillian are speaking, and then Lillian turns toward me and asks, "How are you feeling, Meera…Doña Alicia is asking?"

Even though she asks so gently, a part of me feels like protesting, *You can tell Alicia, I AM NOT OK…that was terrible! What the fuck?* But, as I am thinking what to say, I look around and my aunt and Amanda and Jeff are all beginning to sit up and sort of half-smiling–all are looking so peaceful. I feel like something is wrong with me… maybe I did something wrong? I don't even think I remembered to pray…to the Virgin?

I weakly say, "It was OK…I mean I am OK…I guess I'm just confused right now."

Alicia nods at me, and then she begins to come around to each of us and blows more smoke on us from a fat handmade cigar.

"It's tobacco…to close the ceremony," Lillian says softly.

My mom isn't even here, and yet I'm noticing that I *still* have trouble just asking for help. Or even being honest. I'm always trying to be OK on my own, because then I won't add any snowfall to anyone's sidewalk. I close my eyes and think of my dad. I wonder if something like this would have helped him. It seems like it was very good for the others, even if it wasn't for me. I feel more isolated than ever.

⁓ℓℓℓℓℓℓ⁓

Back in our room, as we prepare to go to breakfast, determined not to keep everything to myself, I tell my aunt all about my terrible night. "I don't even understand what it was all about–it was just miserable. My mom was sad, I was sad, and all of the people I was seeing were struggling. And don't even get me started about the blind woman from our neighborhood....it was...ugh...so terrible."

I'm feeling so overwhelmed and confused.

"Oh Meera, I'm so sorry," Aunt Jill says with worry in her eyes.

"Can I give you a hug?" she offers.

"Yes please," I tell her, softening, and the hug feels so incredibly good. We are heart to heart and belly to belly–there's nothing between us and we stand like that for a long time. I feel our hearts both beating. We've never hugged quite like this at home. It's nice. And it feels so good not to have to be alone.

"What about you?" I ask as we finally end our hug.

I find my hair brush and begin to drag it through my curls.

Aunt Jill smiles sheepishly. "Well...mine was so beautiful. I got to see Lexi...oh gosh."

My aunt continues to smile as she puts a hand to her cheek and tilts her head. "I got to tell her *everything* that I wanted Lexi to know and it..." She pauses as if overwhelmed by the experience. "...and she..." Aunt Jill begins to cry, but goes on to say, "...Lexi told me why she had to leave. She was so tired of fighting. I could see so clearly how hard things had been for her for too long in a way that I never understood before. She had to leave. I'm at peace because I know she is at peace. I still miss her, but I am so grateful for the chance I got to be with her...it was so wonderful."

"OH my gosh...I'm so happy for you."

Hearing how touched Aunt Jill is, I'm crying now too.

"I didn't want it to end it felt so very real," my aunt tells me. "I'm so glad you wanted to come here...but I feel bad it was so hard for you..."

My aunt bursts into heavy tears. They seem to be tears of joy, and I put my arms around her neck and hug her all over again. Even in her sadness, she feels so strong and capable to me. So different from my mom, who feels so fragile.

Though my night was horrible, I am loving this deep and newly tender connection with Aunt Jill that I am experiencing. I want this softness between us to remain. I desperately wish my mom were in this space too. Then I suddenly think about tomorrow—the second ceremony. Immediately, my mind contracts in fear.

I blurt out, "I know we're supposed to stay for another ceremony tomorrow, but there's just no way I can do another one. How this is supposed to help me is beyond me?" My frustrated voice constricts the whole softness of the room. *Gah.* But I can't help it.

I almost wish I hadn't said anything. I don't want the soft and beautiful feeling of Lexi's memory to leave, but it's too late.

"No, no...I understand," Aunt Jill replies. "You had a tough experience, Meera, and I don't blame you one bit. Oh, gosh, I am so sorry."

My aunt furrows her brow and seems to be deep in thought. "Let me see if Carlos can come and get us tomorrow—I'll have Lillian connect with him. I understand if you want to skip the second ceremony…I support you. These old ways can be very challenging. I am just so sorry your experience was difficult for you. You kind of looked like you had seen a ghost this morning. Let's go eat some breakfast. That might help…you know you've been fasting for twenty-four hours now."

I feel relief from my aunt's response. I can't endure that ceremony again. And I also realize I'm not being a hundred percent honest. Because there's also this weird new tenderness that I'm grateful for. I'm also feeling powerfully lucky…to be back to myself again.

Eating a heaping pile of warm scrambled eggs with tomato and onion, along with toasted corn tortillas fortifies me. The food tastes incredible, like I'm eating food for the very first time. Doña Alicia is nowhere in sight, so I feel safe to share. Plus Aunt Jill is there for support.

After I tell Lillian about my experience of the first ceremony, I pepper her with questions. "How is this experience supposed to help me? I'm so confused. And what does it mean? It was so scary, and I felt so alone. Like nobody cared. I wouldn't want to go through anything like that *ever again*." As I plead with her, I wonder why it happened to me.

"I'm so sorry you felt like you were alone," offers Lillian. "We never left you, though maybe you felt that way. Sometimes there are very difficult experiences. This medicine can work in very mysterious ways. Give it some time, and good food and fresh air can help you to integrate this."

I attempt to explain my frustration. "I guess you were there, but it's like I couldn't even think of the possibility of asking for your help–like I was alone, even though you were there? Does that make sense?"

"Yes…do you ever feel like that in your life back at home?" Lillian asks with her eyebrows raised and a gentle smile on her lips.

Wow. Yes, I have to admit it is a pretty common feeling that I experience…especially around Mom. I also find the question a bit annoying. *Is she hinting that it's my fault?* I imagine my dad, for a moment, buried in huge drifts of snow. *I have to deal with everything on my own…I can't afford to be a burden.*

"All the time…" I confess hesitantly, wondering what that means.

"Sometimes the mushrooms show us patterns in our lives so that we can shift them," explains Lillian. "So, tomorrow night, you could set your intention to be able to ask for help whenever you need it–to explore what it feels like to always be able to ask for help."

Ugh. She doesn't get how hard last night was. It's like I'm alone all over again. *No way am I doing that ceremony again.* I feel hopeless. She doesn't understand either. I came here to ask for healing for my eyes…how's this supposed to be helping me?

"Uhm, I don't want to be rude, but there's no way I want to do another night," I tell her. "I mean, at one point, I felt like I had lost my mind and that I would never be normal again. The night seemed like it lasted one hundred years. Is that normal?"

"Sometimes, as I said, the nights are very difficult like that," says Lillian. "But I would encourage you to do the second ceremony–but of course it's up to you."

"I think we're going to try to leave tomorrow," I reply carefully, looking at Aunt Jill, hoping not to sound ungrateful.

"I'm sorry to hear that," responds Lillian with sincerity.

My aunt then explains our need to connect with Carlos to see if he could come earlier to return us to the city. Lillian nods, confirming that she would connect with him that morning.

Then Lillian seems to change gears. "If you're leaving soon, then this afternoon we absolutely must take you to the river for a swim!"

Chapter Seventeen

I get dressed for the river and sit waiting in the courtyard. It feels like summer. It's warming up as the sun rises higher, and there's a breeze. In one of the evergreens, there is a beautiful yellow bird singing. Its deeply melodious twittering and brilliant color mesmerize me. She looks so free and unencumbered. I envy her up there in those branches, dancing around in the breeze. Today, the world feels a little weird, like I am seeing many things freshly, for the first time. I focus on this little bird, and she seems to be staring right back at me. I shake my head, thinking, *I'm crazy.* Then I get an even stronger feeling that she's singing *right to me.*

"Stay. What have you got to lose?" the bird seems to sing, tilting her head.

Listen. *I've got a lot to lose, little yellow bird…my sanity for one thing. It's just not worth it. I will just have to accept my blindness. There is no way I am going back to that place again. You are beautiful, but I just can't.*

Lillian and my aunt appear in the courtyard.

"Ready Meera?" Lillian asks.

The river turns out to be a place that I didn't realize I needed. So very badly. The broad ribbon of crystal-clear water runs through a narrow little mountain canyon, and it is shored up by huge mountain boulders. Dozens of birds roost in the trees and surrounding shrubs. The sun is strong. Rolling up my jeans, I step into the chilly water with my bare feet. The water is cool but not unbearable, and the bottom is filled with smooth pebbles. The stream's coolness reminds me of my favorite spot at the French River back in Minnesota, but the scale of everything here is large–like a fairytale where giants live. The water feels incredible on my skin, plus there is the blue sky, the fluffy clouds, the wise old trees and shining leaves. It's all so alive, somehow.

My vision seems no different, but I have to admit I do *feel* different. My aunt is lying on a warm, large rock a few yards away, and I silently watch the water swirl past my feet in a little part of the flow. I sense Sweetie standing next to me.

Suddenly I think, Sweetie, where did you go last night?

Sweetie replies with her kind eyes: I was there. I'm always with you.

Me: But what happened to me? I couldn't feel you at all.

Sweetie: Your heart was being opened.

Me (pleadingly): What does that mean?

Sweetie nods towards the sparkling light on the water. *Just enjoy the river for now, look for the beauty.*

The sun dances on the water's swirling surface. Everything is definitely better here. I feel grateful. Which makes no sense. *I'm still going blind and I had a horrible night,* I try to remind myself. But, again, I feel lucky to have seen all of this in the first place.

Sitting on a different rock, I grab my pen and journal out of my backpack, and scribble items for my beauty list. I'll add them to my phone when I get back to the house:

Beauty

Water sparkles
Crystal clear water
Underwater mermaid moss
Tender hugs

Lillian suddenly plunks down on a rock a couple feet away from me.

"Are you a writer?" she asks me.

What a funny question? The idea kind of excites me. I know Trevor is.

I reply, smiling, "No, I'm just a list keeper, but I do love books. I decided that I would catalog all of the beautiful things I've seen, to help me remember them?"

"That's so wonderful, Meera," she says, leaning over, putting her hand on mine and squeezing it.

She's so kind. I want to be more loving like her.

With her eyes and nose crinkled into a smile, she asks, "And… how are you feeling after your breakfast and now…being here at the river?"

"A lot better actually," I confess. "I don't know how to say this, but even though last night was horrible…things *do feel better*–like I'm seeing things a little differently."

"That's good. You know, a lot of times, the first night of the *velada*, the ceremony, is very challenging–like the mushrooms kind of 'stir up the mud' so we can see what we need to see," she explains. "And often the second night takes on a totally different quality."

"Hmm...I don't know. I feel confused," I tell her. "It seems like...Doña Alicia...I mean I feel weird about her. Like I don't trust her anymore. Why would she let me have such a bad time?" I'm hoping I don't sound rude.

"If you'd like, you can speak with her," Lillian suggests. "It might be helpful."

"Maybe..." I reply, not sure what I would say to her.

Lillian looks at me with kindness and then changes the subject. "Do you want to go behind the little falls with me?" She nods her head towards the short waterfall filling the swimming hole.

I hesitate, not wanting to get my clothes wet. "Sure, but I'd have to swim in my underwear, so my clothes don't get soaked?" I'm feeling unprepared.

"Oh no, we can't do that here...the people are very modest," she objects. "It's best just to do this with our clothes on, and I have extra garments for you back at the house. Don't worry."

Lillian guides me by the hand up toward the falls. It's not huge, maybe four feet taller than us, but extremely powerful and loud.

As we get closer to it, she tells me, half-shouting, "Hold my hand and you have to trust me. When we get inside—there is a little place where we can sit."

"OK," I say.

As we stand to the side of the falls, with our feet secure on a rock ledge under the water, she yells, "Here we go!" and with that, her whole body disappears, headfirst, into the cascading and powerful wall of water. I am pulled forward, since I'm still holding her hand, but hesitating. Lillian squeezes my hand twice, and I feel my heart pound as I step through the thundering wall of water. For a moment, it feels like the falls is going to spit me back out. Suddenly,

I'm hunched over in a tiny "room" filled with the deafening sound of roaring water.

Lillian is seated on the "couch" made of somewhat slippery stone. She pats the wet stone beside her as if to say, "Come sit." I sink down and slide in next to her, and together we look out through the huge window of illuminated water towards the swimming hole. In this space filled with the roaring fury of water, possibility is palpable. I close my eyes and make a quick prayer: *Please help me. I feel lost. I don't know what's been happening to me or what to do next. If you're there God, please give me a sign. Tell me what to do.* Again, nothing seems to happen.

The water continues its violent cascade, and we sit in the roaring stillness. Lillian turns to look at me, and then she smiles and makes her hands into a prow and dives out towards the light and back into the water from the little room we're in. In a flash of sunshine, she's gone. I linger a few more minutes, alone in the thundering place, and ask once more, *Please help!* Finally satisfied, I dive out through the wall of water and am spit forcefully into the center of the pond, where Lillian is laughing and the sun warms my face.

⟋⟋⟋⟋⟋

We all eat dinner together and share our experiences from last evening's ceremony. It turns out that Amanda had a powerful healing during the first ceremony. She was raped in college and, last night, the mushrooms returned a part of her soul that had been lost. It showed her that she was innocent. It wasn't an easy experience, because she had to relive part of what had happened. But after she realized it wasn't her fault, on a very deep level something changed.

Amanda tells us, "It was like I was swimming in an ocean of pure freedom, and I remembered that no matter what I did–I was loved. It was beyond words!"

She is so happy, and even now retelling the story, tears of joy stream down her face. "I feel much more at peace now..." Amanda says. Then she looks at Jeff quickly, with love, and adds, "Not that I plan on going anywhere any time soon..."

He puts an arm around her and wipes away his own tears.

Listening to all of this, I'm happy for her and a little confused. But I guess that was her intention to have part of herself returned?

My aunt shares her amazing experience with Lexi, and then Alicia asks me, through Lillian, "What about you, Meera? Doña Alicia is asking?"

I remember that Lillian encouraged me to talk with her about it.

"Oh gosh, I hesitate to say anything...you all had such good experiences. Mine wasn't so great–was it my candles?" I laugh nervously, feeling out of place and remembering my wonky, half-toppled candles. I feel bad that I'm not feeling wonderful about the whole ceremony like my aunt and Amanda are...maybe I'm supposed to?

I begin again. "I don't know...but I basically spent the whole night observing the suffering of other people, and I had to see times when I was a terrible person to my mom. It felt pretty bad."

"And how do you feel now?" Lillian presses.

"Well, it was really bad, but I do feel better today, in a way. Mostly, I'm just so happy it's over!" I say truthfully, laughing lightly.

Lillian nods and I continue. "There's something different about today. Maybe it's just that I'm so happy to be alive and be back here on planet Earth? I felt like I was somewhere alone–and so far away from all of you. I was so scared that I had lost my mind–like permanently."

Doña Alicia and Lillian converse for a moment as Lillian translates my words.

Then Lillian shares, "Doña Alicia says that because you made a powerful prayer…to be able to see…the experience that you had is good medicine. You should embrace this…umm…how did she say it?–you should *lean into this experience.*"

I pause. *That's not what I expected to hear.*

"What do you mean 'lean in'…how?" I force myself to ask, realizing that I need the help.

"Try to stay with that experience…to see what it has to teach you," Lillian says with a smile.

I'm baffled and a little embarrassed. *What would such misery have to teach me and what about my vision?* I feel defeated.

"Did you tell her that I don't think I'm up for another ceremony?" I inquire, feeling an ache in my belly growing.

"I will tell her now…"

They continue talking. Then Amanda nods at Alicia and responds to me, "She says, of course, it is up to you. But you have come so far to be healed…why not see what more the sacred *niños* can help?"

Doña Alicia smiles a little at me as Lillian finishes her message.

"I'll think about it," I respond, trying to return the shaman's smile.

After dinner, I help Lillian get more wood for the cooking fire from behind the house. I watch her carefully arrange the wood for the fire. It seems so simple living here. No distractions. I'm curious about how much attention she puts into her fire making.

"What are you doing when you are moving that wood?" I ask her.

"Ahh, this? I'm learning how to tend the fire. Doña Alicia is teaching me," Lillian explains. "This fire is a spirit...and like any other holy being...we believe that it's sacred."

As I watch her blow gently on the small nest of kindling she created, I wonder aloud, "Can the spirit of fire help a person?"

"Oh yes–for sure!" Lillian shares. "It also keeps us warm, brings us together, and cooks our food–so many things. If you like...you can make an offering to the fire, this grandfather spirit."

Then she blows gently on the center of the fire as it begins to grow. The fire now crackles, and the flames lick up into the air from every corner. It does feel fully alive.

"I'd like to try that," I say, interested to see what happens.

"Wait, let me get you something to offer." She walks back into the house and returns with a handful of dried flower petals. "You can ask for its help–after you thank it, of course. It's customary to greet the fire with respect and to say, 'thank you' before making a request...use these."

She places the dried, deep-pink petals into my outstretched palm explaining, "Just hold them in your hand, and think about how grateful you are for your life and for the fire–and add anything else you like. Then, when you feel complete, place the offering into the fire. Then you can ask for the help you need."

Lillian smiles at me.

I hold the petals in my hand and silently thank the fire for all of the fires we had at home and for the hot water for baths and for the warmth he's brought to cook all of the wonderful food here in the courtyard. I express gratitude for my life. I may be losing my sight, but I'm newly aware that I'm not fighting for my life like Amanda is. I drop the petals into the center of the fire. The fire leaps up and dances and sizzles a bit.

Then I ask the fire silently, *Can you help me, or give me a sign? I'm scared. And I don't know whether to stay or to go?*

I'm not sure I'm doing this right…but as I stare into the licking flames, I suddenly notice that below, in the coals, there is a bird forming that looks like the one I saw that morning and the one in my fabric design at home. "Let go!" the little shimmering ember-bird seems to say. The bird is repeating its message from this morning, "What have you got to lose?"

I continue to stare at the fire, knowing that this is most definitely a sign and feeling utterly unsure about how I will respond to it.

"Meera…" Aunt Jill stands in the doorway later that night. I'm lying on the bed.

"Carlos is travelling with another group at the moment and is unable to pick us up any earlier," she says, watching me. "So it looks like we're sticking around for a few more days. Sorry but I don't really want to search for another driver, unless we have to—I really trust Carlos."

"That's fine. I like it here." It's like there is a part of me that knew all along that Carlos wasn't coming back early, so when it happens I'm relaxed.

After brushing my teeth, I suddenly feel exhausted and crawl into bed next to my aunt who is reading.

"Sweet dreams, kiddo."

"G'night."

That night I dream of the yellow bird, and she's up very high… dancing so lightly on the branches of a huge tree in-between the fat glossy leaves that glimmer as they move in the light. She's so bright and beautiful…so impossibly free. I want to be her so badly, and I ask her, *How can I become light like you?*

I wake up with her words filling my head:

Just

let

go.

In the morning after breakfast I decide to fast along with my aunt, partly in solidarity and partly because I don't want to make Lillian work any harder than she already is. She never seems to stop moving. I wonder how Alicia manages when she's not around.

⟨⟨⟨⟩⟩⟩

I'm already hungry as my aunt and I begin our walk around ten in the morning with Lillian to the little store a half-mile away in the village. She needs cooking oil. The people we see along the dirt road wave politely without smiling at us. The store, a 10x10-foot room, is stuffed to the rafters with produce, bags of rice, various household items, sandals and a few canned goods. It has a TV and the only Wi-Fi in town.

Once connected to the Wi-Fi, I scroll through my notifications on my phone, and there's a voicemail on WhatsApp from Trevor. Before I left, he told me to download the app. He'd used it before to communicate with a buddy who was studying abroad in Italy. His message won't download for some reason. I stand there as long as I can, trying, desperately wanting to hear his voice, but my phone keeps saying, "Connection is unstable."

As we walk back to the house, Lillian is clearly frustrated and says, "Have you ever wanted something so badly...but when the opportunity comes, you're too scared to take it?"

"Oh YES...too many times to count!" responds my aunt laughing. "I did that a lot when I was getting started in my textile import business...I never thought I was up to the task. But I've learned that fear is often there with something new...and things are never as bad as I think they're going to be. Sometimes I still do it."

Lillian smiles and then shares exasperated, "I just found out, when I checked my email, that the grant I wanted, but I talked myself out of applying for, just got awarded to this guy in my class who isn't even a C-average student. I'm disgusted with myself. Ha! I'm realizing that I probably could have gotten it." She slaps her forehead comedically. "I convinced myself that I wasn't qualified!"

"Well, what are you going to do about it?" asks Aunt Jill.

Lillian looks over at my aunt, and replies, "That's a really good question. When I get back to university, I think I'll sit with my advisor and ask him for help. I'm so sick of doubting myself." She shakes her head.

Hoping it will be helpful, I offer, "For a long time, I avoided asking this designer at home if I could work for her–always thinking, 'Why would she want to spend time with me? What would I have to contribute?' So I didn't say anything. Luckily, my mom kept pushing me, and finally I got up the guts to write her a letter introducing myself. She called me the day she got my letter. She wanted to hire me on the spot. I was in total shock." I recall the thrill of getting her call.

Lillian smiles and tells me, "You're reminding me, Meera…it's just like the American mythology expert Joseph Campbell says… when you say yes to that thing that scares you–that thing your soul keeps insisting on–doors will open where no doors existed before."

"I definitely felt that way," I reply, hearing her words resonate.

And then I think to myself, *But what difference does it make? My design career is already over, and it never had a chance to really start.*

When we return to the house, I lie on the bed to read and rest and I fall asleep immediately. My dad comes to me in a dream and it feels so real. We're at the old library, and I have a huge stack of books to check out. I'm so excited to get them home, even though I don't know what they are about yet. My dad pulls his library card out of his wallet and shows it to the clerk. As she is checking the books out, Dad tells me how proud he is of me about everything I have been doing. I begin sobbing, and at this point it seems so like real life. I feel like he is right there with me loving me so hard. He tells me I don't need to worry about the future…"That will take care of itself, Meera. All you need to do is trust." And then I wake up. I almost didn't want to. I didn't want to be separated from him again and for a moment we weren't.

～eℓℓℓℓℓℓ～

It is starting to get dark. The birds had all quieted, and you could hear a few coyotes begin to yip back and forth. Lillian comes inside from tending the fire, and she brings my aunt and me both cups of steaming hot herbal tea.

"So, what do you think? Would you like to join Jeff and Amanda in the ceremony tonight again, Jill?" she offers.

"Well, it depends on what Meera is feeling," my aunt says. "I'm really here for her, and I had such a beautiful night the first time. I feel pretty complete as I am…but I'd like to see what more the medicine has to show me."

"What are you thinking, Meera?" Lillian asks me.

"Well, I don't want to go through that again…it scares me," I tell her. "I'm also realizing that I feel a lot better somehow. My vision isn't different, or at least not yet? Not that I can tell. I'm not sure what to expect? I guess I just appreciate everything a lot more…if that makes sense?"

I hesitate a moment as I consider how I'm feeling, then continue slowly. "A part of me is saying, 'Stay safe; you can just skip this ceremony' and another part is saying, 'Trust. It's going to be OK.'"

I add, "I had a little dream last night about a bird…and then I saw–this is going to sound strange–I saw that same bird in the fire today after I made an offering."

"Oh really!" Lillian responds. "Tell us more, Meera." She is smiling brightly at me.

"Well, the bird seems to be telling me that I have nothing to lose and that I need to let go. What do you make of that?"

"Well, the most important thing, Doña Alicia would say, is *what do you make of it?* What you think of everything that's happening is the most important thing."

Chapter Eighteen

As I grip my two candles, my heart, without consulting me, begins thumping away against my chest. I will myself to calm down, which has absolutely no effect. Breathing helps. I watch Doña Alicia carefully sorting out the sacred mushrooms once again, and I'm curious about what she's seeing. I'm still also trying to decide if Alicia is good or not. In her eyes there's a fierceness that makes me uncomfortable. But I'm also trying to remember the immense love the others experienced in this ceremony on the first night. I want her to smile at me or do something else to reassure me that tonight will be OK.

I'm seated next to my aunt, and Amanda and her husband are across from us. The room is illuminated by the many candles on the altar, and long shadows dance on the wall. My intention is the same, to have my vision healed. To be able to see clearly. I remind myself, silently, that I can ask for help if I need it.

Aunt Jill goes to the altar first, and Alicia wafts copal smoke over her portion of mushrooms. My aunt takes her now-lit candles and affixes them to the board. Her candles burn evenly and do not tip.

Lillian prompts me, and I approach the altar next. Tonight I have brought with me the small, beaded deer that I bought on the church stairs back in Oaxaca. I asked Lillian earlier if I could place it on the altar, and she said that it was OK. I hand the tiny deer to

Doña Alicia who takes it into her hands. She sweeps the statuette through the clouds of copal smoke three times and then sets it down on the altar next to one of her statues. Seeing my bright, beaded deer there comforts me.

Next Alicia paints my arms again in crosses with the cool wet paste, chants over me, and begins to hand me my pairs of mushrooms on a leaf.

As I go to take them, I panic and say, "I'd like to take a smaller number of mushrooms tonight. I think maybe I'm just more sensitive to them."

Doña Alicia looks confused and motions to her assistant. Lillian comes over to translate and I repeat my request. Doña Alicia listens to Lillian and then begins to shake her head slowly back and forth. She looks at me kindly but firmly.

Lillian gazes at me softly and then pauses, as if she's thinking of the best way to express something. "She says you just need to trust her, Meera–OK? You don't get to be in control of this."

Ughhh. Right. OK. Deep inside, I know she's right.

Like the little yellow bird said, *I need to let go*. I pause, staring at my beaded deer, and I recognize that he's sitting next to an Our Lady of Guadeloupe figure carved out of wood and painted in muted colors. Her sweet face is calm. I remember the words of the woman at the shop, "If you need a miracle of any kind, she's the one you pray to." Our Lady being there, next to my deer, feels like a sign to reassure me…things are going to be OK.

I begin to return to my seat with my mushrooms and candles, and Alicia touches my shoulder to stop me. She points out one of the mushrooms in my hands, makes a comment, and then motions for Lillian to translate.

"This one…" Lillian points. "…Alicia says it is a very powerful one. It's not a single mushroom but it's a family."

Lillian smiles at me.

I look and notice that this mushroom has multiple little caps and stems that seem to all be coming from one "root."

"*Gracias,*" I say softly to Doña Alicia.

I set the mushrooms down on my blanket, light my candles and then affix them, with great care, to the board with the melting wax. I hold the candles in place for a few moments to secure them and, finally, let go. They do not tip or drip. They burn evenly and perfectly. *Thank goodness.* It somehow seems like another good "sign."

We all chew our mushrooms slowly. As I eat the "family" mushroom cluster, I feel slightly concerned. *Do I really want a more powerful mushroom?*

When all the mushrooms have been consumed, Doña Alicia snuffs out every candle and we're plunged into darkness.

I begin to feel nauseous. Really sick…and I can't help it, but I start to gag. My stomach violently lurches, and I turn away from the circle so whatever is coming up won't land on anybody. Lillian pushes a bowl into my hands in the darkness. As I gag silently into the blackness and away from my blanket–nothing but drool seems to come out into the vessel physically, but I have a clear sense that I am vomiting out my fear. My fear is leaving me. The nausea passes, and I feel much, much better. Suddenly Alicia begins to sing and her song transforms everything.

My eyes are closed, and as I listen, everything is permeated by what I can only say is love…it's so intense. It's as if love itself has appeared or maybe it's God? God is a giant golden retriever puppy licking me–I am being licked to death from stem to stern by this

God-puppy-love. The whole room is. It is overpowering, even obliterating...it's almost embarrassing. Though that's not quite the word. I've dissolved into this love. I don't exist. I begin to laugh softly, and tears run down my cheeks because I am realizing that I am so deeply loved. Everything that has happened...my Retinitis Pigmentosa... my friends...my adoption even...meeting Trevor...it's all somehow part of this absolutely perfectly choreographed dance that is my life. That is love. I am love. I don't fully understand it and I never will. It's simply so damn HUGE I can barely fathom it. Sweetie is part of it, and I am her and she is me. I don't want this song to end. I'm crying and smiling in the darkness as I listen and soak in the love. I want to respond back to this mighty, incomprehensibly grand force. This love. So I begin to whisper very softly, the only thing that makes sense: "Thank you, thank you, thank you." I have the thought: this is prayer too.

Doña Alicia begins a new song, eventually, which is melancholy and filled with so much feeling, and the rich darkness in my mind is planted somehow with the awareness of my mom. I feel *her* love for me–it's beyond comprehension how much she loves me. *Infinite.* I see how I have been so wrong about her and insensitive, and it breaks my heart. I lean forward and place my head on the ground. I'm ashamed. She's loved me no matter what. I could never do anything to stop this love. I hold my head in my hands shaking it, trying to rid myself of this terrible feeling that I should have loved my mom better. As I begin to sob, Alicia comes over, as before, and blows tobacco all over me, and I feel lighter again.

Silences returns, but it is not really silence–it's exquisitely rich, as if it holds, bursting, the possibility of all sounds...or even of all things. It's a heavy sensation. Finally, it's broken as Lillian begins drumming and singing. Her singing voice is sweet and a welcome relief. Like a ringing bell, she's giving structure to this otherwise wildly disorienting ride. After a while, I feel this familiar feeling of lift off... this powerful energetic surge that takes me over, and in the darkness with my eyes closed, I see colored lights swirling behind my eyes.

Alicia is now fanning some kind of perfume in the air, as Lillian continues singing, and suddenly the room is filled by the presence of a huge bird...it's my yellow bird. She has huge loving eyes, and she embraces me in her enormous wings. I can't discern a boundary between me and the love that is her. *I am the bird, and the bird is love and it's in me.* I feel the exquisite softness of her feathers and the absolute power of her wings. This beautiful bird suddenly becomes a woman.

This loving woman is teaching me, without words, about breathing. Being loved is like breathing, she explains, wordlessly. As I breathe in, I fill with love, and as I exhale, I share that love with the world. I feel this ecstasy deep down in my pelvis, as I draw the air deep into my belly. This is how it's supposed to be. I recognize that she, this bird-woman-spirit, is Our Lady of Guadeloupe, and then she fades away and I am aware that I'm holding a baby in my arms.

The baby is so vulnerable and precious, I know that we must take care of her...she's so tiny and perfect and innocent, and then I realize that the baby is me. This is how much my birth mother loved me. *I have never not been loved.* Adored. I am sobbing—not for sadness but for joy as I realize I am loved. Alicia is back blowing tobacco in my heart. I sigh deeply. I always have been loved. *Always.*

At some point, I lie down, curled on my side, exhausted from all of the emotions and experiences. The yellow bird returns to me and gently whispers to me that my purpose on Earth is to show other people their beauty…*to show them that they are loved.* She's giving me a gift that I can share, she says, as she stuffs my heart full of white roses. I can sense each flower's absolute perfection filling the space in my now open heart and the tenderness and heavenly scent of each petal. Yellow bird says that each person has a different sort of beauty inside them, and that I will be able to see that beauty from now on… it's my purpose to show it to them. It, somehow, makes sense. I won't be a designer of beautiful spaces, instead, I will help others to see the beauty and power that's already inside of them.

"But how?" I ask silently. I'm not entirely sure what she means.

Suddenly I am being given a tour of different individual souls. Each is a like showhouse…a beautiful space: an elaborate room with lovely intricate designs and crystal light fixtures and flowers. And there are infinite ones to explore; each person's interior world more beautiful than the last. They are all interconnected by doorways and staircases. My own soul is filled with charming wild-animal figurines, elaborate and gilded Japanese furnishings, brightly colored art, and it has a rooftop garden that blooms with fragrant jasmine. *As I begin to ask more questions, the bird vanishes.* The questions hang in my mind, as I slip back to sleep. And I have a knowing that this bird has been with me for a very long time.

Alicia closed the ceremony hours ago with tobacco, and we have all been sleeping until now. The bright sun is streaming through the windows. Lillian comes over to me and asks me to sit up. Doña Alicia is behind her, and she kneels down and presents me with a tiny perfect yellow feather.

Lillian translates, "This is a gift for you, Meera. Doña Alicia says you are a healer, and this feather is for your medicine bundle."

I stretch my cupped hands out to receive it. The feather is both an unexpected surprise and a remembering. Like home.

Chapter Nineteen

As our car pulls away from Doña Alicia's home, she and Lillian smile and wave from the gate. I put one hand on my heart beneath the sweatshirt I'm wearing. I sense the tender white roses there. The yellow feather is carefully tucked into an envelope in my journal for safekeeping. Alicia also returned to me the beaded deer I had placed on the altar. She wrapped it in brown paper.

Lillian explained to me, "This little deer now carries some of the power of Alicia's healing altar, dear Meera…so keep it in a special place at home. You can pray with it."

I didn't exactly know what she meant, but I knew that praying was much simpler than I had previously thought. It was as easy as "thank you."

Carlos and Aunt Jill catch up in the front of the car as we head back towards Oaxaca. Jeff and Amanda hold hands quietly in the back seat next to me. I began to write a long email to my mom on the phone, apologizing for all the ways I've been difficult. It feels like a relief to get that started.

We stop for a bathroom break about halfway to Oaxaca, and I notice a headache coming on. In the dimly lit, windowless restaurant bathroom, I use my phone flashlight to illuminate the space. It feels harder than usual to be in the dark. Being in the unfamiliar place reminds me, harshly, that I'm still a girl with RP who is going blind.

Tears spring to my eyes, and I strain to recall the yellow bird and that incredible love. But my memory of her feels like it's already fading.

By the time we're back in the hotel and have had our dinner, my aunt and I are exhausted. We watch a couple old episodes of *Friends* on the local TV channel. I ask her for some ibuprofen, which helps with the headache, and I drift off to sleep.

The next morning, I wake up with a colorful new blur right in the center of my vision. I blink and blink and blink, thinking, *This can't be right.* I'm so used to my peripheral vision being limited, but not the center. Suddenly it's like somebody put a splash of rainbow-colored Vaseline on the middle of my vision. *WTF. Why is this happening?* I stand in the shower and cry, feeling so defeated.

I must have been there a while, because my aunt finally knocks softly.

She says warmly, "Meera, did you fall in? I need to get a shower too...we don't want to be late."

"I'm coming," I respond.

I towel dry and exit quickly, realizing I still have repacking to do.

As I reenter the bathroom after dressing, my aunt is still drying off in the shower.

I tell her, "I have something weird with my vision today...I wonder if it started with that headache?"

"What's going on?" Aunt Jill asks, now setting her toiletry bag on the counter. "What are you seeing, Meera?"

My aunt glances over at me, then starts to apply lotion to her face.

"It's right smack dab in the center of my eye...go figure. After all of this 'healing,' my vision just gets worse."

Even as I'm saying this–it feels wrong...as if I am saying something extremely rude and ungrateful, but it's how I'm feeling. I just want to return to that expanse of pure love with Our Lady of Guadeloupe...to go into that ocean of love. This is too hard.

"Worse. How?" asks Aunt Jill. She's got her toothbrush in her hand and she's looking at me, brow furrowed.

I explain, "It's like in the middle of what I'm looking at..." I try to indicate using my hand in front of my face. "It's like there's a new blur and it's kind of flashy with colors...right in the center of the good vision I still had."

I sigh and continue. "I can see your face, but now I have to turn my head to try to see the center of your face...because now in the middle there's a blur."

My aunt cocks her head and puts a hand to her mouth. "Oh gosh, I am so sorry...I'm sure your mom will want to take you in to the doctor as soon as we get back."

Aunt Jill puts her hand on my arm, softly. It feels good. I'm not alone. I'm loved.

"Yeah," I say, "he told me it could get worse...but somehow I didn't think it would happen like this."

I abruptly leave the bathroom.

When we get to the airport in Oaxaca, I finally listen to Trevor's voice on the WhatsApp message. He wished me well and said that he and Eleanor were rooting for me.

I text him back.

Me: Hey, I'm almost back home. Thanks for your message. I can tell you more soon.

The retinal specialist isn't available the week I return home. But the ophthalmologist on call, a gray-haired guy with horn-rimmed glasses, reassures my mom and me during a clinic visit. He tells us that this new change in my vision is just likely a normal part of the progression of RP. With me still being an adolescent, it can accelerate things.

This rapid change has me worried. I share, "I noticed last night that, when I close my eyes, there are more lights flashing. I used to have a little of that, but it's so much more...prominent? Will I always see that?"

He responds, "That's pretty normal too. What you're perceiving is just your brain's way of making up for the vision you're losing. Without that stimulus to the eye, the brain sort of makes something up to take its place. It can shift and change over time...so as the RP progresses, it will change. Or it could stay like this for a while. There is really nothing to do, but enjoy the show, Meera." He looks sheepish as if he's made a bad joke.

My mom looks at me and rolls her eyes, as if to say, *This guy is a real jerk.* It's not his fault but I feel really disappointed.

And I still haven't heard anything back from Trevor. At first, I assumed he had his phone off. But that was two days ago. I double-check and it says, "Text received."

After the clinic visit, I beg Mom not to force me to go to school for the rest of the day, and she obliges. There's a winter storm watch, and school might get cancelled tomorrow anyway. I think she's pissed off about my worsening vision too. Maybe she's realizing, like me, that the doctors really aren't much help...even her beloved science can't save me.

I pull the blinds and crawl under the covers. The disappointment feels like a hundred-pound blanket weighing me down. I begin to sob. Big belly sobs until I am utterly wiped out. Peace finally lands.

Despite my new awareness of how much I'm loved, I still feel alone. Nobody else can do it for me or even understand how it feels. Wrung out from crying, I roll onto my belly and turn my face towards the wall.

Just then, I sense Sweetie there beside me and she asks with gentleness, *So, what are you going to do?*

I'm remembering a dream I had last night. A group of mushrooms, cartoonish and colorful, sang and danced and surrounded me while saying, "Remember, the medicine is in you!" What did it mean? Did this have something to do with what Doña Alicia said to me?

I relax a little more into my bed, and I began to breathe myself back into that space I was in during the second ceremony. That is, in that darkness that was so beautiful...where I could feel that amazing love. As I relax more and more and remember, it isn't quite in the exact same potency that I felt it that night. Still, it's there...this soft peaceful safeness. Like being wrapped in a soft blanket and being held in the arms of something much grander. There, wrapped in peace, I feel a knowing growing in me that I need to choose to love my life. It's up to me. That softness didn't take away my pain, but it somehow lightened it.

❧

Exhausted, I fall asleep and have a bad dream. I'm back in that suffering place, feeling so sorry for myself and all of the people who suffer...it's miserable. I want to get out. Then the shaman Alicia appears and stares at me, while she blows tobacco in my face. She tells me again, "The medicine is in you now." As the tobacco smoke hits me, I feel a strong wave of the love that I felt in the second ceremony wash over me. I don't want it to end. Then there's a huge CRASH and I awaken with a start.

A true blizzard is being stirred up outside, and I realize that the noise in my dream was our back door that's slamming in the wind because it isn't latched. It is so loud and jolting, it feels like it somehow cleared the air. But I still have the soft love buzzing inside my heart, and I don't want that to go away. I get up gently and go latch the door.

When I return to my bedroom, I check my phone: 3 am. Still nothing from Trevor. Maybe I shouldn't have told him so much about what I was going to be doing in Mexico? He probably thinks I'm a freak for wanting to trip on mushrooms.

Chapter Twenty

Two more days. Still no answer from Trevor. Getting ghosted feels horrible, but I remind myself that boys don't matter, and that I have so many good people around me. I try to explain to Penn how horrible and also how wonderful the whole Mexico trip was as she flat-irons my hair and hands me peanut M&M'S. She listens, but I can tell it's not something she can really understand. How could she? And I am noticing that I'm not the same person who went to Mexico. Something has changed. I still have RP and I am still scared, but I feel softer inside.

Like, with Penn, I don't feel as judgy towards her relationship with Jared. It all seems to make more sense. Of course, she and Jared like each other, and they are both just finding their way…it's all happening as it should. I know Penn loves me still as a friend and that hasn't changed.

A weird peace has settled on me in some ways. I keep the yellow feather Alicia gifted me in an old green-painted, wooden cigar box with a beautiful swan swimming on it. The box sits on my desk. Our Lady of Guadeloupe and the beaded deer are nearby, keeping it company.

Since returning home, things are much better between Mom and me. I've stopped calling her Lorraine. Calling her "mom" again feels huge. *I need her.* I think she feels better about things too. While

Aunt Jill and I were gone, Mom set up her painting easel in the living room and started getting ready to paint again. She seems more relaxed too. It's like the ceremonies, somehow, also affected her.

Something else still feels hard. I continue to not fully understand why I had to go through that first ceremony and why it was so bad. Am I a bad person, or doing it all wrong? What was I supposed to learn from that? *How do I lean in?* What am I supposed to do about all the suffering in the world?

It's early morning, and I crack the window in the kitchen to see how it feels outside. It's not safe to say it's spring yet. In Duluth it can snow on into May, but spring feels possible today. The sun is shining, and our yard is filled sweet chickadees twittering and singing.

I knock on my mom's door. "Mom?"

"Yeah, come on in. I'm not sleeping–just lying here."

I go over and crawl in bed with my mom, like old times. I remember as a kid sandwiching myself between my mom and my grandma on Mom's bed. As I get under her covers, it smells like the perfume she wears every day, Clinique's Aromatics Elixir. It's a strange and good smell, which reminds me of moss and roses.

As I settle in next to my mom, she tucks the covers in around me. I nestle closer to her and share, "Something happened to me in the ceremony, Mom...on the first night that I told you was so bad."

"Mmmmm?" she murmurs, squeezing me warmly.

"Well, it's hard to explain, but it was like I was trapped in a...I guess like a maze kind of...or something I'd never be able to escape? And all I could see was how much everybody was suffering, and it was terrible. I was trapped. I mean I don't know if there's a hell for reals—but it felt like that. And I worried the night would never end….it felt like an eternity. When I finally realized the sun was coming up—I cried. I was so relieved it was over and that *I was still me*—and not stuck there. What do you think it means?" I turn my head towards her, hoping she might know.

"Hmm…I don't know, sweetie? I'm so sorry you had to experience that—it sounds awful." She kisses my head.

"Yeah and I have these really strong feelings that I'm supposed to do something about it," I reply, feeling so grateful to be lying there with her.

She yawns a little and then offers, "Well, this astrologer guy I really like, Kaypacha, says that we're constantly being shown reflections of our lives through the planets and their movements. They aren't there to harm us or control us, but they're more like mirrors for us…reflecting. So I wonder if somehow this experience you had might be reflecting something in your own life? That's kind of how I think of dreams?"

That sounds similar to what Lillian said about the ceremonies showing us things about our lives—patterns that aren't working.

Then, changing the subject, she asks brightly, "And how is Trevor? I know you had said you guys were keeping in touch?"

"Ehhh…he kind of dropped off the radar," I tell her, feeling suddenly vulnerable.

"Oh?" she says, sounding surprised.

"Yeah. I don't really want to talk about it."

She turns towards me and hugs me, and I let her hold me for a long time.

I think about those frying-pan-sized ice pancakes spinning freely in Lake Superior with their perfectly polished edges. All that friction eventually gave way to a strange new beauty. It's a little like that for Mom and me. I guess that friction had to happen so we could transform *us*. It feels wonderful in this moment...a little like that spectacular golden morning on one of the coldest days.

"OK, Meera–you ready?" Aunt Jill asks me.

After I spoke with Aunt Jill about my confusion around the ceremony and the meaning of it, she set up a call for me with Alicia and Lillian via WhatsApp. They're going to be talking to us from the little store/bar in the village. I'm hoping to get some advice from Doña Alicia. I feel unfinished somehow.

"Yep. I'm set."

I have a notebook and pen in front of me. My aunt dials them and puts the speakerphone setting on, and then she sets the phone between us on the dining room table.

"Hola," I hear as Lillian picks up.

"Hola! Buenas!" says my aunt kindly. She greets Lillian and Alicia in Spanish and thanks them profusely for helping make the call happen.

Lillian responds and translates. "Hi Meera! How are you now, Doña Alicia is asking and wants to know?"

"Oh thank you! Well...my vision is actually worse now since coming home." I say carefully, being honest, but not wanting to sound ungrateful. To be fair, I want to tell her about the good things too. "You can also tell her that things seem...more calm? My relationship with my mom is better, and I feel a lot more appreciative of life, I guess? The world seems…" I pause trying to find the words. "…more beautiful."

"Oh, I'm so sorry to hear that your vision is worse." says Lillian with kindness in her voice, and then she translates for Doña Alicia.

When she stops translating, I continue on. "In a weird way, it feels OK…I am still sad about it, but more at peace, I guess?" I stop, not knowing where to go from there.

"Meera—why don't you ask your question?" my aunt suggests to remind me why we're calling.

"OK, so Lillian, you remember the first ceremony—my bad one? I spent a lot of that night seeing people suffering, and it was terrible. One of the people I saw was this blind woman that I always see at the bus stop who…oh I don't know—whenever I see her—*I just want to look away.* I worry about her. I mean in winter I wonder if anybody is looking after her. She seems so vulnerable, and I just hate that she's alone. Can you ask Doña Alicia what this all means? I mean—it still bothers me, and I feel like I don't know how to 'lean into it'…as she suggested?"

"Ah yes, OK I understand…let me explain to her." And she begins translating.

After a few minutes of conversing with the shaman, Lillian finally tells me, "Doña Alicia says that because you made such a big prayer, you were fortunate that this was all that happened. I mean you got a brief experience of suffering…a few hours…a small taste of suffering. Do you understand?"

"Yes…" I gulped, "I guess that makes sense?"

"She says that what you need to do is offer a gift to this woman, the blind woman *who you see but who you do not want to see,*" Lillian translates.

"A gift?" I ask, curious what that would look like.

"Yes. Doña Alicia says you will know what to do, or it will come to you," Lillian adds.

"Ahhhh, OK. Thank you," I reply, curious about this assignment.

Days later, as I'm sitting in Art class working on my senior project, an idea comes to me. And I know what I need to do.

Chapter Twenty-One

I'm at Lighthouse for the Blind in the lobby, waiting for my mom to pick me up. I love my teacher, Emily. Somehow, she makes it seem cool and amazing to be blind. Tomorrow she has promised to teach us how to play some good jokes on fully-sighted people.

As I'm staring out the window looking for my mom's car, my phone buzzes.

Trevor: Meera—are you back by now?

Me: Yes...I texted you two weeks ago?

Still feeling hurt by his nonresponse, I feel guarded.

Trevor: So sorry—lost my phone and all my contacts. I got a new phone and then my old phone finally got turned in, so I was able to retrieve your number.

Me: I thought you ghosted me.

Trevor: Ghosted you? No way! So how was everything?

Me: It was a lot. I'm getting in the car to go home with my mom. OK if we just text now?

I climb into the car.

"Hi Meera," Mom says, smiling at me as I slide into the passenger seat and close the door.

"Hey Mom. I have to get back to someone...so I'll be on my phone for a bit."

"Sure." She turns up the volume on her radio news.

Trevor: For sure, texting's just a little bit slower for me.

Me: I'm back and yes–OMG so much happened in Mexico.

Trevor: Are you still planning to come to the U of MN for a tour? I know some girls you could stay with?

Me: Yeah, I'd like that.

Trevor: Just tell me when and I'll talk to my friends. The girls will love you.

Me: When would be best for you? I mean–you probably have class and tests.

Trevor: The next two weekends would work...after that it's closer to finals?

Me: Let me talk to my mom.

Trevor: And call when you can...I want to hear all about Mexico.

It's a warm early spring evening in Minneapolis; you can smell the grass and the earth. The electric green treetops are beginning to unfurl. The sun sets as we enter the city, and Penn and I step off the coach bus around 6:30 pm in Dinkytown near the university. On the way down, she retold the entire torrid tale of her dramatic breakup with Jared. Her mom was the one who finally convinced her that Jared was kind of making her miserable...that you don't change people. I am surprised and happy for Penn. She seems freer than she has been in a long time. Selfishly, too, it is a relief to have Penn all to myself again.

After we both step off the bus, it's so dark outside that I reflexively reach out for Penn's hand as I've done since sixth grade.

"Let's go in here." Penn motions towards a little coffee shop.

We duck in and I text Trevor.

"He's on his way!" I say, with a big smile and my eyebrows raised.

I'm feeling a little nervous. We have texted and talked so much, but I haven't seen him for almost three months. What if it's weird?

"I'm so excited to meet him!" Penn tells me.

Trevor calls. "OK, I think I'm close to the coffee place but I've never been there, so can you meet me outside? I'll be the bind guy with the dog?" He laughs.

"You got it...we'll head out there now," I reply.

"Meera, I see him I think," Penn reports. "He's got a dog right?"

As he gets closer, I see his outline now too as he passes under a streetlight...he's walking slowly, but confidently along with Eleanor. Then, under the lights of the coffee shop's exterior, he looks somehow more handsome and older than I remembered him being. He has on a white U of MN hoodie and joggers that are fitted and show off his muscular legs. His hair is rumpled, in a good way.

I let go of Penn's hand and move quickly toward him, feeling like he's vulnerable.

"Trevor, it's me...Meera! Good to see you."

"Meera!" he says with a huge grin. "Can I give you a hug?"

He opens his arms.

"Of course!"

I move towards him, and Trevor scoops me up in a strong bear hug, which almost lifts me off my feet. He smells like beeswax and woodsmoke.

"I'm so glad you came, Meera!" he says as we separate.

"Can I pet your dog?" Penn asks.

"Oh hey Trevor, this is Penn...Penn meet Trevor!" I am happy that my two special people will get acquainted.

"Hey Penn–great that you could come for a visit too," Trevor remarks. "So awesome to meet you...Meera has told me you're the Queen of Hair!"

We all smile.

"Hopefully you won't judge my mop." He ruffles fingers through his hair. "I mean I can't see so I rely on my roomies to point out when it's not working." Trevor chuckles.

Weirdly, I feel so proud of him.

"Looks like your roommates are keeping you in line–the hair game is strong!" laughs Penn.

"Glad to hear the report is good!" he replies. "And thanks for asking about Eleanor. *I'll give her a pet for you*...because right now she's working. But later you can pet her too."

He reaches down and scratches Eleanor behind the ears, and she looks up at him lovingly.

"Oh sure–that makes sense!" Penn smiles.

"A lot of people don't ask–they just pet her...so thanks," he notes. "I hope you guys are in the mood for a campfire? We have a good one going back at the house, s'mores included! Can I help with luggage–or what did you guys bring?"

"Sounds great and we're good," I say quickly. "We both just brought backpacks and our purses."

"OK–I'll lead the way," Trevor tells us.

We head down the sidewalk. I walk hand in hand with Penn next to Trevor. Between the dark and the new central blur, I'm feeling less sure than ever about navigating this foreign place. We move at a slightly slower pace than usual, which is great for me. Trevor seems so relaxed at the intersection. *What would he and I have done if we were alone?* I wonder. *Would I feel safe in the dark like this, holding his hand?*

"I'm so amazed by you, Trevor. The way you get around…" I smile.

"Lots of practice. Trust me, I've been in a few situations too." He laughs.

At the fire ring, Trevor introduces us to some of his guy friends—Pete, Nick and John—who are all sighted. But my favorite character is Rob. He's blind too and has a white cane leaning on his folding lawn chair.

"Rob just finished his first open-mic comedy gig," Trevor shares, obviously proud of him.

"What??? That's so awesome!" enthuses Penn. "What was it like?"

She is in full-on flirt mode. I haven't seen her like this for a while.

"Well, I was pretty freaked out backstage…I'm not gonna lie," Rob says as he shakes his head back and forth, and laughs. "But the audience was so cool and standing up there felt amazing." He seems to be re-experiencing it all over again.

He continues. "They laughed! Not at everything, but the main thing is that *I got through it*. I loved it and now I can't wait to do it again."

As he shares, I'm in awe and I realize that if he could do that then maybe I could do something scary too.

"So, are you thinking about the U too?" Rob asks Penn.

"No, I'm planning on staying in Duluth and getting my RN degree. I'm kind of a homebody—not like Meera, world traveler here." She smiles over at me.

"How 'bout you, Meera?" Rob seems to be the extroverted interviewer here.

"Well, I applied here to go to the design school but now I'm not sure," I share. "Maybe Trevor told you? I have this eye thing and I'm just figuring things out."

"Yeah he told me a little. You should come here for sure," he says warmly.

"I'm a little overwhelmed at the moment..." I tell him, smiling, not wanting to commit.

"There's a lot of great people here to help you and..." Rob pauses, as if an idea is coming to him. Then he advises, "I don't know if you were thinking of going to like a specialized blind school or something, but my two cents is that you should stay mainstream. I tried blind school and hated it."

"I just started learning a bit of Braille...all I know is the alphabet," I reply.

Nick interjects, changing the subject, "Ha...don't let Rob fool you, Meera. Sure he's a blind stand-up comic, but he cannot cook a s'more to save his life. Here, try this." Nick smiles at his friend as he puts a s'more in my hands.

"Thanks!" I reply, wowed at the hospitality of these guys.

"You got me there!" says Rob.

Wow, what a relief. They all seem so kind and comfortable in their own skin. They make it seem like college and even, being blind, is no big deal. It seems like so much more fun there than in high school.

"The girls just texted me—they're back," Trevor alerts us. "So why don't we head back over there. It's getting chilly."

As everybody is saying good-byes, Trevor asks me more quietly, "Mind if I hold your hand, Meera?"

In that moment, those white roses in my heart blossom even more.

"No, not at all...I mean, yes I'd like that," I stammer.

He reaches out and I put my hand in his. Trevor's hand is so warm, and I am surprised by how much I love walking together with Eleanor on his right and me on his left. Penn stays close to my other side.

Penn shoots Trevor lots of questions about his classes as we walk. The girls' place is just three houses down.

At the girls' house, after introductions, Trevor and I hang out, and we talk on the landing's couch upstairs until a bit after three in the morning. I tell him all about Mexico and the ceremonies, and he seems to honestly enjoy hearing every detail. He asks a lot of questions. Downstairs, Penn watches the TV series *Pretty Little Liars* with the girls, and she gives everybody beachy waves and proper smoky eyes.

Sitting curled up in Trevor's arms is like being in heaven. And it feels like my time with him could only be possible because of the ceremonies...I feel loved...I belong. Despite all the doors that seem to be closing because of RP, tonight I feel full of possibility. And it turns out that you don't need to see a damn thing to be a great kisser.

Trevor picks us up late the next morning, and we grab bagels and coffee. As he and I hug good-bye at the bus stop, it's hard to go. It feels so good to stand there in his strong arms. Like I can do anything. When we kiss one last time, I know that I am, officially, wrecked by this boy.

Penn and I talk on the way home about how excited we are regarding college.

"What do you think, Meera?" Penn bubbled. "Aren't you so much more excited to go to the U now–especially since you know Trevor and all of his friends? I didn't like the U when I toured it with my parents last fall. It seemed so overwhelming. But it was a whole different experience this weekend, like seeing it from a much cooler perspective?"

"Yeah, very cool…" I pause, then confess, "I really, really like him, Penn…is that weird? Girl going blind likes blind guy?"

"But he is so much more than a blind guy, Meera," says Penn. "He's a really special guy–so funny and he's sweet. I guess he seems really great for you because he's real too. All of his friends seem great. And oh my God, that Rob…he was hilarious. I can't even imagine being a stand-up comic much less a blind comic? That takes some serious balls."

"Yeah…he made me realize like–stop putting limits on yourself. If he can do comedy and Trevor can play hockey, and they're blind, then…" Full of thoughts, I look out the bus window at the open fields rushing past.

A moment later, I want to revise what I had just said. "I don't know why I said it like that. *Blind guy.* I guess it's just me still worrying about what everybody else thinks. Truly, I want to pinch myself…

like I can really see being with him—and I haven't felt like that about anybody…ever." I look over at Penn.

"Do you ever feel like a burden?" I ask Trevor on the phone that night after getting home.

"Yeah, but I learned something about that really early in the game," he tells me. "When I feel that way, I know it's a signal that I need to shut down the pity party and hang with friends. I try to let it go and let others help me. You don't really have a choice, you know? I try to help out where I can too. My first hockey coach taught me that when you deny others who are trying to help you—it's a form of selfishness."

"Explain…?" I say, wanting to understand.

"OK, have you ever felt like you really helped somebody?" Trevor asks.

"Yeah, I guess." I think for a moment, and then share, "I redid my mom's bedroom for her…it made her really happy."

"OK—good one…so did you work hard to make that happen?"

I feel like I'm now seeing the "performance coach" side of him.

"Yes—days and days, and then when we actually went to work on the room, it was like twelve hours straight—crazy." I laugh.

"…and how did it feel when you were done?" Trevor inquires.

"Amazing—I mean she loved it so much and still does. It made me realize I want to help more people feel good like that."

"Exactly," Trevor affirms. "And if she hadn't let you help her, I'd argue that you would never have gotten to feel that good buzz… am I right?"

"Yeah, I guess so," I reply, realizing the depth of the exchange.

"So, whenever you allow others to help you–you're actually being generous–because helping you is going to make *them* feel good," Trevor points out. "And whether you're blind or not, my coach says, we all need help."

"I never thought about it like that...your coach sounds awesome."

"Yeah, we're still close," Trevor shares. "He texts me a few times a week, at least...he's one of my biggest cheerleaders."

I confess, "I guess I still worry about how I'd ever be able to make it at the U with everything that's changing for me."

"I worried a lot about that too," Trevor tells me. "But now you have friends here...me and everybody else you met this weekend! You wouldn't be going through it alone. I miss you *already*...when do we get to see each other again? I hope soon?"

"Me too..." I say, smiling to myself.

Trevor adds, "Hey, I was meaning to ask you...did you do the thing you were planning yet?" His voice is warm.

I'm so happy he remembers! It feels so good.

"No, but it's almost done, and I'm putting the final touches on it this week." Talking about it reminds me that I need to finish.

Chapter Twenty-Two

I'm standing at the bus stop in early April. It definitely smells like spring today. Exposed patches of green grass are peeking out from in-between the now-grayed patches of remaining snow. Penn parked half a block down the street, and she is waiting in her car. She offered to stand with me, but I really wanted to do this alone. In my hands, I'm holding the gift I've made. I made it as true to my vision as I could. As I created it, I tried to stay in the feeling state that I was in when she visited me in my dreams and in the ceremonies.

Her wings and body are covered in many scalloped layers of refined and delicate yellow tissue paper and fabric "feathers." I painted in her dark eyes until they felt like the portals I experienced, carrying me into that feeling of being held completely in love. I wanted the recipient to receive that feeling.

I see the receiver coming down the sidewalk now. She's moving slowly and calmly along with her long, white-tipped cane. Her purple-and-gold Minnesota Vikings knit hat is pulled low over her light-brown bobbed hair. Her mouth has a particularly sorrowful twist to it today. She's wearing her oversized dark plastic sunglasses and carrying a huge, overstuffed tote bag. I wonder if the glasses are to dim the light or to keep people from staring at her eyes?

As she approaches, I go inward for a moment, reminding myself what I want to say. Now she's like less than ten feet away and I don't want to startle her, so as quietly as I can, I say, "Excuse me..."

Despite my soft voice, her body jolts–I've surprised her.

"Oh...*sorry*...I didn't mean to..." I start to explain.

She sighs with relief, pausing and putting her hand with the cane up to her heart.

"I *thought* somebody was there and sometimes I'm right about that." She laughs.

"I'm sorry..." I repeat weakly.

"You're fine," she tells me, smiling and relaxing.

She begins to walk a few more steps forward toward the bus shelter.

This is my moment and I launch in. "I know this might sound weird but...my name is Meera, and I made something for you." I hope I don't sound too strange.

"For me?" She appears confused.

Suddenly, I realize how odd this all probably seems.

"Yes..." I continue slowly. "It's a long story, and it might sound weird, but you were in a dream of mine. I'm feeling lucky to be alive, and I wanted to make this gift for you."

This is how Sweetie suggested I say it, and it was true. *I do feel lucky.*

"Oh..?" She's sounding utterly confused.

I just need to press on.

"If it's OK, I can hand you the gift...?" I ask tentatively.

"Oh yes. Sure," she says, nodding while setting her bulky bag down on the sidewalk.

"I can hold your cane for you for a moment?" I suggest gently.

"Sure!" she replies, and for a moment I am realizing how much trust this might require for her.

I take the cane from her.

"If you can put both hands out…?" I ask and she does.

I place the yellow papier-mâché bird into her outstretched hands. She cradles it very carefully and then moves her fingers over it…examining the fine layers of feathers.

"It's so light and…" Continuing to touch it, she suddenly exclaims, "Is it a bird?"

She seems delighted.

"It is. It's a yellow bird," I confirm. Relieved.

Then I feel stupid for mentioning the color.

"Oh it's beautiful! Thank you," she tells me. "What did you say your name was?"

I'm feeling so sheepish and a bit embarrassed at this point. *What was I thinking? She probably thinks I'm a weirdo.*

"It's Meera," I stammer.

"Meera…what a beautiful name. Meera, my name is Phoebe—can I give you a hug?"

"Of course!" I say, surprised and pleased.

She holds the bird in one hand and hugs me tight with the other for much longer than you would ever hug a stranger if you hugged strangers which I don't—at least not until now. It isn't one of those typical Northern Minnesota hugs "lite": squinching up your shoulders for a quick squeeze and release. *It is a heart-to-heart, belly-to-belly hug.* She smells like baby powder.

After a long time, we move apart again.

"Meera, you couldn't have known this…" she shares, her voice quivering with emotion, "…but today is the day that I lost my mother a year ago. She was my *everything*. And today, I was hoping that somehow I would get a sign from her and I'd know she's watching over me, and here you are. You and your gift are that sign." She smiles and wipes a tear away.

"Oh my gosh, I'm so sorry, Phoebe..." I'm temporarily overwhelmed, thinking about what it would be like to lose your mom and that connection.

I hear the city bus rumbling towards us.

"Thank you. Mother was the love of my life and I miss her so much. She loved me so well. I'm OK now, but..."

The bus is pulling up...its hydraulics sigh, and the doors groan and unfolded before us. I wish we had more time.

I offer, "Phoebe, the bus is here...let me put the bird into this bag I brought, so it will be easy to carry."

Moving quickly, I put the cane back into her hands. I take the crumpled plastic grocery bag, that suddenly seems inadequate, out of my pocket. Feeling anxious, I take the bird from her and place it into the bag. In no hurry, she slowly moves to pick up her tote bag with one hand and takes the grocery bag and bird from me with the cane hand.

"Well, I guess I better hop on this bus," she tells me. "Um... can I give you my card? Maybe we could have coffee some time, and I could tell you about my mom and you could tell me more about this dream? And to thank you properly for this wonderful gift you've given me?" Her eyebrows are raised above her sunglasses.

"I would love that," I say, relieved that we would have a chance to connect again.

Setting the tote bag back down, she fumbles in her coat pocket and hauls out a single card and reaches her hand out. I take the card from her.

"Thank you so much. God bless you Meera."

After retrieving the tote bag, Phoebe boards the bus.

As I stand there, the bus groans and rumbles away.

I stare at her card. "Phoebe Kincaid PhD, Biofeedback Specialist." The backside of the card is embossed with Braille. All this time, I figured she was the one who needed help. I smile to myself and look up to the sky. I whisper, *"Thank you, thank you, thank you"* as I move towards Penn's car. I know I'm loved.

I get in the car with Penn and buckle my seatbelt. She sets down her phone and puts the car in gear.

"You're back. How'd it go?" Penn asks as she pulls out into the road.

"It was absolutely perfect."

Chapter Twenty-Three

Having received my acceptance a while ago, I withdrew from the College of Design and applied to transfer to the College of Liberal Arts at the U of MN, also in Minneapolis. I received my official transfer letter in mid-April, and then the date came and passed that I was supposed to send my deposit to the U of MN. Despite all the good things that had happened since the ceremonies—such as my new sense of inner peace—I'm still struggling with imagining myself on that campus. I know I could count on Trevor, but I can't expect him to be there every time I need to navigate things. Plus, a second Vaseline-like smear has appeared in my left eye's central vision, and I'm feeling a bit more hesitant about everything.

Penn is down, and I'm kind of worried about her. She and her mom, who are normally really close, are struggling. After I got back from Mexico and told Penn about the ceremonies, she confessed to her mom that she's been wanting to search for her birth mother. Before now, she'd been too scared to bring it up. When she finally told them, her dad was supportive, but her mom got pretty defensive and withdrawn.

While brushing out her hair on my bed, Penn says, "It's like no matter what I say to her, she's hurt and thinks it's all about her—like she's a bad mom— but it's not that at all."

"She *will* come around Penn...it'll probably take some time," I offer.

"Yeah, I know...and really, no matter what happens, I'm glad I did this–even if I don't find my birth mother. No matter what comes of it, at least I will have tried."

She had been in contact with the Children's Home Society, and they were beginning her paperwork to open up a search for her birth family in China.

All these years I had believed Penn was judging me for wanting to know about my birth family. Now it turns out she wanted to know too.

Penn starts braiding my hair. "Meera, did you decide to accept the U offer?" she asks, changing the subject.

"Still not sure...I'm chicken of navigating that place," I confess. "Right now, so much is changing for me. Even knowing Trevor is there and could help me out...I just don't know if I'm ready."

I start thinking anxiously about navigating in the dark.

Penn grabs a rubber band and begins wrapping it around the end of my braid. "I've been thinking...now I don't want to crowd your party bus, but..."

"But?" I ask her, confused.

"You're my best friend, Meera..." says Penn.

"And you're mine..." I echo her back, curious what she's getting at.

"What if I said I was going to the U? We could room together?" Penn smiles wide.

Still confused, I reply, "But why would you...go to the U? I thought you were set on Lake Superior College for nursing?" I feel concerned about her change of heart.

"Well, the deal is that I can really get the same degree at the U, and after being there with you, and sitting around that fire? That whole weekend really changed something for me. The U of MN seems less scary and more real. And I would LOVE to be there for you–to be your eyes when you need them?"

She sits back and looks at me with a smile.

"I didn't even know you applied!" I say surprised.

I begin to smile thinking of the possibilities.

"My dad made me apply because he's an alum, and…unlike my mom, I think he wants me to go away for school," Penn explains.

This new idea of going to the U of MN in Minneapolis with Penn would have been a dream before, but now I'm not so sure.

Chapter Twenty-Four

I text Trevor.

Me: I have some news.

Trevor: Don't leave a man in suspense...I'm calling you–hang on.

My phone immediately begins buzzing with a phone call from Trevor.

"I've decided to stay home in Duluth and go to the UMD campus here for my first year," I confess.

Before I can explain, Trevor interrupts me. "So what changed, Meer? I'm so bummed you're not coming down here–what happened?" He sounds a little wounded.

Haltingly, I share, "Well...Penn decided she wanted to go to the U too...and I thought if she would be there with me...then I would feel better about everything." I pause, then confess, "Only... as I thought about it...I didn't feel better. It was weird."

I continue carefully, wanting to reassure him. "I do want to be close to you. But with all of these new vision changes happening, I'm feeling like I need to keep the focus on my Braille, and I can do that really easily here in Duluth. You said yourself that Braille is really important. And my mom and I are really doing well right now. She's supporting me, and there's a part of me that just knows this is where I'm supposed to be for a while anyway. Penn was disappointed, but she's decided she's still going to the U. So, with both of you there, I'm planning lots of weekend trips to Minneapolis. I can just take the bus down...." I'm anxious to hear what he thinks of my decision.

"And I'll be here for you too–you know that," Trevor responds with kindness.

"I know–and I also am aware that you have a 'life' too," I tell him.

"I do, but Meera...and I hope this doesn't sound stalkerish, but...I hope you know that you're a part of that?" Trevor confesses.

My heart swells and I let out a sigh. "Thank you. That means so much," I say. "I miss you! I'm really grateful to you for the thing you told me about letting people help. It's helping me."

I feel this sweet contentment rise in my chest. I feel free and connected all at once.

"Can I say something right now?" asks Trevor. "It might sound weird, but words are becoming more and more amazing to me lately. They express so much feeling, if that makes sense?"

"Yes..." I respond, and then think, *I haven't lost all of my sight, but I don't ever remember experiencing so many feelings as I have this year.*

"Meera...to me you are...wait...have you read *Charlotte's Web?*"

"Yes, my mom read it to me when I was a kid. *It's so sad!* I cried at the end when the spider died."

I'm curious what he's getting at.

"OK...well, I just finished reading it in Braille so it's fresh in my mind." He laughs. "You Meera...you're...radiant! You're a real light in my life."

Hearing this, I start laughing inside. I remember that love, *that light,* flooding my body in the ceremony and in my dream. I wonder if, somehow, it *actually* lit me up somehow. I'm also laughing now, about the connection to the story.

"Trevor, are you saying I'm kinda like Wilbur, a State-Fair prize-winning pig?" I tease, laughing out loud.

"No…Ha! But he is my second favorite character, Charlotte–the amazing web-spinning spider–being number one." Then in a now-lowered voice, he adds, "What I'm saying is that I'm really glad you're in my life."

"Thank you, I feel the same about you, and as mad as I was that day my mom ambushed me with you, I'm so grateful she did!" I reflect on how much has happened since that awkward moment at the Edina Grill.

"Hey, now that I know you're a fan of spiders, I have to read you something from *my favorite book,*" I tell him. "Would you believe me if I told you that the creatures in our life might have messages for us?"

I grab my well-worn *Book of Beasties* off the shelf.

"I'm ready for a message from a Spider, hit me," he replies with a soft laugh.

I begin to read to him. "OK, here you go: *If Spider has appeared in your life, you can be assured you are being called to create. The medium doesn't matter; try whatever sounds fun. Try them all! Spider reminds you that any creative process is the result of many tiny undertakings. She won't ask you to do too much too fast. Don't resist, Spider implores you; simply put one leg in front of the other, and soon you'll turn around and be astonished at what you have accomplished.*"

"Hmm…that really makes sense," he replies, reflecting. "I've been thinking about working on writing my story of losing my vision–maybe even to publish it one day. My advisor thinks it could be an important part of my coaching practice somehow. Wow. Interesting!"

I'm smiling ear to ear. I love that he's open to making these wild sorts of connections.

Trevor jumps in with enthusiasm. "And, back to *Charlotte's Web*, the Minnesota State Fair is another one of my favorite things—will you promise to be my date in September? We can pet the goats, get *Hippo Campus* tickets, and eat frozen deep-fried Snickers on a stick."

"Yes, Trevor, I will go to the fair with you," I say, smiling.

I don't know where this is all going. But lately, I've been feeling my trust in myself growing. And, little by little, I'm learning to trust in the unknown. In that darkness that holds so much potential.

I dream of the yellow bird again. She wraps me gently in the infinite softness of her wings and stares intently into my eyes. Yellow bird floods my whole being with a love that is light. Together, we explore the upper branches, way up high, of an ancient white pine. I am completely free. Wordlessly she tells me that I'll be on a journey to learn from many different teachers and that she will be with me each step of the way. So will Sweetie. *But how?* I ask. She tells me that I am a healer being born. There are people waiting who I can help. I know she's going to lead me where I need to go.

About the Author

I was born of two rather Bohemian individuals and raised in the harsh and tundra-like (warmish for six weeks in the summer) conditions of Northern Minnesota with my only sibling, Maria Bamford, a successful stand-up comedienne. I am a fourth-generation physician and I practiced as a board-certified physician specializing in surgical pathology in a multispecialty group known for excellence in the Midwest. Although I thoroughly enjoyed my wonderful practice and partners, after 20 years in the world of allopathic medicine, I felt a strong pull to do transformative work and to be creative again. By that time, I had four children and my life had become "complicated." I got coached and found it life-changing.

My husband and I decided to right-size our lives by selling off our vacation home and decamping from a 6000-square-foot house into a lovely, more modest one. Then I took a six-month sabbatical from my job as a physician. I found myself wandering deep into the woods. I was re-awakening my own deep connection to nature and to myself. At the end of the sabbatical, I determined that my path was to continue in the field of personal transformation. If you're curious about my vocational transformation from MD to shamanic healer, I wrote *Swimming with Elephants: My Unexpected Pilgrimage from Physician to Healer* for you.

I have a deep appreciation for nature and use many different methods to help others connect to their own brilliance, including animal totems (and other shamanism-based tools, such as journeying and divination), surfing, and forest bathing. I believe that forging a connection to a spirit animal is powerful and wrote *The Book of Beasties: Your A-Z Guide to the Enlightening Wisdom of Spirit Animals*.

Part of being me involves having many, many interests and an *extreme* curiosity about many things. I was diagnosed as an adult with Attention Deficit Disorder, inattentive type. <u>Getting that diagnosis was a gift,</u> as it helped me fully embrace my irrepressible *muchness* and my special talent for taking seemingly unrelated ideas and creating something new. I have the ability to hyperfocus and, as a result, enjoy transcendent experiences on a pretty regular basis, which is pretty cool! I also have to be sure to get support and lots of rest so I don't become overwhelmed. I think nature holds the cure to whatever seems to be causing us to struggle, suffer, or feel stuck. I wrote the book *Born to FREAK: A Salty Primer for Irrepressible Humans* to help others diagnosed with ADHD, Asperger's, depression, anxiety, bipolar, and addiction.

First and foremost, I encourage you to re-discover your own FEELGOOD and follow it. It will take you to good places.

With love,
Sarah

Acknowledgements

Thank you Mother Earth, Father Sky, Grandfather Sun and Grandmother Moon from the bottom of my heart. And thank you to each of my helping spirits, but especially Charlotte, who introduced me to Meera and let us converse directly. I am so grateful for all the coincidences, synchronicities and chance meetings you spirits placed on my path to remind me to get back to writing this book. You didn't give up on me! Thank you also Meera for encouraging me from the realm of spirit. My prayer is that the book pleases you tremendously.

Thank you to Molly Burke, amazing YouTuber and motivational speaker. I've been stalking you lovingly for four years now, and I'm so grateful for your grace, authenticity and honesty. You are an incredible teacher, and I'm so grateful you had the courage to begin sharing your medicine with the world.

To London, thank you doesn't approximate the feeling I had when we connected by phone for the first time. Meeting you and hearing your hero's journey firsthand was a great blessing to me. In a way, immersed in research for Meera's story, I knew something about your history before we met, but encountering your courageous soul directly was something different entirely. To use your expression, I felt "shot right out of a canon" as I listened to you recount your epic tale: your incredible challenges, your stubborn and fiery spirit that never gave up, no matter what challenges came. I can't wait to see what you create next, and I am forever grateful for Sheppard who brought us together!

Thank you Aaron Reitstad for your writing! Knowing you through your words left me in awe. You are a fine human with such a beautiful message.

Thank you Suzi for being the first reader of the rough draft. Of course, Meera needed a love interest! I'm so damn grateful to know you and to occasionally be able to mine your wise and infinitely creative brain for literary and decorative insights! Your support means the world to me.

Thank you, Mom. You are gone now, but forever with me. It was hard to trust your kind words about the manuscript because you already knew you were dying when you wrote them. I'm forever grateful for your words and for your final physical act of loving editorial assistance. They bless this book. Without your prayers and love, I would not have written it. You live in my heart now and make me stronger and better than I was before. I miss you.

Sheppard Lake, thank you so much for being a first reader and giving me such wonderful and helpful input! Thank you for being the amazing open-hearted and take-charge/fearless human that you are!!

Gini Breidenbach, when you left that voicemail in tears after reading the draft, I felt the kind of profound joy that a writer dreams of feeling. *There is no higher praise.* I'm so grateful for our ongoing journey together in life on this sacred path. Thank you.

Nancy Schoenheide Phares, thank you for being a supportive early reader and making the absolutely critical suggestion that Meera needed a Beastie!

Thank you to my daughter Katherine–for reading this book! And for setting me straight on how youth text and so much more.

You are amazingly meticulous and going to make the world's most AMAZING nurse. I love you!

Thank you to Kris McGuffie; your editing is so good, it's embarrassing. You understand story and character like nobody else I know, and I can't thank you enough for your help. I wouldn't have been able to complete it without you.

Thank you to Robin Quinn! A series of magical coincidences led me to you so I was not surprised when you arrived to help me polish this book and whip it into submission condition! Thank you for your incredible attention to detail, nuance, character and timelines. I am forever grateful!

Thank you dear reader for being here and witnessing Meera's story. I hope it gave you something that you needed.

While writing this book, I became an enormous fan of guide dogs…those magical furry beings who change the lives of so many people! London Pickett introduced me to Southeastern Guide Dogs, an amazing organization that shares tips about how we can support these special dogs and the humans they serve.

Respect the Harness: Guide Dog Etiquette

When a guide dog is in harness, it is working and you should do everything you can to not distract it.

Guide dogs are highly trained to know the difference between "harness-on" and "harness-off." When the harness is on, the dog is focused and working. When the harness is off, it's time to relax or play like any other dog. Humans, please respect the harness and ignore a working dog!

When navigating with a guide dog, a person with a visual impairment relies on the dog to avoid obstacles; stop for curbs and crossings; find objects such as doors, exits, and stairs; and generally, help the person arrive safely to their destination. A working dog is alert and busy concentrating on commands. Distracting a working dog can be frustrating to the handler and may put both dog and human in danger. Follow these tips for proper etiquette when encountering a guide dog.

Guide Dog Etiquette Do's and Don'ts:

- **Don't** interact with a working dog by petting, calling out the dog's name, or giving the dog commands. A guide dog should only hear commands from its handler.
- **Don't** allow children to interact with the dog. **Do** teach children the difference between a pet and a service dog.
- **Don't** allow your pets to interact with a working guide dog.
- **Don't** feed the dog anything without the handler's permission, especially not table scraps. Guide dogs must maintain an ideal weight and fitness level, not to mention food being a natural distraction from work.
- **Don't** attempt to guide, steer, or hold a person navigating with a guide dog. **Do** let the dog work.
- If the dog is out of harness, **do** ask permission to pet the dog or to allow children to pet the dog. If the dog is resting, **do** allow it to rest without disturbing it.
- Walking together? Right-handed handlers often work their dogs on their left side. **Do** walk on the handler's right side, a few paces behind. Walking on the left side (the dog side) may distract the dog.

You should always ask before petting another person's dog.
The handler will tell you if it is OK.

Republished with permission by:
Southeastern Guide Dogs
4210 77th Street East, Palmetto, FL 34221
www.GuideDogs.org

HELLO DEAR READERS!

I'd be so grateful if you'd be willing to leave a brief review at Amazon, share the book with your beloveds on Goodreads, or gift a copy to somebody who you think would enjoy it.

Thank you so much for your support!
It means the world to me.

With BIG love,

Sarah

P.S. On my website, you can learn about how we can work together one-on-one (I offer shamanic healing and life coaching virtually and in person) and about my trips and events.

FOLLOWYOURFEELGOOD.COM

*"The basic difference between an ordinary
[wo]man and a warrior is that
a warrior takes everything as a challenge
while an ordinary [wo]man takes everything as a blessing or a curse."*
–Carlos Castaneda

SARAH
SEIDELMANN M.D.

FOLLOW YOUR
FEEL GOOD

CPSIA information can be obtained
at www.ICGtesting.com
Printed in the USA
LVHW011149231121
704187LV00002B/9